A MOMENT IN TIME

Racquel went to Sean, intending to give nothing more than a quick embrace, but his arms wrapped around her like twin bands of steel, and he pulled her to him and held on for a lot longer than she had envisioned. Strangely, she experienced no need to struggle. In fact, she felt safe there, with his arms about her—safer than she'd ever felt before.

She rested her head on his chest, and a hand came up to gently stroke her hair. He was so warm, and solid, so well-suited to her physically. They almost seemed to fit together, like two pieces of some inscrutable cosmic puzzle.

She raised her head to look at him. His eyes were deep and dark, and very gentle. She sensed a hesitance in him, and knew instinctively what it was. It was completely natural, in this moment, to want more than she was giving. She raised herself onto her toes, and without saying a word, he lowered his lips to hers. He kissed her, slowly, slowly, holding her as though she were the most precious cargo in the world. Her hands went around his back, and she felt more than heard him moan.

He deepened the kiss in subtle movements of his head.

For Sean, time had gone away. It had no meaning anymore. All that mattered was here and now, and holding her this way. When she attempted to move away from him, he shifted her mouth back, with the muttered protest, "not yet." *He'd waited so long for this. Almost an entire lifetime.*

BOOK YOUR PLACE ON OUR WEBSITE AND MAKE THE ARABESQUE ROMANCE CONNECTION!

We've created a customized website just for our very special Arabesque readers, where you can get the inside scoop on everything that's going on with Arabesque romance novels.

When you come online, you'll have the exciting opportunity to:

- View covers of upcoming books

- Learn about our future publishing schedule (listed by publication month and author)

- Find out when your favorite authors will be visiting a city near you

- Search for and order backlist books

- Check out author bios and background information

- Send e-mail to your favorite authors

- Join us in weekly chats with authors, readers and other guests

- Get writing guidelines

- AND MUCH MORE!

Visit our website at
http://www.arabesquebooks.com

DISTANT MEMORIES

Niqui Stanhope

ARABESQUE
★BET
BOOKS

BET Publications, LLC
www.msbet.com
www.arabesquebooks.com

ARABESQUE BOOKS are published by

BET Publications, LLC
c/o BET BOOKS
One BET Plaza
1900 W Place NE
Washington, D.C. 20018-1211

First Printing: December, 1999
10 9 8 7 6 5 4 3 2 1

Printed in the United States of America

For my wonderful parents, Malcolm and Joyce.
My brothers. Leticia Peoples of Odyssey Books.
My two adorable nieces, Abina and Chante.
Thank you for everything!

Also, to Sean and Allison.

Prologue

It was a few minutes since the electricity had returned, and Racquel Ward maneuvered carefully about the rambling farmhouse, flickering candle in hand. The place was still in darkness, because a fuse had blown. Outside, the wind howled and rattled at the ancient window shutters. And, every so often, a jagged flash of lightning pierced the darkness to reveal a sodden glimpse of the hulking hillside.

On the winding, gravel-strewn road leading to the property, under the lacy boughs of a large oak, a car stood with its engine running. A man in a heavy coat sat at the wheel, his face smooth and saturnine in the darkness. He watched the house with quiet intensity, his brows knitting into frown lines as he followed the bobbing candlelight from room to room. There was an air of bottled excitement about him. A certain quality of waiting.

Suddenly, without warning, the thick greenery above the car moved in a strong gust of wind. Heavy rain slashed at his windshield, and for a moment he allowed his eyes to wander from the house. He wiped at the glass with the edge of a sleeve, then paused to watch with a rapier sharp gaze when a stocky, cloaked figure bent against the wind, appeared out of the night. The other man made his way up the driveway, slipping a bit on the smooth black stones.

He watched as the figure pounded at the door, and a smile sloped across his lips when the solid wood sprang back to admit the visitor.

A sudden fit of wheezing overtook him, then, and it was several minutes before the life-giving blast of the inhaler in his top pocket made his breathing less labored. He wiped his forehead free of the beaded spittle of perspiration, reached a rock-steady hand toward the glove compartment, and pulled it open to reveal the well-polished glint of a handgun.

He would wait until 9:00 P.M., but no longer.

One

"We've been over all this many times before," Racquel said, turning from the window. Already, she was beginning to wonder if she could go through with it. She had dreaded the very thought of seeing him again, dreaded it all the way down to the core of her soul. But, if she was to get away from him for good, it had to be done.

She had made painstaking plans, looked into every detail of her escape. She was packed and ready to leave for Los Angeles that very night. She had to be sure that he wouldn't find her too quickly. She knew that he would look for her no matter what she did. If she got lucky, though, he might not discover exactly where she had gone for a few months—maybe longer. Once he did know, once the farce was revealed, he would do all in his power to find her. That, she knew.

She tried to make her lips smile at him, but found that they were stiff with fear.

"Why won't you believe that I've changed . . . that I'm not the same man you married two years ago?" he asked. Her ex-husband came toward her, and instinctively Racquel took a step backward. His temper was often quite unpredictable.

She gripped the windowsill behind her with a hand and attempted to steady herself.

"It was never any good between us, Ralph . . . you know that."

His chest rose and fell for several beats, and the flash of hatred in his eyes sent a genuine lance of fear through her.

"That's only because you never gave us a chance, woman. Didn't I share everything I had with you? Gave you everything you wanted, didn't I? Expensive vacations to—Mexico? New York? But you weren't satisfied with just that, were you? You had to have more. You wanted to be a modern woman . . . have a *career.*"

He spat the words at her, and an involuntary spasm clutched at her throat. Whenever he had struck her in the past, she had never fought back. She had taken the abuse quietly, ashamedly, disguised her bruises with makeup and colorful scarves. Always forgiving him, when later he was filled with remorse. Always believing him when he told her how much he loved her. Irrationally, she had never doubted his promises that it would never happen again. She had always managed to convince herself that, somehow, she had been to blame for his behavior—that, somehow, she had deserved it—until one particularly severe incident had landed her in the hospital with a badly bruised face and a fractured collarbone. She had made up her mind to leave him after that.

"I don't want to fight with you, Ralph. We've done more than enough of that. I want us to be friends . . . to like each other. We did share a life—"

"Friends?" he growled, cutting her off before she could finish. "We'll never be friends. Understand me? Never."

Racquel took a breath and tried to control the fierce

battering of her heart against her ribs. "You said you wanted to clear the air between us . . . make things more normal . . . remember?"

He smiled, but continued to watch her with the glassy-eyed gaze of a predator. "Yeah, I remember, baby. I remember. Things will be good between us again. I've learned how to control my anger now. See?" He stuck both hands into his pants pockets. "Even right now I feel like wrapping my fingers around your pretty throat, but because you're afraid of me . . . I won't. I'll never hurt you again. Never. I promise you. You've got to believe me."

Racquel nodded. There was a dry, bitter taste in her mouth, and her breath came in short, shallow little bursts.

"I love you so damn much," he said softly. "So much that the thought of another man . . . even touching you . . . makes me crazy." His hands came out of his pockets, and he took another step toward her. "You don't want to make me crazy . . . do you, baby? You don't want to hurt me anymore . . . surely? Not after all I've done to make you happy?" He spoke to her as he would to a particularly backward child, and Racquel trembled.

"I don't want another . . . another man. I promise you. I just . . . just want to be left alone, to have a career. To leave something good behind . . ."

He looked at her for several beats, his eyes flicking over her tall slender form. Quickening anger caused his nostrils to flare, and for a moment Racquel was sure that he would strike her.

"You want to leave something behind? You can stand there and say that to me? How many times did you refuse to bear me a child? How many times?" His voice rose to something just short of a bellow. "And now . . .

and now, when you've decided that you no longer need me, want me, you decide to take up a career—where you'll probably meet men who make ten or fifteen times as much money as I do."

"I'm not interested in men," she repeated in a soothing tone. "I promise you." She willed him to believe her.

"Maybe so," he said after a long perusal. "Maybe so. But I want you to understand one thing." His leathery hands took hold of hers. "You made a promise to me years ago—a promise before God and all my friends—and I intend to hold you to that. You are mine forever. And no piece of paper can change that."

He tilted her slender chin up with a thick index finger, and the expression in his eyes made her feel like a trapped animal. She fully realized it now. He would never let her go, never allow her to find happiness. He meant to hound her for the remainder of his days, even if it meant the destruction of his own life. He would never allow her to live life on her own terms.

Her throat clenched painfully, and the words she had spent several hours rehearsing seemed lodged in the narrow confines of her throat. "I . . . I'm thinking of closing up the house. Going somewhere else for a while."

The hands holding hers tightened, and a pulse began to beat somewhere along his left temple.

"Closing up the house? Going somewhere else?"

Her heart pounded heavily at her ribs. This was why she had forced herself to agree to a face-to-face meeting. He believed that she could tell only the truth if he was standing right before her. She was counting on this. She had, after all, never had the courage to lie to him before.

She took a breath to steady her nerves, then said a

prayer that the words would come out without so much as a quiver.

"I'm going to move out to New York. I always liked it there . . . whenever we visited."

There were several beats of silence, during which time she wondered if he would be able to tell that she was lying. She met his eyes directly, and after a moment he released her hands and crossed to the window.

He stood there for long moments, watching the rain come down in heavy sheets. Then, when it seemed that he would say nothing at all, he turned back to her. "New York," he said. "You would leave Idaho for that place? Acting, I suppose?" He spoke almost as though she were not there at all. "I never could understand that desire in you, never could. Why weren't you happy with the life I gave you? A farmer's life isn't such a hard one, after all. And we weren't that bad off."

A tear pooled in the corner of Racquel's eye, and she brushed it away with stiff fingers. She had promised herself that she would be strong throughout her little talk with him. She knew better than anyone how much of a manipulator Ralph Penniman was.

"You hit me," she said, and her voice cracked a bit. They had never really acknowledged his abuse of her—not in so many words.

He gave her a pained look. "Does a parent love the child he chastises?"

She gritted her teeth. and spoke sternly to herself. No matter what he said, she must not say anything in anger that she would later regret.

"I am a grown woman," she said, "not a child. And . . . you, you had no right, no right at all, to raise your hand against me. No matter what it was you might have thought I was guilty of."

"Well," he said after a moment of surprised silence.

"The rabbit has a voice. Who would have thought it?" His eyes rested for a moment on her bosom, and a note of suspicion crept into his tone. "I haven't noticed any men hanging about here. So who could have taught you to defy me like this?" His eyes narrowed to slits. "Have you finally found that no-good, little orphan runt you were so attached to as a child?"

Racquel flinched as though he had struck her. "No . . . of course not." It had been years since she had given up any hope of ever seeing Stephen again. She had openly adored the lanky adolescent boy, following him around her parents' farm, watching with admiring eyes as he helped birth calves, foals, and sometimes even sheep. Theirs had been an instant bonding, like two kindred souls coming together. Whenever she had fallen, he had always been there to pick her up and dust her off. If ever she cried, he was never too busy to listen, and to wipe the tears away. Most nights, they sat out under the stars, and dreamt wonderful, grown up dreams. She was going to become a famous actress, he a country vet. It had been a wonderful time; a happy respite from the daily battles between her parents.

By the time she was eleven, she had decided that when she was old enough she would marry him. It didn't matter a bit what everyone else had to say about him—that he was a troublemaker, and would never amount to anything good. She had known better.

But, one day, with no prior warning, Stephen had disappeared. Many years later, and quite by accident, she had learned from her father that he had been adopted, and that his adoptive family had taken him away to live in another state—which one, she had never discovered. It still bothered her, even now, to think that he had not thought enough of her to say good-bye, or to even write.

"Are you listening to me?"

Racquel blinked at the man standing before her. "I'm sorry. I didn't hear you, Ralph."

"If you go to New York I'm going with you."

Racquel gritted her teeth. She had expected something like this. "There's no point in your going to New York with me. You hate it there. Besides, we're divorced. We have to learn how to live separate lives again."

She could tell that he was working himself into a grand passion again, so she shifted smoothly into phase two of her survival plan. "I'll be staying with Great-Aunt Ada, and you'll remember that she doesn't have much space." Her great aunt was the only woman whom Ralph Penniman appeared to fear, and her reason for making her part of the plan. She was a tall woman, six feet at the very least, and built like a very sturdy, weathered old oak. Her fiery tongue had been known to reduce the most worthy of opponents to fits of stammering incoherence.

"Maybe, later, when I get my own place in the city, you . . . you can come up for a visit." She swallowed, and without conscious volition her fingers bunched into fists at her sides.

"Well, you've made up your mind about it, I can see that," he said, and his forehead creased into frown lines. "Is there anything I can say to make you stay here—in Idaho?"

She shook her head. "No. Nothing."

He returned to the window he had been walking back and forth in front of for some minutes now, and for a long while he just stared out at the inky darkness.

Finally, he turned to look at her, and there was a

certain hollowness in his eyes. "OK. Go to New York, if you must. But, remember this—I did give you a chance. A fair chance. Whatever happens now, you have only yourself to blame for it."

Two

After he had gone Racquel dead-bolted the front door, carefully locked all the windows, then collapsed into a chair in the sitting room. The blood sang madly in her veins, and a strange feeling of exhilaration made her feel as though she would never stand again. She had done it. He had actually believed her little story. Of course, she knew that it would only be a few days before he discovered that she had left immediately following their little meeting, and maybe a week at most before he worked up enough courage to buy a ticket to New York. He would not call Aunt Ada before embarking, because he was well aware that the old woman did not like him. What he would do is skulk around the outside of the exclusive apartment house in New York once he got there, scouring the faces of all the women who came and went. Eventually, it would dawn on him that maybe she was not staying there, after all; a process that would take several weeks or more. He would then begin searching the city of New York. Several months more would be lost in this undertaking. Finally, he would be forced to give up, forced to come to the realization that New York was a large enough city for one solitary woman to get lost in, especially if she did not desire to be found.

The howling of a dog somewhere off in the distance penetrated the euphoric haze. She had arranged with the local taxi service to be there at 9:00 P.M. sharp. Her flight to Los Angeles from Boise Municipal Airport did not leave until well after midnight, but with the heavy rain and slushy conditions on many of the rural roads she wasn't taking any chances at all that she might be late. She was already packed and ready. Rental arrangements had been made with the local real estate office. There was really not much left for her to do now but wait, and maybe make herself a warm mug of tea while she did so.

The lights flickered as Racquel poured a good quantity of water into the teakettle and set it to boil on the stove. Strangely enough, she had never felt any apprehension at all, staying alone in the roomy farmhouse. But now, with the heavy wind and rain, the almost unearthly howling of the dog, and the precarious nature of the electricity, it suddenly dawned on her how very isolated she was, how very easy it would be for someone to break in if they really wanted to—maybe through one of the windows in some distant part of the house. If that happened, who would be there to hear her? To help her?

The whistling of the kettle caused her to start violently, and she gave herself a good talking to. She was being silly. This house had been her parents', and there was absolutely nothing to be afraid of. She had inherited it at their deaths. It was quite probably one of the few really good things they had ever done for her. So wrapped up in the private misery of their own lives, they had never had the time or the inclination to nurture. She was over all that now. She had forgiven them, had even come to pity them, in a way. They had both been so very unhappy. Why that was, she had never really understood. She had finally settled on the only reason that made sense to her: They were just two completely incompatible personalities who should probably never have married each other. They had made a mistake, just as she had in her choice of a life partner. But she had realized her error early in the marriage, and was determined to do all in her power to correct it. In less than half an hour, she would be on her way to the airport, on her way to an entirely different life, so it was just plain idiotic to work herself into a high state of nerves just because she happened to be alone.

She took a deep sip of the warm tea, and forced herself not to think of the wayward window shutter in the dining room, the one she had somehow forgotten to secure. The wind was playing merry havoc with it, slapping the ornately carved frame back and forth against the wooden sidings. If she had any sense at all, she would put down her tea, walk into the dining room, open up the window, and close the shutter properly.

A trident of lightning, followed closely by a roll of thunder, suddenly rent the night, and in that moment of clarity Racquel was certain that she saw something move just beneath the window. She placed the mug on the counter. It was quite probably one of the dogs from the next farm over—maybe the same poor creature she had heard howling just minutes before.

She made herself walk to the window. The only thing that would adequately calm her jittery nerves was the solid reality of familiar, nonthreatening shapes.

"See . . . there's no one out there." She spoke to herself in the exact tone her mother had used with her whenever she'd had one of her childish nightmares.

"No one at all. Just the trees . . . and the wind."

Even to her own ears, her voice sounded hoarse and frightened.

The lights flickered again, and Racquel forced herself to walk into the dining room. She would close that window shutter, and stop behaving like a complete fool. Besides, the taxi would be here very soon, and she did want to make certain the house was all closed up before she left.

The dining room was almost directly opposite the entry hallway, and Racquel hesitated for a moment. Should she go out into the wet and take a look? Maybe there was some poor animal lurking about out there, soaking wet, cold, scared.

The ringing of the telephone prevented any further thought on the matter, and she walked across to answer it.

"Yes. Hello?" It was the cab company ringing to let her know the car would be at her door in less than five minutes.

She thanked the man, hung up, and went to get her luggage. She was traveling very light—just two bags, both of which she would take on board the aircraft. Once she got to Los Angeles, she intended to buy a completely new wardrobe. She would spend the first week looking around for a place. Arrangements had already been made to stay at the Sheraton Hotel. She had reserved one of the more plush rooms. For once in her life, she would really pamper herself: Room service, in-room massages to keep her muscles supple, manicures, shopping. She had more than enough money to last her the entire year, though she did intend to start auditioning as soon as she got herself settled. It might take several months before she got a part, but she was up for the challenge. In fact, she was looking forward to it.

Racquel was humming happily when bright head-lights came slowly up the drive, and ready at the door with her bags when a fist pounded on the wood. She opened it up, and shivered a little at the wet blast of air.

"Sorry to make you come out on a night like this," she said, smiling and rubbing her hands together.

The man was tall, and possessed a rather solemn face with eyes resembling twin pairs of sunken black prunes. "These all your bags?" He motioned to the two at her feet.

She nodded. "Yes. Just these." She was suddenly happy, exuberantly so. By tomorrow she would be in Los Angeles, mere minutes away from Hollywood, and Ralph Penniman would no longer be a factor in her life. Finally, finally, she would be free.

Racquel settled into the back of the car, smoothing her long ebony tresses behind both ears. The first thing she would do after she unpacked was find a good hair-dresser. She had been thinking of changing her hair color now for the longest while. Honey-brown with golden highlights had always fascinated her. It would be a different, more glamorous look, well in step with her new image.

"Airport, right?" The driver's voice seemed strangely hollow in the tiny confines of the car.

"That's right," she said, and gave her watch a glance to make certain that they were still on schedule.

They pulled slowly out of the drive, and Racquel gave the house a final look. She wasn't sorry to leave. Idaho held very few happy memories for her. There were no friends to leave behind or to miss. Ralph had more or less seen to that. He had prevented her from making friends with the other women in the community, had even appeared jealous of them. She unfastened the top button on her jacket. Ralph Penniman was a queer fish. She could only hope that in her absence he would somehow become a little more normal.

"The planes might be late."

"Excuse me?" Racquel said, glancing into the rear-view mirror and meeting the dark sunken eyes. The lack of expression in them made her look hurriedly away.

"Wherever you're going, I'm sure your flight will be late. Not a good night for flying." Racquel made a non-committal sound and turned to stare after a yellow taxi-cab that was slowly making its way up the narrow gravel road.

"Strange," she said, more to herself than to anyone else. "He must be lost. Is that one of your cars?"

She turned back to the driver. The shoulders shrugged. "Could be."

"Maybe you should call him up . . . let him know he's going the wrong way. My house is the only one up this road."

"He'll find his way. Don't worry."

She sat back in silence until they were out on the main road. "Do you mind if I smoke?"

Before she could think of a polite way to say that she minded very much indeed, he had placed a cigarette between his dark leathery lips and was preparing to light it. Racquel inched her window down a crack. It wasn't very far to the airport. She could hold out until then.

"So," he said after taking a deep draw, "is this a vacation, or something else?"

"I'm leaving Idaho . . . for a while, at least."

The driver tossed the half-finished cigarette out the

window, wheezed a bit, then lit another one. "Where're you headed?"

The plumes of smoke were beginning to irritate her nostrils, and Racquel gave a tiny cough before remembering to say, "New York."

The driver flipped the butt out the window, then met her eyes in the mirror. "There's an old cemetery a few miles up the road, an ancient forgotten place where no one ever goes anymore. Lots of weeds and moss about the place. I heard a woman was buried alive up there a few years back. They packed in dirt and everything on her. Can you imagine lying in that box—arms cramped, feet cramped—air just fading away? Terrible way to go. Her husband found out she was cheating, you see . . . and instead of telling him the truth, she lied. Husband broke down and confessed to it later. Interesting stories you hear when you drive these cars."

Racquel shuddered and huddled lower in her jacket. What a horrible man. How could he possibly find anything even remotely interesting about that story? And why had he thought she needed to hear it now? There were no other cars in sight, and nothing but the wind and rain to separate them from the inky darkness and the lurking predators of the night.

A sudden thought occurred to her, and her heart gave a thick thud in her chest. Could the driver be a maniac of some sort and—sensing that she was all alone in the world—have decided that she would make the perfect victim? Was he intending to take her off to some far-flung, absolutely secluded spot to hack her to pieces? Or maybe strangle her? He did have big hands, ideal for wrapping about the width of just about any neck, and squeezing all of the life out.

She stared at the back of his head, and made a valiant attempt at controlling the rapid beat of her heart. She was being paranoid again. Not everyone was out to get her. This driver was no threat. He was just a strange man with a warped sense of humor. But, just in case, she would keep a very close eye on where they were headed. If need be, she could bash him on the head with something, then mace him.

She felt around in her purse, and her fingers closed around a sizable container of cold cream. She tested its weight in her palm. It was good enough to do significant damage. Never again would she allow herself to be brutalized by a man.

She remained silent for the rest of the journey, her eyes glued to the highway signs. At the airport, she hustled out of the car, shoved some money at the driver, and walked rapidly off into the terminal building without saying much of anything in parting. She looked behind her as soon as she was at a polite distance. The man still stood where she'd left him. He rested casually on the car door, arms folded, eyes on her. She turned around quickly. God, she was making herself crazy. The man was just looking at her. There were several possible explanations for that, surely?

She didn't feel quite safe until she was onboard the aircraft, and even then she couldn't allow herself to settle in for the flight until she had studied all of the faces around her.

Later, on the way to the hotel in Los Angeles, she had a good laugh at herself. This time, she was completely animated with her cab driver, peering out the window at the city lights, asking the questions tourists usually do. She cranked the window down, letting the damp night air whip through the car. The driver watched her for a while, thinking how very beautiful she was.

"Here on vacation?" he asked.

Racquel laughed. "Oh no. I'm here to work. I'm an actress, you know."

The man seemed suitably impressed. "One of the studios brought you out to test for a part, huh?"

"I wish," Racquel sighed. "I have to do it the hard way, I guess. Auditions."

The taxi driver nodded. He had ferried many a hopeful starlet from the LAX airport. They were invariably upbeat on their trip out, but not so when he drove them back to catch their planes to Small Town, USA.

At the hotel Racquel paid the fare and gave the man a very generous tip. He wished her good luck, even though he wasn't much of a believer in luck, good or bad. Racquel waved him off with a smile and a polite thank you. She walked into the hotel, her face aglow. She was happy. For the first time in a very long while, she was truly happy. And free.

Three

The next several days passed in a blur. She did all of the things a tourist would. She visited the La Brea Tar Pits, Hollywood Boulevard, and the Mann's Chinese Theatre. She stood in the footprints of the stars, and unashamedly stopped passersby to ask their help with taking a picture or two. She spent half a day shopping on Rodeo Drive, where she bought herself several low-cut, strapped dresses that cost outrageous sums. With her guidebook in hand, a fashionable straw hat atop her head, and dark sunglasses perched jauntily on her nose, she threw herself wholeheartedly into the exploration of LA. By the fifth day of her arrival in the city she had dyed her long sweep of ebony hair honey-brown, and changed her look entirely.

During her running around, she had also managed to pick up a daily newspaper, and the latest copy of *Auditions* magazine. She sat on her bed now, in the spacious hotel room, giving first the newspaper, then the magazine, a very thorough going over. On a pad provided by the hotel, she very neatly made a list of apartments she would see the next day and, finishing this, made another list of possible auditions. She was in the middle of a very thoughtful consideration of a general casting call for a big-budget movie when the phone at the bedside rang. The sudden noise in the quiet of the room startled her, and for a minute she made no move toward the instrument. When it continued to ring, she leaned over to lift the receiver.

"Hello?" Her voice was cautious. She knew no one in Los Angeles, and there was no one in Idaho who would call her, except her ex-husband.

The voice on the other end of the line was well-modulated and crisply professional. "Ms. Ward, this is the hotel concierge."

There was a slight pause, and Racquel relaxed and spoke warmly into the phone. "Oh, hello, David. Is something wrong?"

The man seemed a bit unsure of how to say exactly what he intended, but finally he managed, "We've had a request from one of our . . . guests. He noticed you walking through the hotel foyer and would like to know if you would consider meeting him in the bar for a drink."

Racquel laughed. Before she had married Ralph she had never had any trouble attracting men. In fact, she'd had considerably more trouble keeping them away. After getting married, she had of course never looked at another man, even though Ralph's opinions on the matter were to the contrary.

"Thank him for me, David. Tell him I'm very flattered, but not interested."

She detected a very audible swallow on the other end, and wondered briefly what it was that had the usually unflappable David so very nervous.

"Our gentleman—that is to say, our guest—would like to discuss some business with you. He's in the movie industry, you see, and—"

Racquel's interest quickened. "The movie industry? Are you certain?"

The concierge cleared his throat. "Very certain. He's one of the hottest producers around today. I'm sure you may be familiar with a lot of his movies." He proceeded to run through a short list of recent box office blockbusters.

By the time he was through, Racquel's heart was beating in thick, heavy thumps in her chest, and she was so excited she could scarcely breathe. Her hands were ice cold, and suddenly, holding onto the receiver was a chore.

"He wants to see me?" she almost stammered. "You couldn't have made a mistake, could you?"

"No mistake. You're the one he wants . . . to see."

Racquel weighed the odds quickly in her mind. She had nothing to lose, after all. The hotel bar was a public area. There would be lots of people all around. What harm could possibly come of it?

"OK," she said with a hint of breathlessness in her voice. "I . . . tell him I'll be down in a few minutes."

She hung up, then scurried about the room. She would wear one of her new spaghetti strap dresses—the burgundy, crushed velvet number with the high front and deep scoop in the back should be appropriate. Matching shoes and the old, loopy gold earrings which she'd had for years would complete the picture of fashionable sophistication.

In less than ten minutes, she was giving herself a final very critical look in the mirror. Her now honey-brown hair fell thickly to just below her shoulder blades, and the dress followed the curve of her waist and hips as though it had been custom-made just for her. She gave her flat abdomen a pat and muttered, "I guess I'll do."

She picked up a clutch purse she had chosen for the occasion, dropped her room key, a canister of mace, and her only credit card into the soft interior and snapped it shut. In another minute, she was clopping smartly down the hallway and entering the elevator. She found her way to the bar without much difficulty, and stood for a moment in the entryway listening to the soft music, the clink of glasses, and the general hum of voices. She was really beginning to love Los Angeles and everything about it. It was as though she was just awakening from a very long and deep sleep.

A hand touched her elbow, and Racquel moved to one side of the doorway with a quick apology. The man standing beside her was middle-aged, with the slight beginnings of a paunch, and was dressed in an expensive-looking suit and tie.

"Are you waiting for someone?" he inquired.

Racquel flashed a quick look in his direction. "Yes. Yes, I am." Before anything more could be said, she had walked away from the doorway, and entered the bar. She immediately recognized the man sitting on a stool at the bar—the balding head, thick glasses and florid, jowly face. He turned when he saw her and clambered off his stool with what appeared to be great difficulty. Racquel extended her hand as soon as he was close enough. "Mr. Jacques. I can't tell you how nice it is to meet you."

Her hand was enveloped by both of his. "Thank you for coming down." He raised a chubby hand and clicked his fingers. Within seconds, a waiter from the adjoining restaurant was standing at his side.

"We'd like a table now," Jacques said, and Racquel was impressed with the speed at which they were shown to the best table in the room. The maître d' came over and personally saw to the seating arrangements, pulling out chairs and waiting with proper deference while they were adequately situated. He handed them both wine lists and stood back a few paces to await their order.

Racquel's eyes quickly skimmed the list of wines, champagnes, and Bordeaux. She wasn't much of a drinker, so she had little idea of what choice to make. Jacques put the menu down and peered at her through his thick glasses.

"What would you like?" he asked.

"Well . . ." Racquel began. She had fully intended to pay for everything herself, but felt that saying so now could possibly cause offense. "What do you suggest?"

Jacques gave the maître d' rapid instructions, and when the man was gone he sat back with a smile. "I think you'll really enjoy my choice."

Racquel returned his smile. It was almost incredible to her that only a few days before, she had been living the life of a lonely recluse in an old farmhouse in Idaho. Now, she was sitting at a table in a fancy restaurant in LA, casually chatting with one of Hollywood's biggest film producers. Sometimes miracles did happen.

The man in question leaned forward to give her a very direct look. "You're very beautiful," he said. "But, I'm sure you already know that." He sat back again. "Hollywood is full of beautiful people. Did you know that? I think there may be more beautiful people here than anywhere else in the world."

"Well . . . beauty has its place, I guess," Racquel said, "but I don't think that it ever helped any actor win an Academy Award."

Jacques grinned. "Maybe so, maybe so. You're interested in acting, then?"

Racquel nodded. "That's why I'm here in LA. It's something I've always wanted to do."

Jacques ran a palm along the side of his jaw. "This town is filled with hopefuls. Seems like every waitress is an actress, every gas station attendant an actor or director."

A waiter arrived, wheeling a linen-covered trolley with a sizable bucket of ice atop. There was a large bottle of fine, golden champagne nestled amongst the crushed ice. Jacques waited until the sparkling amber had been poured into two fluted glasses before saying, "So, what have you done?"

Racquel's throat constricted. For a moment, she was tempted to fabricate a long list of accomplishments, but after a flash of weakness she plunged in and gave him the truth.

"I did a few plays in high school. And I was a member of an amateur theatrical group in Idaho. We used to do monthly plays in Boise." *Before I married Ralph.*

"Hmm," Jacques said. "Pity. I'd hoped you might've been right for a part in my next movie. We've been trying to cast it for the past year. Just haven't found the right girl yet, though. It's not enough to be drop-dead gorgeous, you know. You have to be able to act, too."

Racquel burst into immediate speech. "I know I don't have an extensive resumé yet, but I can act, I assure you. Maybe if you'd let me read for you?"

Jacques shook his head. "I . . . don't know. We really need an experienced actress. Someone who knows what to do once she's before the camera. I don't have the time to teach you."

Racquel knotted her fingers together, and prayed that she'd be able to convince him. "Let me read for you. I promise you I can do it."

Jacques gave his watch a glance. "OK. But if you're no good, you'll have to accept that . . . agreed?"

Racquel was enthusiastic. "Oh, yes, you don't have

to worry about that. I'll be fine with your decision, whatever it is."

Jacques stood. "Good. The script is in my suite. We'll have the waiters bring the rest of the champagne up. We can finish it there. OK?"

Racquel blinked. "Your suite?"

Jacques motioned for a waiter. "If you're not comfortable coming up, that's fine. As I said before, the part is really for a much more experienced actress."

Racquel rose slowly. This was a once in a lifetime opportunity, and she would not throw it away foolishly because of any silly puritanical notions.

"I'll read for you," she said.

They were away from the table and in a private elevator going up to the penthouse floor before she even had a chance to possibly rethink her decision. The elevator opened directly into one of the most massive hotel suites Racquel had ever seen. The doors pinged open, and the trolley with the champagne was wheeled out by a waiter dressed in a pristine white jacket with gold buttons running down the front. Jacques pointed the man in the direction of a very well-appointed bar.

"You can leave everything there," he said. "If we need anything else I'll let you know." The waiter nodded, and with a "Thank you, sir," and a deferential bob of his head, he was gone.

Jacques waited until the doors were closed before he turned to his guest. "Come on, come on," he said to Racquel, who still stood in the middle of the shiny parquet foyer, a bit in awe of the palatial surroundings. "Make yourself at home while I go up and get the script."

Racquel followed his portly figure up the curving staircase to the second level. Her heart was beginning to thrash at her ribs again. She took a steadying breath. This was her big chance. She could do this. There was no need to be nervous. She would get the part. She would.

By the time Jacques had returned, Racquel was seated on one of the massive overstuffed sofas and was almost in full control of her nerves. Armand Jacques was now wearing a deep mauve smoking jacket and matching pants of pure silk. He came to sit beside her on the couch, resting an arm along the back. Racquel gave him a hesitant smile.

"I know you're not certain that I can do this, but I want to thank you for at least letting me try."

Jacques removed his arm from the back of the couch and gave her arm a little pat.

"Let's have some more champagne before we get started. OK?"

Racquel nodded. Maybe the drink would help her completely relax.

"To us," Jacques said, and he raised the glass of sparkling liquid, and swallowed it in one gulp. He poured himself another while Racquel gingerly sipped at hers. His obsidian eyes observed her from behind thick glasses while he quickly quaffed the second drink and poured himself yet another. "You don't drink much, do you?" His eyes wandered her face while he sloshed the drink around in his mouth.

"No. I've never really developed a taste for alcohol."

Jacques laughed. "That will change, believe me. Once you've lived in this town for long enough, everything changes. There'll be lots of parties all the time, and lots and lots of booze. If you don't drink, you don't fit in. And if you don't fit in, your career will go down the tubes. Trust me."

Racquel took another swallow of her champagne. She was beginning to feel slightly woozy, so she put the glass down on an oval center table with ornately carved legs and tried to get her eyes into proper focus.

"I . . . I don't think I'd better have any more."

Jacques pressed her hand. "Finish the glass. You'll feel much better." He sidled a little closer to envelop her with a chubby arm. "I won't give you the script unless you finish the glass," he coaxed softly.

Racquel stiffened, and prepared to stand. "No," she said with a hint of frost in her voice. "And if you won't let me read, there's no reason for me to be here." She shrugged out of his embrace and pushed herself to her feet.

For such a portly man, he surprised her by moving with a burst of sudden speed. He grabbed her about the waist, and yanked, hard, and before she could even think to react she was lying on her back on the sofa and he was attempting to clamber atop her. For an instant, her brain stopped cold. It refused to believe what was happening. This was Armand Jacques—one of Hollywood's biggest producers. She was here to get a part. Nothing else. Surely, he couldn't have misunderstood her intention. Surely, he didn't think that she actually wanted this.

She began to struggle as his soft wet lips began pressing kisses against her long, elegant neck.

"Please stop," she said between gasps for breath. "You've misunderstood me, I'm not interested in this—"

"Oh, relax, baby," he purred wetly against her skin. "Don't you want to break into the movies? One word from me, and you could become the next hottest thing out there. Millions of dollars, homes all over the world. Be sensible. It's not so much to ask of you."

Racquel pushed at the spongy flesh that was very close to smothering her, and twisted her head violently from side to side. Flashes of memory came and went before her eyes. It was no longer Armand Jacques atop her, it was Ralph Penniman, and his hands were wrapped about her neck, and he was squeezing and squeezing, trying to cut her breath off, trying to kill her.

She began to fight like a wildcat—kicking, clawing, biting, and even using the blunt of her forehead. Jacques let out a grunt of rage as one of her blows landed somewhere close to his groin. He raised a hand to strike her across the face, but Racquel managed to twist free of him and scramble to her feet. She had lost one shoe, and the straps on her dress were torn and hanging. She lunged for her purse, and pulled out the canister of mace. She held it in front of her.

"Get back," she said, "or I'll use this."

Jacques made another grab for her, but she dodged the bulk of his body, standing aside while he crashed to the ground. Strangely, she felt no fear now. She had made herself a promise when she was back in Idaho— that she would never again allow a man to brutalize her. She meant to keep that promise.

But Armand Jacques was fueled by passion, and too many glasses of liquor. He was also surprisingly resilient to physical pain. He was on his feet in an instant, and before Racquel could make it halfway to the door he was upon her again. She struggled with the mace, pressing the top of it in desperation. She had never used it before, and in her panic she had turned the spray nozzle in the wrong direction. A stream of liquid shot out of the can, but missed Jacques entirely. He knocked the can from her hand, pressed her up against the elevator doors, and fastened his lips to hers. One hand held her steady, while the other grappled with the hem of her dress. With a strength born of true fear,

Racquel managed to get one of her legs between his. She brought it up sharply and felt him grunt, sag away from her, and collapse to the floor. She stood there for long seconds, shivering violently, and taking long, deep breaths. There was a large tear in the front of her dress, and her pantyhose was riddled with runs.

Jacques looked up at her from his position on the floor. Between gasps, he said, "You'll never get an acting job in this town, my girl. I'll see to that."

Racquel trembled, but forced herself to speak bravely. "I'm going to report you. You're . . . you're sick, and shouldn't be allowed out among decent, God-fearing people."

Jacques rolled onto his back and began to chuckle. "You really think anyone'll believe you? A tramp? A starlet? Everyone saw you leave quite willingly with me. I didn't put a gun to your head. This was your decision. In fact, as I remember it, you almost forced yourself on me. You wanted to come up here. You wanted to be with a famous producer. You wanted to use me to further your career." He cackled again. "But I showed you, didn't I? Not quite what you were planning, was it?"

Racquel took a shuddering breath, and pressed the elevator button. The doors opened immediately and she hobbled inside and watched them close. Her eyes were flushed pink, and already there was a tear rolling down the flat of her face. She was not a tramp. Why did all men think she was? Ralph had treated her like one, had called her one. What was it about her that prompted all men to behave so?

How she made it back to her room, she would never know, but once she was back in her little sanctuary, she walked woodenly to the bathroom. Like an automaton, she stripped her ruined dress and hose off, leaving them in a crumpled pile on the floor. Then she stepped under the steaming hot shower and scrubbed her skin until it was almost raw. Over and over again, she passed the bar of soap across the spots where Jacques's lips had touched. She felt violated and unclean, and even after a full hour of scrubbing she couldn't get rid of the feel of his soft lips.

Finally, when her fingers were all pruney and shriveled, she stepped from the cubicle to wrap her body in a large, soft white towel. She went to stand by the window. Her room was on the fourteenth floor, and the lights of the city were spread out before her like a blanket of diamonds. She stood there for a long while, eyes huge, body trembling. Why was she being punished in such a way? What terrible sin had she ever committed to warrant such cruel treatment by fate?

"Oh, God," she said, and hot tears streamed down her face. "Why won't you help me? Acting was the only thing I ever really wanted. Now, it's been taken away."

She stumbled to the bed and pulled open the bedside table drawer. Her eyes fell immediately on the black-bound Gideon Bible. She picked it up and began to read some of the scriptures. The words settled the roiling fear in her, and as she turned page after page a certain calm came over her. She read for hours, and finally fell asleep sprawled on the bedspread, still wrapped in the thick white towel.

She was up and dressed by nine. Somehow, during the night, she had regained a bit of spunk. In the light of day, she was able to analyze with better clarity what had happened to her the night before. Jacques was a predator. The fluid ease with which he had enticed her up to his suite indicated that he must have used that very ploy with many other hopeful actresses. Men like him were the scum of the earth, and she was angry with herself for being so very stupid. She had walked willingly into his clutches. It didn't justify his actions by any means, though, and she wished that there was something she could do about it. He was a very powerful man, undoubtedly, so reporting him to the authorities would do little if any good at all; not without substantial proof of assault. If there had been a witness to what occurred in the suite, she would've been in a much stronger position. As things stood, it was just her word against his.

She sat on the side of her bed, chin cupped in hand, lost in thought. The sound of knocking on the room door brought her back to life. She uncoiled from her sitting position with a certain amount of unconscious elegance, her thick sweep of hair sloping silkily to her shoulders.

"Who is it?" Yesterday, she would have opened the door without making such an inquiry.

"Bellboy," the voice said. "I've got a delivery for you."

Racquel slid the chain into place. "I'm not expecting anything." She opened the door as far as the chain would allow. "You have the wrong room."

The man on the other side of the door grinned at her. From behind his back, he produced a huge bouquet of pink and white roses. "Mr. Armand Jacques sends his compliments."

Racquel felt the muscles in her jaw clench. She couldn't believe the nerve of the man—after what he had attempted to do to her. She felt very much like taking the entire collection of flowers, vase and all, and breaking the arrangement over Mr. Armand Jacques's head.

In a voice that was supremely controlled, she managed to say, "Take them back to Mr. Jacques and let him know that I do not want his flowers, or anything else he might care to give me. And please tell him that if he tries to contact me again, I will be forced to file charges of harassment."

With that, she closed the door, leaving the bewildered bellhop to make what he would of what she had just said.

Four

Two days later, Racquel was snapping her suitcases closed once again. She had found herself a cozy little cottage in the Hollywood Hills, right off Hargrove Drive. It was a wonderful little place which she had leased for surprisingly little money. The owners were off to Paris for a year, and had wanted to get the property off the market quickly. Racquel had fallen in love with the place almost immediately. It was a two-story, with three bedrooms. The kitchen was large and airy, with a stylishly curved center island, and the master bedroom came equipped with its own bathroom and huge, wood burning fireplace. It was the little yard out back, with its orange and lemon trees and finished deck that had finally sold her on the property. She had signed the lease agreement, handed over her deposit, and promised that she would start moving her things in right away.

Shopping for furnishings and other knickknacks had been a pleasurable exercise. She had bought sofas, love-seats, padded wicker chairs for the deck, a huge, four-poster bed, pots and pans, and a collection of other things which she felt would make the cottage seem more homey and lived-in.

She had arranged for all of the big items to be delivered by the end of the week, so she was in a great hurry to ensure that she was there before the trucks started arriving.

She walked across to the phone now, and dialed O for the front desk.

"I need a bellboy, please."

In less than five minutes, there was someone knocking at the door. She had acquired a few more things since she had first checked into the hotel, so she now had two additional bags.

"I'll carry this one," she said when the man attempted to put her handbag atop the pile of cases on his cart. She was not about to let the bag holding the canister of mace out of her sight. Not that she really expected Armand Jacques to accost her in the hotel lobby, but knowing that some manner of protection was close at hand did make her feel considerably more secure.

In the lobby, David, the concierge did his utmost to avoid her gaze, and Racquel was convinced that he had known of Jacques's intentions all along. She tilted her chin a little higher, and followed the luggage cart out the door. The bellboy pushed the luggage to the lip of the curb.

"Do you need a taxi?"

Racquel nodded. "Yes. Thank you."

The man raised an arm, and a green cab sitting at the head of a row of cars started its engine.

Racquel opened her purse and handed the man a generous tip. He opened the car door for her, and very politely guided her in. He was just about to close the door when he paused. "Oh, I almost forgot," he said, and his hand groped for a second in the top pocket of his tunic. "I've a note for you."

Racquel wound down the window, and looked up at him. "A note?"

The bellboy nodded. "It was left in your mail slot."

Racquel accepted the sealed envelope and looked at it for a second, turning it over and back, searching for signs of identification. "It can't be for me," she finally said. "No one . . . I mean, I don't know anyone here in LA." There was only Armand Jacques, and she was reasonably certain that he would not have left her a note of any kind, not after the very brusque manner in which she had returned his flowers.

The bellboy stepped away from the car and gave the roof a little pat. "I'm sure it's for you. Have a safe trip." Before she could say any more, the car was pulling away from the curb.

Racquel waited until they were on the freeway before carefully tearing open the white envelope and extracting the folded piece of paper. It was typewritten, and read simply: *Be Very Careful. I'll Be Watching.*

There was no name. No initials. The stationery was completely devoid of any identifying marks.

Racquel crumpled the paper into a ball, and dropped it into her handbag. She was very glad that she had left the hotel. Again, she had misjudged Armand Jacques. Maybe he derived some sort of demented pleasure from tormenting his victims. She sat back, and passed the back of her hand across her eyes. Suddenly, she felt tired. Why was it that no matter where she went men always felt the need to mistreat her? Or was she being paranoid? She didn't know anymore. The attempted assault was definitely real, and now, this note. What did it mean? Be careful of what? Maybe she *should* go to the police, at least let them know that she had been attacked. But, would they believe her? Wouldn't they just think that she was a disillusioned starlet vengefully getting back at a famous producer who had spurned her? She had no proof, after all, just a typewritten warning of some sort.

A shiver rippled across her skin, and the long, elegant fingers of one hand lifted to massage away the goose-flesh. A thought suddenly occurred to her, and she spun around to look behind. Were they being followed? She peered at the cars directly behind, but could see no one who appeared to be paying particular attention to her. She sat back against the seat and closed her eyes for a moment. Her nerves were beginning to get the better of her. This was probably exactly what Armand Jacques had intended, but she wouldn't buy into his game. There was no one following her.

She forced her eyes back open, and for the remainder of the journey she stared out at the towering skyline of Los Angeles until all the images blended together, and the fear receded to the edges of her mind.

Later that afternoon, when all the furniture had been delivered and everything nicely arranged, Racquel finally allowed herself time to relax and enjoy the soft beauty of the cottage. It was really quite a nice little place now that all the things were in place.

She stood looking around the living room. The only things it needed now were a few potted plants, an aquarium with colorful fish, and a great big, shaggy dog to fall asleep at her feet in the evenings.

Her eyes misted over for a moment. She had always longed for this cozy scene of domesticity. In her girlish daydreams, Stephen had always been the man she had imagined sharing the rest of her life with, but he had gone away. And now, she was destined to spend the rest of her life without love, completely alone, because she found that she could no longer put her trust in men.

She walked slowly up the short flight of stairs. What she really needed was a group of friends—people to hang out with, people who shared at least some of her interests. She wouldn't be so prone to melancholy if she had at least one person to talk to, and, maybe, a dog to keep her company whenever she was alone.

After indulging in a long, hot shower, she sat on the four-poster bed wrapped in a terry cloth bathrobe. She flipped through the phone book until she located the local pound, then spent a bit of time circling various numbers with a fluorescent orange pen and marking a small asterisk beside the ones of particular interest. Tomorrow she would get a dog, and some fish. Next week, she would begin the arduous process of auditioning.

Racquel fell asleep that night with the TV playing, and was unaware when a shadowy figure entered the house just after midnight. The man spent a long while exploring the first floor. He took note of the large butcher's block on one of the counters in the kitchen, and paid particular attention to the many sharp-bladed knives sticking out of the wooden apparatus.

By the time she awoke in the morning her visitor had departed, leaving her none the wiser about his nocturnal visit.

Five

Over the next several days, Racquel found herself falling into a pleasant routine. She awoke just before six, went for a three-mile run, then returned to eat a breakfast of Shredded Wheat cereal, fruit, and nonfat milk. She then spent the remainder of the day going through the auditions magazines, ticking off the projects that caught her attention.

She hadn't quite gotten around to buying the fish yet, or picking out a dog from the pound. She had promised herself that she would before the close of the week. She had also decided to start a flower garden in a patch of dirt just beneath the front window. So, in the evenings, she contented herself with weeding and troweling the tiny patch of earth.

It was on one of these evenings that a neighbor came jogging by. The tiny blonde woman noticed Racquel's solitary figure bent over the flower bed. She continued to run in place for a moment, then decided to go over and introduce herself.

She came to a running stop just behind Racquel, cleared her throat, and spoke. "You must be the new tenant."

Racquel turned, with trowel still in hand. She had been

so engrossed in her weeding that she had not even heard the other woman's approach.

"I'm Morganna," the woman said. "I live just up the hill, at the house on the corner. I've seen you go running by in the mornings."

Racquel wiped her hand on the seat of her trousers, and beamed a welcome. "Racquel," she said. "I'm afraid I'm a bit filthy."

Morganna laughed. "Yes, you are, but I'll forgive you if you invite me in for something to drink. I'm really thirsty."

They shook hands briefly, and Racquel had the immediate impression that they would be friends. "Sure," she said. "I'm glad to take a break from all of this, anyway." She stuck her garden tools into the soft earth and stood gracefully.

"Wow," Morganna said. "You're a beauty. Very lucky thing my Charley is in love with me, or I might be a bit worried."

Racquel grinned at her, taking the compliment in the spirit in which it was meant. "If you only knew the kind of trouble I've gotten myself into because of it."

They entered the living room, and Morganna drew in a breath. "Oh, you've done wonders with the place. I always knew this house could look like this."

"Thanks," Racquel said. "I haven't quite finished decorating yet, though."

Morganna followed her through to the kitchen. "You're not from LA, are you?" she asked, seating herself comfortably at one of the padded stools positioned next to the center island.

Racquel smiled. It was so nice to have someone to talk to. "No, I'm from Idaho. Have you ever been out there?"

Morganna grimaced, shaking her head of short blonde

curls. "God, no. I'd hate to live out in the boonies. No offense meant," she said, darting a quick look at Racquel, "but country life is not for me. I have to be where the excitement is."

"So you're from LA, then?" Racquel asked while pouring two large glasses of pink lemonade and setting down a sizable platter of sugar cookies.

Morganna took a deep drink from her glass before replying. "I'm a Valley girl. I was born in Sherman Oaks. My husband's an attorney for one of the big studios. Warners."

"Wow," Racquel said, impressed. "And what do you do?"

Morganna selected a cookie and took a large bite. Between crunches, she said, "I haven't quite decided yet. I've done a little of everything, but I've never stuck at anything for too long." She leaned forward in a conspiratorial manner. "I think I really prefer just being a housewife. I know that view isn't very popular these days . . . with all the career women on the loose. But"—she shrugged her shoulders—"I like it."

Racquel nodded. "Doing what makes you happy is the important thing. I know . . . believe me."

"Listen," Morganna said, "we're having a party next Saturday night. Why don't you come? There's usually an interesting mix of people. You're an actress . . . right?"

Racquel wrinkled her nose. "Well, not yet. I haven't really done anything major."

Morganna gave an airy wave of her hand. "Don't you know what the credo is in this town? Everyone is a little richer than they really are, a little more accomplished than they really are. It's all image. Nothing more complicated than that. Trust me."

They shared a laugh, and Racquel took a thoughtful

sip of lemonade. "I'd love to come, of course. But—will there be lots of single men at the party?"

Morganna gave her hand a squeeze. "Lots. But don't worry, I'll point out the fakers so you don't waste any time on them."

"Actually, I'd like to stay away from the single ones entirely. I don't want to get involved with anyone right now."

Morganna gave a thoughtful, "Hmm," and shot a speculative look her way. "Let me guess. You've had a run of bad luck with men?"

Racquel swept her long hair back behind both ears. She was undecided about how much information to share with her new friend. It was obvious that Morganna was an extroverted type, and it might very well be that whatever was shared with her would ultimately be passed along to a multitude of others.

"Well, I'm recently divorced, and it's too soon for me to get back into the swing of things."

"Oh." Morganna said, and clasped her hand warmly. "I'm so sorry. Do you want to talk about it?"

Racquel stood and went to the sink. She put down the empty platter of sugar cookies, and turned on the tap.

"It was a bad relationship. I wasn't sorry to see it end. It's made me cautious about getting involved with someone else. I'm not even sure that I want to go through all that ever again. It doesn't seem worth all the trouble."

Morganna frowned. "I guess I've been lucky with Charley. A lot of my friends are on their second and third marriages. But the thing is"—she brightened considerably—"you can't give up just because you've had one bad experience. You have to be willing to take a chance again."

Racquel wondered what her bubbly neighbor would have to say if she knew that her ex-husband had more or less threatened to do her injury should she become involved with another man. She was certain that Morganna would have something bright and brave to say about restraining orders and things of that nature, but she didn't know Ralph Penniman. She wouldn't understand the great lengths to which he would go to prevent her from finding happiness with another man.

"I suppose I'm just a coward," Racquel said.

Morganna came to stand beside her. "Well," she said, "coward or not, you have to come to my party. Look"—she turned her face so that Racquel could see her profile—"can you tell that I've had a lift?"

Racquel gave her a startled glance. "A lift?"

Morganna grinned at her. "A face-lift, silly. Everyone here has one sooner or later. Charley gave me one for my thirty-fifth. What do you think? Pretty good work, huh?"

Racquel blinked, momentarily wrestling with embarrassment. She had never before run into such an utterly candid person.

"I'd never have guessed if you hadn't told me," she finally managed, and it was the truth. Morganna's face was smooth and completely wrinkle-free. Had she not been told to the contrary, Racquel would have guessed her age to be no more than twenty-five.

She nodded. "Dr. KirPatrick's work. He's one of the best plastic surgeons in Beverly Hills. It's almost impossible to get onto his client list, of course. He's booked for years. All the stars use him." Morganna gave her a conspiratorial wink. "He's not married, by the way . . . and he's rolling in dough. There are very few single females in Hollywood who haven't thrown themselves at him. Some married ones, too."

Racquel wondered briefly whether Morganna was one of the married ones. She did seem like such a social gadfly, constantly in search of one excitement after the next.

"I'm not one of them, of course," Morganna was saying, and Racquel gave her a slightly guilty look. Her face was always so readable. Ralph had always said so.

"Oh . . . I didn't," she stammered, "I didn't think you were. Really."

Morganna chuckled. "If something did go wrong between Charley and me, though, I'd be first in line."

Despite herself, Racquel laughed. It was absolutely impossible not to like the woman. "You are crazy," she said. "You must have a whole pack of friends, huh?"

"A few, a few," Morganna said. "Listen, I've an idea—why don't we go running together in the mornings? It'll be much more fun than running on our own, don't you think?"

"Sure," Racquel agreed. "But, I have to warn you, I get up kind of early."

"Perfect. So do I. I'll meet you at your front door tomorrow at six-fifteen. OK?"

And with that, she was gone, breezing through the kitchen doorway. She paused on the stony drive outside to give a cheery little wave, then continued her jog up the hill.

Racquel went back out to finishing up her weeding. Things were looking up. She now had a friend. Life was wonderful, indeed.

Later that afternoon, she finally decided to get a dog. Her old yellow Volkswagen bug, which she had bought at the local used car dealership, performed marvelously. Although it did exhibit a tendency to backfire rather loudly whenever they were going up steep hills, she wasn't considerably worried. She had paid a relatively paltry sum for it, so a few fixable flaws were to be expected.

She had spent no more than fifteen minutes walking between the many cages at the pound before a huge, shaggy, black-and-white dog caught her attention.

"What kind is he?" she asked, pointing at the massive animal which sat rather forlornly within the confines of the tiny cage.

The attendant took a look, scratched his head, then said, "Dunno. It could be a Saint Bernard mix. You don't want this one. He'll eat you out of house and home, and . . . see those hairs, you'll spend a fortune keeping your carpets clean."

"Hmm," Racquel said, "is he sick? He doesn't seem to have much energy, somehow."

"He's OK. He probably knows that he's next in line to be put down. Animals sense these things, you know." The man proceeded to bang on the bars of the cage with a thick stick. In response, the big dog's ears lifted, then flopped back down again.

"I'll take him," Racquel said. There was no way on earth she was going to walk away from the cage now, knowing that the poor animal was going to be euthanized.

It was a bit of a struggle to get the massive dog into the tiny car, but after a lot of coaxing, pushing, and shoving she and the attendant finally managed to get the animal situated in the passenger seat. All the way back home, Racquel was forced to steer with one hand, and control the dog with the other. Having been liberated from the cage, he was intent on lathering her face with a rash of very wet kisses.

Once she had safely made it back, she pulled slowly into the front yard and threw open the passenger door.

With no encouragement whatsoever, the dog sprang from the car, and proceeded to tear about the yard, trampling all over the neat little flower beds on which Racquel had spent so much time that very afternoon. After ten very unsuccessful minutes of chasing him around trees and other shrubbery, Racquel decided to give up. She sank, panting, onto one of the stone stairs leading to the front door of the cottage.

"OK," she said, "you win. I can't chase you anymore." The dog flopped onto its paws a short distance off, watching her with bright eyes. Every so often his tail gave an encouraging thump on the grass.

"You think it's all a game, don't you?" Racquel said softly. "You're just a big puppy. Just a big playful baby. How could anyone have let you end up in the pound?"

She stood, brushing her hands against the seat of her pants. From her pants pocket, she produced a set of keys. She jingled them in her hand. "I'm going inside now. Wanna come?" She opened up the front door, walked in a few paces, then poked her head out again. "Come on, I won't hurt you."

The dog stood, wagged vigorously, took a couple of very cautious steps toward the door, then sat again. Racquel decided to just leave the front door open for a while. She was certain that eventually the poor animal would work up the nerve to come in. She had already decided on a name for him. Since he was so very hairy, Shaggy seemed very appropriate.

She headed straight for the sizable freezer in the kitchen. She opened up the lid and peered in. Before deciding to get a grown dog, she had stocked up at the local butcher shop on cheap cuts of meat. She selected one of these now, and put it to thaw under the hot water tap. With that taken care of, she went upstairs to the master bedroom suite to change into a pair of sweats.

It was while she was going through one of her dresser drawers that she caught sight of the object. Her hands paused in their busy activities, and she straightened slowly. A music box. There were two intricately fashioned figurines poised atop the lid. One was holding a sharp dagger to the throat of the other.

She reached out a hand hesitantly, and lifted the box from the top of the dresser. Her fingers were ice cold as she lifted the lid. There was nothing inside, and no music came. She turned to look around the room. Someone had been in the house while she'd been out, and they wanted her to know it.

Racquel backed slowly from the room. Maybe they were still in the house—hiding somewhere, waiting until she was asleep in bed. Something fuzzy pressed at her from behind, and she narrowly managed to still the high-pitched scream that rose in her throat by clamping a hand across her mouth.

"Shaggy," she said with a tremor in her voice. "God, you scared the life out of me."

The dog thumped his tail, then sat heavily on her feet. She reached down to scratch him behind the ears.

With the dog there beside her, she felt brave again. She went across to the phone and dialed the local police station.

"Someone's broken into my house," she told them. She answered a few routine questions, then a tired sounding voice said, "OK, ma'am, we'll send a detective over."

Several hours later, after answering a lot of questions, Racquel sat in bed absently channel surfing. She couldn't seem to focus on anything at all. Two detectives had shown up and had given the house a very thorough going-over, but had found nothing particularly significant to report.

They had taken the music box along to the station for fingerprinting. She had also told them about the note which the hotel bellboy had given her. They had taken a look at that, and then taken it along, also. The only recommendation they offered upon leaving was that she get the locks on all the entry doors changed right away. The senior detective had appeared a bit regretful when he'd finally said that there was nothing else they could do.

Racquel called the locksmiths as soon as the two policemen had gone. She had them install some of their best locking devices on all the doors. They put dead bolts on the front and kitchen doors, and assured her that no one would be able to get through the locks. The only way in would be by blast force.

She had thanked them nicely, but had still experienced a shiver of fear once they had driven off and she was alone again. Who was stalking her and why? Why had they left her the music box? Was it Armand Jacques? Surely not. The man was nothing more than a cheap pickup artist, masquerading as a Hollywood producer. But, if it was not Jacques, who could it be? Her ex-husband was still in Idaho. He could not have discovered that she had intended to go to LA, and not New York. Could he? She had been so careful.

She sat for several minutes staring into space, her forehead furrowed in thought. Maybe she should have told the police about him, but she hadn't really considered Ralph as a possible suspect—until now. Her hand hovered over the telephone. She was tempted to call his number in Idaho, just to see if he was there. But if he was at home, and he did answer, his Caller ID would pick up her number, and then he just might figure out where she was.

She sank lower in bed, pulling the covers up around her chin. She was glad of one thing, though—she did have a very huge dog in the room now. If the intruder, whoever he was, did return, he'd be in for a very unpleasant shock.

She patted the bedcovers beside her. "Come on up, Shaggy." After a brief hesitation, the dog sprang agilely onto the blankets and settled down with a contented sigh, directly on her feet. Within an hour, she had drifted off into a fitful sleep.

Just before midnight, a silent figure clambered over the fence and headed toward a window on the bottom floor of the cottage. Skillful hands worked silently for several minutes. Once entry had been gained, he padded on soft feet to the kitchen. For what he intended, he would need the use of a very large knife.

Six

If there was one thing Sean KirPatrick could not stand, it was shopping at the local grocery store. He usually tried to do his shopping late at night, when there were few people around. Although he was not a celebrity by any means, his face was well-known in certain circles and he was well aware that among the Hollywood jet set he was considered one of the most eligible bachelors around.

He didn't have any illusions as to why he was so very highly sought after, of course. It was a simple matter of finances. Once a woman got to a certain age she began, quite naturally, to look around in earnest for someone to settle with—someone to provide her with love and security.

He didn't have anything against marriage as an institution. He just was not ready to get seriously involved with anyone yet. His last few relationships had run their course, then naturally fizzled when it became apparent to the women in question that he had no intention of proposing. He was in no great hurry to jump back into a dating situation, either. He was quite content to return to his lonely bed each night after spending most of the day working in the well-equipped surgery unit at the private clinic where he practiced his craft.

There was something about plastic surgery that had always attracted him. It had been the ideal choice of specialty as far as he was concerned. It was a unique combination of art and medicine, of light and the absence of it. Every day his patients expected him to work miracles. And in every instance, he did. From one case to the next, his level of skill continued to climb. It was comforting to know that he was not required to make any life or death decisions. He did not have to face the kind of pressure that a heart surgeon was routinely under, nor did he want to. Holding someone else's tenuous existence almost literally in the palm of his hand was the kind of responsibility he hoped he would never be faced with.

"Dr. KirPatrick?"

The light, inquiring voice caused a feeling of dread to settle in the pit of Sean KirPatrick's stomach. He had thought himself safe. He had almost made it through the entire store without running into a single woman who wanted his advice or counsel, or more. He turned from his contemplation of a large spread of succulent peaches, a polite smile stretching his lips. The tiny blonde looked familiar, but he couldn't quite place her.

"Hello," he said. "Doing some late shopping, are you?"

The blonde gave him an exuberant grin. "Milk. Charley goes through the stuff like there's no tomorrow."

Sean returned the smile while wondering how he might get out of the current situation without being absolutely rude. She, at least, appeared to be involved with someone, so she was obviously not in search of a late-night conquest.

"You don't remember me, do you?" the blonde said after a moment of silence.

Sean turned back to the peaches. Over his shoulder, he said, "I'm embarrassed to say I don't."

"Morganna O'Bannon." She held her face in profile. "Two years ago, I was under your knife."

A chord of memory twanged, and Sean flicked a quick look at the woman's jawline. His meticulous eye followed the soft lines of her face, running over the nose, the mouth area, and then drifting to the ears. A face-lift, he decided.

"You look very good," he finally said. "Not thinking of having anything else done just yet, I hope." He never encouraged his patients to overdo it. In fact, he would only agree to perform surgery if, in his opinion, it was really needed. The woman standing before him was quite youthful in appearance. With the tightening of the skin, the average layperson would probably guess that she was in her twenties.

Morganna selected a huge peach and handed it to him. "Oh, no. No," she said. "I don't intend having anything else done for years yet. But you can be sure that if and when I do, I'll be coming back to you. I think you're a wonderful doctor. Try this, too." She handed over another peach.

Sean accepted the fruit, since there was little else he could do. He considered the selection of peaches a very personal undertaking. He never allowed anyone to do this for him. He had, after all, developed an almost foolproof technique of determining just the right quality of ripeness. If a peach did not have that certain, indefinable texture and freshness, he would not eat it.

"Doctor KirPatrick," Morganna continued while earnestly selecting yet more fruit. "I never really got a chance to thank you for the brilliant job you did on me—"

Sean stayed her hand. "That's quite enough peaches for me, I think."

"What about some apples, or maybe strawberries?" she asked, and before he could reply she had torn off another plastic bag and was busy in the selection of an assortment of other fruit.

Despite himself, Sean found that he was struggling against an almost overpowering desire to laugh. The woman was virtually unstoppable, and he didn't have the heart to tell her that he had no intention of eating any of the fruit which she had so willingly selected.

She handed him another bag filled to the brim, and Sean obligingly dropped it into his cart. "I'd like you to come to a party I'm throwing on Saturday," she said, giving him a quick look.

Sean scratched the side of his jaw for a moment. It was a policy of his to never socialize with any of his single patients, and he was not overly fond of attending parties where he, as a matter of course, was a part of the evening's menu.

"Miss O'Bannon—"

"Oh, I'm married, you know," Morganna interrupted. "So, you don't have to worry about me flinging myself at you."

Sean blinked at her, momentarily embarrassed. "Well, I didn't think—"

"Not that I wouldn't if I were single, you understand? You are very good-looking," she rushed on, a note of apology in her voice.

This time, there was no way of controlling the humor that consumed him. Sean threw back his head and laughed. She was actually apologizing for not being able to throw herself at him.

"You're quite a woman," he said. "Your husband's a lucky man. But . . . I don't really attend many parties. They're not my favorite thing to do."

"Hmm," Morganna said. "I've heard that before. You know, you're too young to be so stodgy. Listen"—she whipped out a business card and pen—"here's my address. It's just going to be a barbecue type thing, nothing formal. Steaks, hamburgers, roasted corn . . . music. If you decide to come, make sure you get there by about eight." She pressed the card into his hand. "I'd be so happy if you could make an exception, just this once."

Sean was uncertain of what to say in response, so he just said nothing at all. He watched her walk away. Then, when he was certain that she was nowhere in sight, he began returning the bagged fruits to their respective bins.

Racquel's eyes sprang open as soon as the heavy weight on her legs lifted. She reached for the base of the lamp and turned the small knob. The dog was standing near the door, its large ears at rigid attention.

"Shaggy?" Racquel whispered. "Is there someone out there?"

The dog sniffed at the crack beneath the door, backed up a bit, then released a volley of bloodcurdling growls.

Racquel's heart began to beat in heavy thumps against her breastbone. Someone was in the house again. Not only were they in the house, but they appeared to be somewhere right outside her bedroom door. She reached a trembling hand for the phone, and whispered her need for help into the mouthpiece.

"Tell them to hurry," she said, "please."

From her position in the middle of the bed, she honestly expected to see the golden door handle begin its slow, inevitable turn. The door was locked from the inside, but what if the man had a gun? The thought of it made her tremble. Why in the name of heaven was she being tormented by this person? What did he want from her? Was he trying to scare her to death? Was that it? Did he just want to keep her in a state of constant fear? Or was his intention decidedly more sinister?

After a few more growls, the dog returned to sit on the bed. Racquel reached out a hand and ran it up and down his huge back.

"Good boy," she said, and she bent to rest her face against his furry neck. She had never been more glad that she had decided to bring him home from the pound.

Minutes later, there were flashing red and blue lights outside, and someone pounding at the front door.

With the dog at her side, she opened the bedroom door, took a quick look around, then darted down the stairs. What followed was a situation much like the one earlier in the day. The police officers took a look around the house and searched the yard and perimeter, only to return with the news that there was no sign of anyone at all. In fact, they told her, they could find no evidence that anyone had been on the property, at all.

Then came the questions. This time, they were a lot more suspicious.

"Do you have a boyfriend, miss?"

"No . . . no I don't. But, I have an ex-husband."

"Where?"

She told them.

"Have you ever lived on your own before?"

"Yes, of course I have."

It suddenly struck Racquel that they did not believe her story. They didn't believe that anyone had been in the house, at all. They probably thought that she was some hysterical female, fearful of every squeak on the staircase and every shadow in the hall.

"I'm telling you there was someone in the house," she said, and she willed her voice not to quiver. "I'm not imagining things. The dog—he woke up first. He started barking . . . and snarling at the door—"

The police sergeant looked at her with disbelieving eyes. "Did you see anyone?"

Racquel shook her head. "No . . . but I know he was there. I know. If it wasn't for the dog, I'm sure he would've broken the door down. I'm sure he meant to do me harm this time."

Detective Joseph shut his notepad and rose to his feet. He wasn't unfamiliar with cases of this type. Maybe there was someone stalking her, maybe not. It was very hard to tell sometimes without hard evidence. It could be that she was suffering from nothing more serious than a severe case of loneliness. Solitude sometimes did strange things to people.

He handed over a business card. "Maybe you should get to know some of your neighbors, Miss Ward. Maybe help organize a neighborhood watch group. In the meantime, though, I would recommend that you install a burglar alarm. It should make you feel a lot more secure."

Racquel accepted the card, and assured him that she would look into installing an alarm system on Monday. She was beginning to feel quite the fool. She hadn't seen anyone at all, after all. Maybe she had let her nerves get the better of her. It wasn't possible for someone to slip in and out of a house without leaving a trace of physical evidence behind, was it?

She stood at the window and watched the car drive away. There were no flashing lights now, since there was no emergency.

Before going back up to bed she checked all the doors and windows. Everything was as it should be, except for a slightly loose latch on one of the front windows. She would also get that fixed on Monday, she decided, and she *would* get to know her neighbors. Until now, she had been uncertain as to whether or not she should attend Morganna's party, but there was little point in hiding from the world any longer. If she was going to at least try to have a normal life, she would have to interact with men again. They couldn't all be like her ex-husband.

She settled back against the pillows, and spent the next several hours planning how she would spend the upcoming week. She had two auditions scheduled for Monday. One was for a recurring role on one of the daytime soaps, and the other a bit part in a sitcom. She had managed to secure both auditions without the services of an agent, but she was beginning to realize that she might need one of those, too.

She drifted off to sleep just before daylight, and came sharply awake a mere hour later, to the insistent sound of the doorbell. She gave her watch a lightning glance, then sprang from beneath the covers. She had overslept. She swept her hair back, and leaned out of the bedroom window.

"Morganna," she called out, "I'll be right down. Wait for me, OK?"

Morganna gave her a cheery wave. "Thought you might have gone without me."

"Not a chance," Racquel said, "I just overslept. I'll be right down."

She rushed into the adjoining bathroom, gave her face a good dousing with ice cold water, then swept her hair into a ponytail and secured it with a barrette. She creamed the skin under her eyes, got into her black stretch pants and gray jacket, then slid her feet into her old worn-out sneakers. She spent only a moment tying the laces. Then, with Shaggy at her side, she went springing down the stairs. She was glad it was morning. The events of the previous night still had her feeling a bit jittery, but daylight made her feel safer.

She pulled open the front door. "Sorry to keep you waiting out here in the cold."

Morganna wrinkled her nose at her. "I'll forgive you this time. What happened? Couldn't sleep last night?"

Racquel nodded. "Yeah, I sometimes suffer from insomnia. I'm often awake for hours during the night." She didn't want to tell Morganna about the break-in, just in case she had imagined the entire thing.

"Hmm," Morganna said. "Ready to go?"

They started off at a slow trot.

Morganna gave her a sidelong look. "How far do you usually run?"

"Usually three miles. Sometimes four, if I really want to press myself."

"Good," Morganna grinned. "Do you mind if we take a different route today?"

"No," Racquel said, "I don't really care too much where we go. As long as I get my exercise in."

After they had covered a few hundred yards, Morganna said, "You'll never guess who I ran into last night."

Racquel picked up the pace a bit, and Morganna followed. "Last night?"

"In the grocery store," Morganna said with a somewhat smug look on her face.

"Oh, God, Morganna," Racquel groaned. "You're not

thinking of matching me up with that doctor you were telling me about, are you?"

"Sean KirPatrick. He's gorgeous, I promise you. And a really nice guy."

Racquel patted the sweat away from the space just above her top lip. "My ex-husband was supposed to be a really nice guy, too. I found out a little too late that he was more image than substance."

"Dr. KirPatrick is different. I know you'll like him."

"I'm sure I won't."

They turned down a long, winding, two-laned road with large leafy trees shrouding either side of the street. The houses on the street were huge, and set quite a distance back from the roadway.

"We call this area Millionaire's Row. Nothing here costs anything under two million."

"Wow," Racquel said in response. She was genuinely impressed by the well-manicured lawns, and the enormous size of each house. "Do movie stars live around here?"

Morganna shrugged with the true nonchalance of an LA native. "A few." She pointed to a pink house on the corner. "That one used to belong to a British pop star. Nice guy. I would see him every morning as I went running by."

"Listen," Racquel said, after a few more minutes had passed. "I'm sorry if I sounded kind of abrupt about this Sean Patrick . . . or whatever his name is."

"KirPatrick," Morganna corrected obligingly.

"OK, Sean KirPatrick. It's just that I don't really feel that there's anyone out there for me. There was someone once. A long time ago. But that was . . . was when I was a kid . . . just a foolish daydream. And, nothing ever came of it."

"What happened to him?"

Racquel shrugged. "Who knows. No one thought he'd ever amount to anything. I always thought they were wrong, but maybe . . . they were right, after all. He left Idaho years ago."

"Oh," Morganna said, "puppy love. We all have one of those experiences. Trust me. It's never the real thing, though. You find that out once you're an adult."

"Maybe." It was Racquel's turn to sound noncommittal.

They turned down another rather exclusive-looking lane and Morganna said, "I have a confession to make. I hope you don't get mad at me but we're running in the direction of the good doctor's house right now."

"We're what?" Racquel's footsteps faltered a bit.

"He leaves for work every morning at around six-thirty. I wanted him to meet you."

Racquel gave her jogging clothes a quick glance. "Oh, no . . . not like this. Not that it matters of course, but, I'm—I'm not prepared. Maybe tomorrow."

Morganna grabbed her by the hand. "Come on, you look fine. Better than most women look all day."

"I don't want to meet him," Racquel said, and there was a trace of stubborn resistance in her voice.

"We'll just say 'Hi.' He's as regular as clockwork. He should be walking out to his car right about now." She glanced at her watch, and then back at the large house which they were rapidly approaching. Almost on cue, the front door swung open and a tall man emerged. He was dressed in business attire, and to Racquel's keen eye he appeared more suited to the business world than to the friendlier world of medicine.

"We'll run up slowly . . . then pause at the head of the drive. Jog in place for a moment—you know, as though we're trying to get our breath back. OK?"

"He'll know what we're up to for sure," Racquel whispered fiercely.

The doctor came slowly down the walkway to where his black Jaguar was parked. His head was slightly bent, and he obviously had not a clue that there was anyone else in the vicinity.

"Let's just run on by," Racquel pleaded. "He doesn't look as though he wants to be bothered."

Morganna ignored her and called out a very cheery, "Good morning, Doctor."

The man's head came up immediately, and for some reason which was unclear to Racquel he gave her a very pointed stare before turning his attention to the woman who had called out to him.

"Good morning," he said, coming forward. "Morganna O'Bannon, isn't it?"

"That's right," Morganna said, and she gave Racquel a discreet shove with her arm. "We were running by and noticed you coming out. Heading to work, are you?"

The doctor looked at Racquel again, and a strange tightness grabbed hold of her vocal cords.

"Have we met before?" he asked, and his very direct eyes met and held hers.

Racquel blinked a few times before managing a rather strangled, "No. I don't think so. I'm Racquel."

He smiled at her. "You must remind me of someone."

Racquel, who was never at a loss for words around men, found that she could think of nothing intelligible to say.

Morganna cast a worried look in her direction, then plunged in to the rescue. "So, have you decided whether or not you'll come to my party Saturday night?"

"If time permits, I might." The doctor glanced at his watch. "Well, I have to get off to the office now. I have an early consultation." His eyes flickered over Racquel once more. "It was very nice meeting you," he said. "See you later," he said to Morganna.

After he had driven off, Morganna gave her a very satisfied look. "I had a feeling about both of you, and I'm never wrong about these things. So what do you think of him? Not too shabby, huh?"

Racquel swallowed away the dryness in her throat. "He's not . . . what I expected. He's very handsome. And, he has . . . kind eyes."

"Glad I made you come, then? Not mad at me?"

Racquel laughed. "I should be, but I'm not. He's probably deeply involved with someone right now, though. Men like that always are."

Morganna broke into a trot again. "He's not. I did some checking."

"God, you're incredible," Racquel said. "Are you sure you're not with the CIA?"

For the remainder of the run they joked back and forth, and a burst of unexplainable happiness was glowing in the depths of Racquel's eyes by the time they were back at her doorstep.

Morganna flopped down onto the front steps and began to fan herself vigorously. "Whew," she said, "it's going to be warm today. Kind of hot for February."

"Come in and have something to drink," Racquel said, opening the front door. They were immediately greeted by a flurry of welcoming barks. Racquel whistled and clicked her fingers. "Here, Shag," she said, "here, Shaggy boy. It's me." The dog trundled forward and plastered her hand with kisses.

Morganna gave the animal a dubious glance. "Whoa. Where did that monster come from?"

Racquel bent down to give the dog a hug. "Picked him up at the pound. Isn't he beautiful? And very protective too . . . aren't you, Shaggy boy?" She scratched him under the chin. The dog gave a deep bark, and seemed to understand every word she was saying.

Morganna looked him over with a critical eye. "He needs a bath and a trim. Why don't we take him to be groomed later on today? Unless you've got plans?"

Racquel glided easily to her feet. "Nope. No plans. Sounds like a great idea."

"Maybe, we might go shopping, then? Ever been to the Redondo Beach Pier? They sell some of the best seafood I have ever tasted. They have all sorts of fish, crab, lobster—you name it."

Racquel smiled, and for some reason silly tears clamored at the backs of her eyes.

"Thank you," she said, "for being . . . so good . . . and so friendly. You can't imagine how alone I've been. You just can't imagine." She clasped Morganna's hand, and the other woman enveloped her in a quick hug.

"Come on, come on," she said after a bit, "I'm pretty sure you would do the same for me, if I was the one who was new in town."

Racquel sniffled and removed several squares of Kleenex from her pocket. She dabbed at her eyes, then gave her nose a good blow. "I'm sorry. I'm not usually so emotional. It's just that I've been under such a strain for such a very long time."

Morganna gave her back a pat. "Listen. I'll run home, clean up a bit, maybe grab something to eat, and meet you back here at about noon. We'll take my truck, OK? I don't think we can all fit into your Volkswagen bug. We definitely won't be able to get him in." She jabbed a finger at the dog.

Racquel beamed. She was over the little bubble of emotion now. "Yeah, I didn't figure on owning such a big animal when I got the car. But"—she gave the dog a hug—"I love him."

"Well, see you in a little bit," Morganna said with an airy wave.

The remainder of the day passed quickly after that—much too quickly, as far as Racquel was concerned.

Morganna was back, as promised, by midday. She helped Racquel coax the dog into the backseat of her 4X4 truck, then screeched away from the gateway and accelerated down the hill, barely giving Racquel enough time to safely belt herself into the passenger seat.

They stopped at the groomers first, and Racquel spent a bit of time explaining exactly what she wanted done. Once she was convinced that the dog would be well taken care of, they decided to take a window shopping stroll down Rodeo Drive. Morganna dragged her from store to store, insisting that she try on this or that item of apparel.

"We have to find you something for Saturday," she said.

"But I thought it was going to be casual—you know, jeans and a T-shirt? Isn't that what you said?"

"For everyone else. Not for you. The doctor's going to be there."

"Listen," Racquel said, "Doctor KirPatrick may not even be there. He seemed very uncertain about coming. And, besides, even if he does show up I'm still not interested in—"

"OK . . . OK," Morganna said, whipping a long floral dress from the rack and holding it up before the mirror. "Let's just find you something nice, then. You don't have to wear it on Saturday if you don't want to."

Still protesting, Racquel was hustled into a changing room. From the space just above the door, Morganna continued to hand her garments. Every so often she called out, "Do you have that one on yet? You do? Great, come on out."

It soon became very clear to Racquel that they were attracting quite a bit of attention. The other patrons in the store had actually paused in their browsing to observe the rather unexpected fashion show. Somewhere near the end of it, the store manager came down from his office, and Racquel was certain that they were going to be asked, quite politely, to leave the premises. He surprised her by asking in a very pleasant manner, "Which magazines have I seen you on the cover of?"

Before Racquel could utter a single word, Morganna was saying, "Do you mean recently?"

What transpired thereafter was the most incredible recitation of bald-faced lies that Racquel had ever been witness to. At one point during the lengthy discourse Racquel attempted to restrain Morganna by giving her a none too gentle prod in the side, but it had little effect. The outcome of the entire tangle was that Racquel was invited to appear on the cover of the store's fall fashion catalog.

Once they were out of the store with their purchases cradled beneath their arms, Racquel finally let go: "Oh my God," she said. "How could you tell that man all those lies? And why did he even believe you?"

"Oh, take it easy," Morganna said cheerily, "he'll never check on any of the details. He won't even remember half of what I told him about you, anyway. All he really cares about is whether or not his clothes sell. And, judging by the way everyone stopped to look when you tried on a few items, he knows that you can help him sell them. That's why he came down to talk to you. He was hoping that you were a professional model. I just gave him exactly what he wanted."

Racquel shook her head. "You're incredible. I think you may have finally found your niche."

Morganna grinned at her. "Would you like to be my first client? I'll get you tons of work. Modeling and acting. I do know all the right people, after all."

"I'd take you up on that if I thought you were really serious," Racquel said.

Morganna gave her a speculative look. "Really?"

Racquel nodded. "Why not? I don't have an agent yet. You don't have a niche yet. Sounds like a good combination to me. Especially since you're so darn good at it."

Morganna dropped her packages in the back of the truck, then turned to give Racquel an exuberant hug. "OK. Let's do it," she said, her eyes shining with enthusiasm. "Charley can take care of all the legal stuff for me, and . . . oh, I don't know why I never thought of this before. This is going to be great."

All the way back to the groomers they chatted animatedly about the new idea.

"Maybe I'll rent a little office somewhere," Morganna said. "I'll call it the C. Morganna Talent Agency. How about that? C for Charley."

"Sounds catchy," Racquel said. "I like it. When am I going to meet Charley, anyway?"

"If you invite us over for dinner, you'll meet him tonight."

Racquel laughed. "You have to be the most direct person I have ever met."

"So what does that mean," Morganna asked, "are we invited or not?"

Racquel shoved her with an elbow. "Of course you're invited. Maybe I can prepare some of that seafood, if we ever make it to . . . where was it again?"

"Redondo Beach," Morganna said, opening the door

to the groomers and ushering Racquel through in a mother-henlike fashion.

They collected Shaggy, who now looked like an entirely different animal, then headed down the freeway to the beach. The remainder of the afternoon was spent scouring the many tiny shops scattered along the Redondo pier. With the dog tethered to a retractable leash, they walked in and out of makeshift galleries, trinket stands, and interesting little sweet shops where the candy was made while they watched. They even stopped at a little curio shop where they both had their fortunes read by a colorfully dressed woman of indeterminate age.

As the afternoon began winding down, they stood for a while at one of the wooden rails, watching as scores of people dangled their fishing poles in the ocean. The wind whipped the hair about Racquel's face, but she made absolutely no attempt to tame it. For the first time in her life, she felt completely free. Life was vibrant and full of exciting possibilities.

"You know," she said, turning to Morganna, "I don't think I've ever felt like this before. I feel as if something wonderful's about to happen to me. You know, almost as though I know that from now on everything's going to be all right."

"Your ex-husband must've been a real creep," Morganna said. "Maybe you should talk about what happened when you were with him . . . it might help you to get all that stuff off your chest."

"Maybe," Racquel agreed. All day long she had been trembling on the verge of telling Morganna about the strange things that had been happening to her over the last few days: the note, the music box, the break-ins. She still wasn't sure yet if she should. Morganna didn't know her well enough yet. She didn't want her to think that she was in the process of befriending a blossoming nut case.

"Let's go get that fish," Morganna said after a long span of companionable silence. "The wind's beginning to get cold."

By the time they made it back to the cottage, the first flush of twilight was already beginning to drift across the sky. Racquel carted her load of packages indoors, then collapsed on the couch in the living room.

"What a day," she said.

Morganna came to sit beside her. "Are you thinking what I'm thinking?"

"Rain check?" Racquel asked, pulling her feet up onto the couch and stretching back to rest her head on the thickly padded arm.

Morganna nodded. "I don't think I'm up for any more entertainment tonight. Do you mind?"

"Mind?" Racquel yawned. "I could almost kiss you, but I'm too tired to even move."

"Well, I'm gonna go home," Morganna said, standing. "Charley usually gets in by about seven. I'll whip some food together for him, and turn in early."

"Don't forget to talk to him about the agency thing," Racquel said. "It's a good idea."

"Oh don't worry, kiddo"—she winked—"we'll make a lot of money together."

Racquel walked her to the door and stood watching as she drove away. Then she went to the kitchen and spent several minutes putting away all the things she had bought. The fish she put in large, ziplock bags before stacking them neatly in the freezer. She was in the middle of steeping the shrimp in spicy vinegar when the phone rang. She ran hot water on her hands, wiped them on the front of her apron, then picked up the phone and said, "Hello?"

There was a short silence. Then a raspy voice said, "I saw you today . . . did you like the music box?"

She gripped the phone a little tighter and asked in a firm voice, "Who is this?"

"You looked lovely in that running suit. Long legs . . . beautiful face—"

Racquel slammed the receiver into the cradle and stood there for a long moment, taking deep, almost painful breaths. Her heart hammered at her ribs, and it was quite a while before she could still the trembling in her limbs. When she was calmer she walked around the house, shutting and locking every open window. She knew one thing for certain, now—it wasn't Ralph Penniman who was tormenting her. It was someone else entirely—someone she didn't even know, a faceless maniac who intended to do her harm.

She made herself walk back into the kitchen and, very deliberately, she spent a long while putting the rest of the seafood away. She would not let whoever it was scare her any longer. Tomorrow she would get the burglar alarm, and everything would be fine. This was probably the way this particular man got his kicks. She had heard all the stories about the weirdos in Los Angeles. It was just unfortunate that she seemed to be running into more than her fair share of them.

When the phone began to ring again, she ignored it. She needed a Caller ID box. That way, she'd be able to know exactly who was calling before she picked it up. She stretched out on the living room couch, listening as the answering machine picked up. There was a pause, and then a voice said, "Ah . . . Racquel, this is Sean—Sean KirPatrick. We met this morning—"

Racquel sat up, her attention riveted. She listened as

the doctor left his message, and reached immediately for a notepad and pen to scribble down his number. He had called her. How had he gotten her number? Her brow furrowed in thought for a minute. Then she remembered that her number was listed.

She decided to go up and take a shower first before calling him back. In the shower she stood beneath the spray, wondering what she would say to him. Maybe he had not called to ask her out on a date. Maybe he'd been trying to get hold of Morganna to let her know that he would not be attending the party. Maybe that was it.

She spent a few minutes blow-drying her hair while Shaggy snoozed at the foot of the bed. Then she slid into her white cotton pajamas and picked up the phone. She dialed slowly, spending long moments over each digit. When she hit the final number, her heart thudded heavily in her chest. She leaned back against the pillows and gave herself a very stern talking to. What was the big deal, after all? There was nothing so very special about Sean KirPatrick. So what if he was tall and handsome, and almost every living female's dream man?

After a couple of rings, a woman answered, and Racquel felt her heart plummet.

"Sorry, wrong number," she said, and hung up without further inquiry. So, Morganna had been wrong about him. He was involved with someone, after all. Not that she should be so surprised. Men like him very often were taken. The kind intent she had seen in his eyes had fooled her into thinking that he might be a different kind of man—one who would at least have some morals, one who would not play fast and loose with someone else's emotions.

She clicked on the TV and settled lower in the bed. The sad truth of it was that Sean KirPatrick was probably no better than her ex-husband. In the beginning, she had thought that Ralph Penniman was something special, too. Everyone had. But, oh, how wrong they had all been.

She got tired of watching the flickering images, so she closed her eyes. Soon, she was asleep.

Outside, a man watched from a parked car. He hadn't counted on her getting a dog, but that situation could be easily remedied.

Seven

The week began with a fine drizzly rain, which continued intermittently for the next several days. By the end of Monday Racquel had arranged for a very high-tech burglar alarm system to be installed, and had requested a Caller ID unit from the local phone company.

She spent the next few days driving to different parts of town, showing up for open auditions for a string of low-budget B movies. By Thursday evening she was telling Morganna on the phone, "Trying to break into this business really sucks. I need an agent like yesterday. Imagine being turned down for a nonspeaking role in a movie about killer tarantulas from outer space. Any idiot can lie in the road and play dead."

"Welcome to Hollywood, kiddo," Morganna said. "It's really true when they say, 'it's not what you know in this town, but who you know.' "

"In just one week I've been told I'm too tall, too short, too ethnic. One casting director actually told me I needed to lose ten pounds."

Morganna laughed. "Well, don't do that. You're skinny enough, already. I think you need to gain five pounds or so, definitely not lose any."

"Humph," Racquel said, "why did I ever decide that this was what I wanted to do?"

"You surely didn't think it would be easy, did you? That in your first week you'd be offered the lead role in a multimillion dollar movie?"

Racquel sighed. "No . . . but I'd hoped to get at least a small part in some kind of movie."

"Listen," Morganna said, "I spoke to Charley about becoming your agent. And he's all for it. I've invited a lot of studio people from Warners to the barbecue on Saturday. You know, people who really have some clout at the company. I'll introduce you around. I just hope this darn rain lets up by then."

"Do you want to come over for dinner tonight? You and Charley?"

"Sure. What're you having?"

"I thought I might do a pickled shrimp salad, fried fish, potato salad, white rice . . . you know, that sort of thing."

"Umm," Morganna said, "sounds great. I'm hungry already. I'll bring the wine and the dessert, OK?"

"Fine. See you at about seven-thirty, then?"

She rang off and went to the kitchen to begin the preparations. She put the fish in the microwave to defrost, drained the vinegar from the shrimp, and began looking around for her large-bladed knife. The last time she had seen it, it had been sitting in the wooden carving block, where she kept all the knives.

She spent several minutes pulling open drawers, checking the bottom of the dishwasher, and opening up various containers of food in the fridge. She finally gave up in frustration when she couldn't locate it, selecting a smaller and duller knife. It wasn't like her to misplace things. She was usually very careful with everything she owned.

She was still thinking about the missing knife when the doorbell rang. She took a quick glance at her watch, rested the knife on the cutting board, and went toward the front door. It would be just like Morganna to be extra early.

She opened up the door without checking to see who it was, prepared to launch into a friendly tirade, but the humorous words she had been about to say stalled in her throat at the sight of the man standing on her doorstep. Sean KirPatrick. He smiled at the sight of her standing in the doorway wrapped in a stained pink-and-white apron.

"I hope I haven't caught you at a bad time," he said.

Racquel blinked wordlessly at him for a few seconds. What a very bold man he was. He was living with one woman, and openly courting another.

"Doctor . . . KirPatrick," she managed after a stretch of silence.

"May I come in?" he asked, hunching his shoulders against the rain. "It's a bit wet out here."

Racquel stood in the middle of the doorway, riddled with indecision. She couldn't very well be rude and shut the door in his face—even though he didn't really deserve the consideration of polite behavior.

"Well . . ." she said, "I was in the middle of preparing some . . . some dinner." Maybe he might take the hint, and just go away entirely on his own.

He disappointed her by breaking into an even friendlier smile. "Oh, good," he said, "I came at the right time, then. I can help."

Racquel's mouth opened, and she struggled for the right thing to say. "I'm . . . sure you don't want to help me. Besides, it's fish. And . . . and I wouldn't want you to—"

"Oh, don't worry about me," he said, "I love fish." And before she could get another word out, he had somehow pushed by her and entered the cottage.

Racquel watched in disbelief as he removed his coat and hung it on the coat stand in the passageway. Her brows knitted in consternation as he continued to move about as though this was the most natural thing in the world for him to do. He bent to remove his galoshes, then placed them neatly on the thick, fiber welcome mat.

"Look," Racquel began again. There were no two ways about it. She was just going to have to be rude to him. "I'm expecting company in about an hour. I'm not sure what it is you want, but I'm going to have to ask you to—"

She stared after his retreating back. Where in the name of heaven was he going? She followed him through the living room, around the corner, and into the kitchen.

"Doctor KirPatrick?"

"Sean," he said, opening up the microwave oven and removing the now defrosted fish.

Racquel took in a tight breath. "What do you think you're doing?"

He rested the fish on the center island, folded his arms, and subjected her to a very direct look.

"Why didn't you return my call?"

She opened her mouth, started to say something, then closed it again with a snap.

"Yes?"

"Do you usually do this? Break into other people's homes and harass them in their kitchens?"

He raised an eyebrow at her. "I hardly broke in."

"I would like you to leave now," she said. "Why did you come, anyway? How did you find me?"

"Wasn't hard after I got your number."

"Did Morganna—"

He raised a hand to wipe a trickle of rain from his

brow, and Racquel cowered away from him before she could prevent herself. In the instant that his hand had flashed upward, memory of another time had come upon her: She and Ralph were engaged in an argument and without warning he had lashed out at her, knocking her viciously to the ground.

A puzzled frown came and went like quicksilver in Sean KirPatrick's dark eyes. What in the name of heaven had happened to her in the years since he'd last seen her? Sweet Racquel. She had always been such a spunky little thing. When he had seen her again a few days ago, standing at the head of his driveway, he had thought for a long moment that it was just the morning sun playing tricks on him. Her hair had been a different color—brown, not the rich ebony he remembered. She'd been taller, and differently proportioned, but there was no way on earth that he would not have recognized her—the wonderful shape of her face, the large, black eyes that could once have made him do almost anything at all, the soft, dewy mouth he had longed to kiss in adolescence but had never dared.

He had written her letters for years after leaving Idaho, but every single one had been returned to him, unopened. Finally, he had given up and stopped writing altogether. He had gone into medicine, just as he had once promised her he would. And, when it came time to choose a location for his practice, he had settled on Los Angeles, knowing instinctively that one day—despite every effort made by her father to prevent her—she, too, would find her way there. She had always wanted to become an actress.

Now, she was here, and there was no way on God's earth that he was going to let her go again. Fate had given them another chance. She didn't recognize him. Maybe she didn't even remember the teenage boy who had been so smitten with her. But he was a man now, and even if she had never cared for the boy, she would learn to love the man.

"Doctor KirPatrick?" Racquel was saying, and there was a slight furrow between her brows. She didn't understand at all why he just stood and stared at her without uttering a word.

Sean unfolded his arms. "I really wish you wouldn't call me that."

"You don't like being called doctor? Isn't that what you are?" Racquel approached the center island, and took a quick peek at the fish. It was perfect for breading and frying. All it needed now was a little seasoning.

"I don't like you calling me that. I do have a name, you know."

She looked up and met his eyes. "Sean. I know." A cold shiver went through him at the quick meeting of their eyes.

"Who are you cooking dinner for tonight?" He prayed that he didn't have competition, that it was just her friend, Morganna.

Racquel gave the fish a prod with the tip of her fork. "I guess if you're not going to go like I asked you to, you might as well help me with the cooking." She looked at him again, as if to ascertain his level of agreement. "You did offer, remember?"

"I remember," Sean said. "Where's my apron?"

Racquel waved a hand. "In the corner behind the door."

Sean fetched the frilly bit of fabric, and returned to stand before her. "How do I put this on?" He wanted to feel her hands on him. For years, he had dreamt of her hands.

Racquel took the fabric from him. "Bend," she said. He did so obligingly, and she slipped the loop of the apron over his head and stood close to him to fasten the solitary button in the back.

Sean barely dared breathe, lest she hear the violent pounding of his heart. He longed to touch those perfectly formed, shell-shaped ears, stroke the fine golden skin of her cheek.

Racquel looked up at him when she was through. There was something about those eyes of his that looked very familiar. A slight furrow rippled the soft skin of her brow. She was quite probably beginning to crack up. "Can you make a salad?" she asked when he continued to stand before her without making any attempt to be helpful.

He felt very much like saying: *I was the one who taught you to make your first salad. Why don't you remember? Why don't you remember me?* He held his tongue.

"Green, or shrimp?"

Her head flashed up, and she gave him a quick look. "Shrimp."

"Spicy or bland?"

"Spicy. I hate bland food." He remembered that very well. She had asked for pepper on just about everything. Some things hadn't changed, after all.

He went about the kitchen, pulling open drawers and lifting down bowls. When he had gathered all the utensils, he pulled out the meat board and inquired over his shoulder, "Can you hand me the onions and shallots? Oh . . . and the mayo. Give me some honey, too, if you have it."

Racquel handed him the items he requested, then went back to preparing the batter for the fish. Every so often she looked up at him. He did seem to know what he was doing. Not very many people knew how to make a shrimp salad—at least, not the way she liked it.

Sean chopped and tossed, mixed and blended. When he was through, he emptied the appetizing salad into a glass bowl, covered it with plastic wrap, and settled it in the fridge to chill.

"How're you doing with the fish?" he asked once the fridge door was closed.

Racquel turned her head aside to sneeze. A whiff of black pepper had become airborne and had found its way to her very sensitive nose.

Sean pulled out a white cotton handkerchief. "Here," he said.

Racquel accepted the offering without protest and sneezed again, burying her nose in the square of cloth.

Sean took control of the batter. "I'll finish the fish . . . is there anything else to prepare?"

Racquel nodded, while making a valiant attempt not to break into another spasm of sneezing.

"Rice . . . potato salad. Hors d'oeuvres."

"OK," Sean said easily. "Why don't you get everything else started, while I do the fish?"

They worked in silence for a good while, with nothing more said between them. The kitchen was filled with the wonderful aromas of good food and the sounds of frying and chopping. At about seven-fifteen, everything was prepared, and Racquel paused to look at their handiwork.

"Well," she said, "we seem to make a good team. Everything looks great."

Sean smiled. "Since I live alone, I have to cook for myself." That wasn't exactly true. His housekeeper did most of the cooking. But he did want to make a favorable impression on her.

"I wouldn't have thought it," Racquel said. "When

did you find the time to learn to cook like this? I've heard you're a pretty good plastic surgeon."

Sean shrugged. "I guess I'm just good with my hands." His dark eyes looked directly into hers and suddenly, Racquel was uncomfortable.

"Why don't you wash your hands? Morganna should be here soon. I guess we have to think of a reason why you're here."

Sean turned the tap on and let the cold water wash over his hands. He was pleased, very pleased. The fact that she was having dinner with her friend meant that she didn't have a serious love interest.

"Why do we have to tell her anything at all?" he asked.

Racquel swept the hair back from her face. "Because . . . she knows that we only met a few days ago. She'll think that I've been—"

"Been what?" Sean quirked a brow. "You never finish your sentences . . . anymore." The word escaped before he could restrain himself, and he wondered if she would notice, but after a moment of waiting he realized that she hadn't even heard him. She was too busy bothering about what to tell her friend.

"I know," she said after a bit, "we'll tell her that you . . . that you were on your way to see her . . . to ask a few questions about the barbecue . . . and you noticed me in the yard with Shaggy, and decided to stop by for a visit."

"Who's Shaggy?" Sean inquired. He'd never considered the possibility that she might have a son—a son with someone other than himself. A wave of jealousy rippled through him, and he made an effort to control the feeling.

"My dog," she said after a moment. "He's upstairs

in the bedroom. I had to lock him in. He gets into everything if I don't."

"Oh," Sean said. The relief in him was so strong it was almost palpable. "If we're going to tell Morganna anything at all, why don't we tell her the truth?"

Racquel frowned. "The truth? I don't even know what that is, remember? You haven't told me why you're here."

"I came here to see you."

"Why?"

He straightened. "I'll leave you to figure that one out. Now"—he walked into the dining room—"Do you want to set the food up on the table out here?"

Everything was nicely spread when the doorbell chimed at almost exactly seven-thirty. Racquel had gone upstairs to change, so it was Sean who actually opened the door and ushered the guests in.

For the first time, maybe ever, Morganna O'Bannon was at a complete loss for words. Her husband, however, was not similarly bereft, so he took over, shaking hands warmly with Sean and proffering the bottle of white wine in his hands.

"Come in and have a seat," Sean said, trying his damndest not to laugh at the expression on Morganna's face. "Racquel will be down in a minute."

Almost on cue, the lady in question came hurrying down the stairs. She was dressed in a flowing turquoise gown, her hair was swept up, and tiny, honey-brown tendrils escaped in flowing ringlets at her temples. Her beauty was so striking that both men stared wordlessly at her for a moment—one stunned, the other very favorably impressed.

Racquel rushed into a burst of speech. "Oh . . . Morganna, I'm sorry I wasn't down to let you in. Long story. Believe me." She gave her friend a hug, then extended her hand in Charley's direction. "It's such a pleasure to finally meet you." She gave Morganna a wink. "I've heard lots of interesting things about you. But Morganna didn't tell me you were this good-looking."

Charley O'Bannon laughed. "I think I'm going to like you." He'd been called a thing or two in his time, but never had it ever been said that he was good-looking. He stood at just about six feet tall, and had very average features. His once lustrous black hair was beginning to recede, and he had been asked by more than one of his clients if he had ever engaged in the sport of boxing before embarking on a career as an attorney.

Morganna placed a hand on Racquel's arm. "We'll leave you men to get acquainted while we get things ready for eating."

Once they were in the kitchen, she placed the chocolate cake on the center island and closed the door. Her eyes sparkled. "I can't believe you didn't tell me about him. Here I am trying to think of ways to get you two together, and little do I know an affair is going on right under my nose. I almost keeled over with shock when he opened the front door."

Racquel pulled out a stool and sat. "There's no affair. He just showed up here this afternoon . . . out of the blue. We . . . I can only guess what made him do it."

"Hmm," Morganna said in agreement, "I can only guess, too. Have you seen the way he looks at you? I knew it wasn't my imagination a few days ago."

"Oh, be quiet," Racquel said. "There's nothing strange or unusual about the way he looks at me."

Morganna rolled her eyes. "What's the matter with you? Are you blind? The poor guy's probably out there right now trying to think of the best way to get you into his bed."

Racquel giggled. "You're crazy. Besides, I think he's living with somebody."

Morganna shook her head. "He's not living with anyone. If you passed by his house and caught sight of a woman going in there, it must've been the housekeeper. Trust me."

Racquel blinked at her. "Oh." She could think of nothing else to say.

Morganna stood. "Let's put the food out. I'm starving."

Racquel went to the stove and removed the nicely garnished platter of fried fish. "Can you get the salad in the fridge, and the punch . . . oh, but you brought wine."

"Don't worry about it," Morganna said. "We'll have punch and wine."

It took several trips back and forth to lay everything on the table, but once they were finished the spread looked festive enough to please the most discerning of epicureans.

Morganna sampled a spoonful of shrimp salad. "Mmm," she said, "this is delicious. You have to give me the recipe."

"Doctor KirPatrick prepared it," Racquel said, and left the room before Morganna could ask any of the questions burning in her eyes.

In the sitting room, both men were deeply involved in a discussion of some sort, but all talk ended once she appeared. Sean rose to his feet in an expression of polite gallantry, and a feeling of pleasure ran through Racquel. It had been years since she had received such considerations.

"Dinner," she said. They both followed her into the dining room. Morganna was back in the kitchen, so Racquel saw to the seating arrangements. "Let's see," she said. "Sean . . . why don't you sit in the middle there? That way you'll be able to talk to both Morganna and Charley, and I'll sit on the other side of the table."

Morganna appeared with a huge bowl of punch, and both men rose again to help her set it safely in the center of the table.

Charley picked up his napkin and was preparing to tuck it beneath his chin, but a glare from Morganna made him reconsider. Instead, he rested the square of linen on his lap.

"Well," Racquel said, "everyone help yourself."

Throughout the dinner there were exclamations of how very tasty the food was, and repeated requests from Morganna for one recipe or another. Sean spent most of the time attempting to bring a smile to Racquel's face. He was quite a raconteur, and Racquel found herself listening with great interest to the many amusing stories he had to tell. Apparently, he had been an army brat, traveling from one base to the next, attending more than three different high schools.

At one point she said, "It's incredible that you did so well in high school . . . well enough to get into college. I mean . . . you did travel around a lot as a child."

Sean shrugged. "If you want something enough . . . you often get it. And I was never a stranger to hard work."

Charley nodded. "I can attest to that. My folks weren't rich, so I had to put myself through college and law school. And it wasn't easy, believe me. I used to work at Chippendale's."

"That's where I met him," Morganna chimed in.

Racquel blinked. "Chippendale's? You mean, as a dancer?"

Charley threw back his head and roared. "Unfortunately, no—though I would've tried my hand at that had the manager thought my physique good enough to get the ladies all riled up. No, I worked security."

The conversation continued along those lines, and very soon Morganna was beginning to complain that she was bursting out of her breeches. "No dessert for me, thanks," she said when Racquel began to slice up the nicely iced devil's food pound cake.

"Sure?" Racquel asked.

Morganna patted her stomach and said, "You're too good a cook. I'm gonna have to run ten miles tomorrow to work all this food off."

Sean and Charley accepted huge slabs of cake and wolfed them down, assuring the women that they were not even halfway to being filled yet.

Racquel stood and began stacking the dishes. "Morganna, why don't you take everybody out to the living room. You guys can watch TV or something. I'll be done with this in a moment."

Sean stood. "I'll help you."

Charley was about to say the same, but was quickly hushed by Morganna and hustled out of the room.

Racquel continued to stack the dishes. "I'd feel much better if you didn't," she said.

Sean rocked back on his heels, hands in pockets. "What are you, a reverse chauvinist?"

Racquel looked up at him. "What?"

"Do you think this is woman's work?"

Racquel felt a flood of heat rush to her face. Maybe that was the reason why she didn't feel comfortable with him helping her. Ralph had always refused to give her any assistance at all with domestic activities. He had always claimed that it wasn't the manly thing to do.

She allowed a long sweeping curtain of hair to hide

her face from him. "Well if you really want to help. Go ahead." She knew that she sounded much less than gracious. In fact, she was treating him rather badly for someone who had obviously gone out of his way to be helpful.

She burned with the need to apologize to him, but couldn't think of an appropriate way to do it, so she picked up a pile of dishes, and headed into the kitchen. She felt him just behind her, and a flicker of worry coursed through her. She was far too aware of him. A strange happening, indeed. Whatever was causing her to feel the way she did, she was just going to have to ignore it. She absolutely did not want to get involved with anyone at the moment, regardless of how very pleasant he might appear. She knew all about nice guys, and she wasn't at all certain that she liked them very much. They were invariably something other than they claimed to be.

She rested her dishes on the side of the sink, turned, and collided with the rock-hard muscles of Sean's chest. The sudden impact knocked some of the wind out of her, and his hands came out to steady her.

"Are you all right?" he asked.

Racquel swallowed, and nodded. "Fine . . . I'm fine."

When he continued to hold her, she looked up at him. "I'm really OK," she said. The eyes looking down at her were deep and dark, and seemed to see right into the hidden parts of her. She swallowed audibly, and he raised a finger to gently stroke the elegant curve of her brow.

"Are you afraid of me?"

She shook her head and squeaked, "No . . . of course not. Are you dangerous?"

His finger traced the line of her cheek. "Not to you. Never to you."

She lifted a hand and stilled the movement of his finger. "I don't want to get involved . . . right now. Do you understand?"

A ripple of jealousy ran through him. "Is there someone else?"

"No. There's no one. I'm just getting my life back together now. I'm . . . I'm recently divorced."

That took him by surprise, and he stepped back. Somehow, he had never imagined her married. The truth of the matter was that he had never been able to imagine her with anyone but himself.

"Children?" he inquired in a voice that was a little cracked.

Racquel turned back to the sink and turned on the water. "No children."

He relaxed again. He could tell that something terrible had happened to her. He would find a way back to her. He would help her remember him, remember them as they had been when they were children.

"I'll get the rest of the dishes," he said, and was gone before Racquel could say anything more. He walked back and forth between kitchen and dining room, carrying bowls and dishes and other utensils. Racquel kept her head bent over the sink. She was trying desperately to quiet the voice in her head that chided her for her cowardice. *Take a chance. Take a chance,* it said. *He might be different.* She scrubbed at a pot, and answered the voice: *What if he's not? What if he's even worse than Ralph? What if he likes hitting women, too?*

She was so involved with her internal debate that she didn't hear him speak. She suddenly looked up, and found that he was watching her. "Did you say something?" she asked, mildly embarrassed.

"I wondered whether you'd go with me to the bar-becue on Saturday?"

"Oh . . . I . . ." she stammered. "I don't know," she finished quite lamely.

He moved in closer. "What don't you know?"

"I don't know if that's such a good idea," she said.

He leaned on the side of the sink. "You don't even have to stay with me all evening if you choose not to."

"There must be other women . . . you could ask."

"Plenty. But I want you."

Racquel swallowed the dryness in her throat. Well, that was plain speaking for you.

"Well, if we agree that it's for this one time only."

Sean held up both hands. "This one time—only." He experienced no qualms about twisting the truth a bit. He had every intention of spending more time with her, of course.

"Shall we kiss to seal the bargain?" he asked, and proceeded to stare at her with those deeply hypnotic eyes. A feeling of panic spread like wildfire through Racquel.

"No," she said. "I . . . I can't."

Sean took a few steps away to give her a little more space. "OK," he said. There was an expression of un-derstanding dawning in his eyes. He could only guess at what had happened to her, but he knew that it had been something violent and traumatic. He turned away to hide the flash of anger that ran through him. If he ever got his hands on the man who had done this to her, all of the civilized urbanity which he had learned to cultivate in the past years would be completely stripped away.

He turned back toward her, and found that she was watching him with a slightly fearful expression in her eyes. "No one will ever hurt you again, Racquel," he said. She blinked wordlessly at him, and he knew she was trying to understand why he had just said what he did.

For a long minute, he trembled on the verge of telling her who he was. Yes, his name might be different— Sean now, instead of Stephen—but he was the same boy who had spent a good portion of his early teenage years working on her parents' farm in Idaho. He was the same boy who had done all in his power to hide his true feelings from her.

"There's something very strange about you," she said finally, and turned back to the dishes in the sink.

Sean picked up a dishtowel, and began to dry. "Strange? How do you mean?"

She scrubbed at a bowl for a good long while before answering. "Why do you speak as though you . . . you know things about me."

Oh, did he know things about her. He knew that Sundays were her favorite days. That she liked poppy seed muffins and chocolate milk. That she had a distinct fondness for riding horses bareback.

"I guess it must be the doctor in me. Maybe I'm treating you like a patient. Do you think so?"

She gave a short laugh. "If you treat all of your patients like this, you're going to be in deep trouble very soon, Sean KirPatrick."

So, he had made her laugh. He liked that. She looked as though she hadn't had very much to laugh about in a long while, a very long while. Well, he was here now, and he was never going away again. Never. No matter what.

"Why don't you leave the rest of this stuff to the dishwasher?"

Racquel turned on the tap to rinse. "It leaves streaks on the glasses."

A smile twisted the corner of Sean's mouth. She was

just as meticulous as he remembered. Everything had always had to be just so.

"Put the dishes in then, and hand wash the glasses."

She turned on the hot water tap full blast. "You're very bossy, do you know that?"

Sean flipped the dishcloth across one shoulder and leaned on the counter.

"Do you like my face?" he asked.

Racquel gave him a sidelong glance. "Your face?"

"My face," he said, and turned sideways so that she might see his profile. "What do you think of it?"

Racquel chuckled. "You're a lunatic. If your patients really knew how crazy you are, they'd never let you anywhere near them."

Sean laughed, and the sound of him caused a chord of memory to vibrate somewhere deep in Racquel's mind. She felt as though she knew him. She *felt* it.

"You have a nice face," she said. *And a nice laugh. And kind eyes. She especially liked his eyes.*

"Thank you," he said, and smiled at her.

Racquel bent her head, and began to wash furiously.

"I wonder what Morganna and Charley are doing," Sean said after a moment of observing her.

Racquel's head bobbed up, and she rubbed a soapy hand across her forehead. "Oh . . . no. I forgot all about them."

"I'll go check," he said.

He was gone, and suddenly the kitchen seemed gapingly empty without him. Racquel began stacking the remaining dishes in the dishwasher. She had to get a grip on herself. One single evening spent in his company, and already she was beginning to experience feelings that she'd sworn off forever.

He was back in less than five minutes. "They're

gone," he said. Racquel straightened from her position before the dishwasher. "Gone? Why would they go?"

"Morganna left a note. It's addressed to you. I guess she didn't want me reading it." Racquel took the folded piece of paper from him and read it quickly. A wave of heat crept slowly up her neck, and she crunched the paper into a ball and dropped it in the garbage bin.

"So, what did she say?"

"Oh, nothing much. She just thanked me for dinner, and promised to call me tomorrow." *She had also wished her a passion-filled night spent in Sean KirPatrick's arms, but there was no way on earth that Racquel was going to reveal that bit of information to him.*

"Well," he said, after a moment of staring at her. "It's just you and me, then."

She was nervous again, and desperately trying to think of a polite way to suggest that maybe it might be time for him to go.

He moved to a cupboard. "I'll make us some hot chocolate, OK?" He was tempted to ask her if she still enjoyed poppy seed muffins, but decided not to. It was too soon.

A frown rippled across her brow, and she said, "You like hot chocolate, too? Not coffee?"

Sean put the kettle on, and tried to hide the smile he was feeling. "I never outgrew the taste of it, I guess. I drank gallons of it as a kid."

"Hmm," Racquel said. "So did I."

Within a few minutes the chocolate was ready and waiting in two steaming mugs. Sean opened the fridge and removed a can of whipped cream and a bowl of cherries. Racquel watched him in silence as he garnished the tops of both mugs with cream, then settled a ripe cherry atop each peak of white.

"There," he said, when he was through. Unless her tastes had changed, this was just the way she liked it.

She accepted the mug with a hand that shook a little. "Thank you."

He longed to hold her in his arms, and take away the sadness he sensed in her. He knew, though, that if he attempted that now she would retreat from him. "Let's go into the sitting room," he said. "Maybe there's a good movie on."

He stood aside to let her pass and Racquel walked ahead, bending every so often to take a sip from the warm mug. She seated herself on the large sofa facing the TV set. Sean came to sit beside her, but not very close.

"What kind of movies do you like?" she asked.

"Horror," he said. "Sweet romantic movies, westerns, action . . . other kinds."

She gave him a quick look. "Just about everything, then?"

He nodded. "So you can take your pick. Whatever you choose, I'll like."

"OK." She leaned forward to pick up the remote. "I never thanked you for helping me prepare dinner. You cook pretty well for a brilliant surgeon."

He smiled at her. "Do you like skiing?"

Her brows crinkled. "Skiing?"

He stared directly into her eyes, willing her to remember him. *You used to like the outdoors, and I promised you that one day when I was all grown up I would take you camping and boating and skiing. We said that we would rent a cabin, and spend months at a time there just having fun. Remember?*

"Don't tell me you're one of those city girls who'd rather spend her free time jostling hundreds of other people . . . in the malls?"

A smile drifted into Racquel's eyes. "I'm not a city girl at all. I'm from farm country, in Idaho."

He put his mug down and came a bit closer. "I've a small clinic up in the mountains. I often take my serious cases there—the mountain air helps them recuperate. Would you like to go skiing up there one weekend?"

Racquel drew her feet up beneath her. "I can't ski. I mean, I never learned how. So—"

"I can teach you."

"Well, maybe if you invited other people, too."

"Other people like Morganna and Charley?"

She nodded, assuming that he probably would not agree and that the idea of the ski weekend would most likely be dropped, but he surprised her by saying, "Well, we'll have to talk to them about it. Maybe at the barbecue on Saturday."

She barely managed to prevent her mouth from sagging open. "You mean . . . Charley and Morganna . . . you don't mind them coming?"

"No, why should I mind? They're your friends, and if they'll help you have a good time, then that's what I want."

She turned blindly to the TV set and stared without any comprehension at the passing images. Why was he trying to be so nice to her? What was it that he wanted? Sex? Surely he could get that easily from a whole horde of other women. What did she have to give him, after all? Just a pretty face, and a severely broken psyche. Once he discovered all of her many problems, once he learned that she had no interest in being touched or held or anything else along those lines, he'd be sure to leave her alone. Any normal man would.

"Are you cold?"

Racquel turned to give him a frosty look. So, he was

finally going to make his move. It *was* sex he was after. All of the pretense this evening—the cooking, the wiping of dishes, the gallantry—it had all been leading to a roll in the sack.

"No, I'm not cold."

"You're shivering," he said. "Come over here, and I'll keep you warm." He patted a spot right beside him.

Her eyes battled with his for a minute. *OK, she would move closer to him. He would soon discover that she had absolutely no interest in anything he might be planning. She would sit beside him as stiff and unresponsive as a piece of board. After five or so minutes of that, he'd be sure to get up and leave.*

She drained her mug, got up, and sat rigidly next to him. She knew that it was a trifle immature to behave so, but at the moment she found that she just didn't care too much. She turned to look at him, and the expression in his eyes had her turning hurriedly away. How dare he look at her as if he understood her? He didn't know a single thing about her, not a single thing. Did he know that there was a spot along the length of her collarbone that would quite probably ache for the rest of her life? Did he know how she had gotten that? Would he care even if she told him? No. Of course not. He was just in search of a little light fun, and for tonight at least she was the flavor he desired.

She stiffened even more when one of his hands came to rest on her arm.

"Relax," he said. "This isn't going to hurt."

Racquel gritted her teeth. She didn't want to relax. She didn't want him to touch her at all. He was obviously very accomplished at the art of seduction, the way his long fingers moved in slow sinuous strokes, smoothing away the goose bumps on her arms, making her feel warm and safe and loved, despite every effort she made to control herself.

He repositioned her against him, shifting so that she could rest comfortably against his chest. And, lord, did her limbs betray her. No matter how hard she tried to remain wooden, they would not. His fingers were magical, wonderful, strangely therapeutic. It must be because he was a physician, she decided. He knew all the right spots to touch, since he'd been taught this in school.

"Does that hurt?"

Racquel found herself nodding. How had his fingers made their way up her shoulders to just the right part of the crescent-shaped bone that ran from shoulder to shoulder?

He turned her so that she was now almost lying in his arms. His thumb and forefinger ran gently across the bone, tracing out the unevenness, softly massaging the spot that always brought her pain.

"How did you break it?" He looked down into her eyes, and saw the frightened memory of something terrible there.

"I . . . it was a long while ago."

His jaw tightened. Someone had brutalized her, and he wouldn't rest until he found out who. Her father had never had two kind words for her, he remembered. It was almost as though he had blamed his daughter for not being a boy.

Racquel closed her eyes, and gave herself up to the wonderful massage of his fingers. She didn't care to fight it anymore. She was weak. Maybe she was a coward, too. But she had suffered so terribly for such a long time. Ralph Penniman had not only broken her body—in many ways he had also broken her spirit.

Sean looked down on the face beneath his, and for several minutes he fought the urge to bend and rest his lips against hers. She had such a sweet, trusting face. How could anyone have done her injury? The very thought of it made him viciously angry.

"Why haven't you married? Everyone says that you're such a good catch. I would've thought some smart girl would've snatched you up years ago." Her eyes were open again, and she was speaking to him.

He hesitated, then decided to give her the truth. "Once there was a girl I loved . . . a long while ago. But I was poor, and her family did not think I was good enough for her."

"Oh."

He smiled down at her in the dim half-light. He knew that he had caught her attention with that.

"But they must—I mean, now that you're a doctor?" She paused, and her brow wrinkled a bit. "Why didn't you marry her, anyway?"

"I would've. I wrote her letters. Many, many letters. But she never answered, not even once. I gave up after a while. I figured that it was just a childish infatuation for her, not something real as it was for me."

Racquel gave his hand a consoling little pat. "Never mind. She probably wasn't even really worth the effort, anyway." She had decided that maybe she would like him, after all—even if he was after her just for sex. There was something infectious about the way he smiled.

He linked his fingers with hers. "Do you like poppy seed muffins?"

Racquel gave him a genuinely confused stare. "Muffins? Yes. Most people like them."

His lips curled. "That's what I thought."

She sat up slowly, and almost without conscious thought his hands reached out to keep her with him.

"You ask the strangest questions sometimes."

He grinned. "That's what you keep telling me." His hand lifted to brush the hair back from her face. "I don't have any cases scheduled at the clinic tomorrow. Why don't we pack a picnic lunch, maybe take a ride up the coast?"

A troubled little look danced for a minute in her eyes. "As friends?"

"If you like."

"OK, then. Where shall we go?"

He stretched, and for a brief instant his shirt pulled open at the neck. "Let's be really adventurous. How does San Diego sound?"

Racquel's gaze quickly followed the length of muscled chest. Then, very deliberately, she turned her eyes away, but not before Sean could notice a flicker of interest in them.

His skin burned at the thought of her hands on his chest, and he was of a mind to unbutton every single fastening on his shirt so that she might see more of him—maybe even touch him, if she could only overcome her fear.

"Isn't San Diego far from LA?"

"Just two hours or so. We can take my Range Rover."

"I'll have to bring the dog," she said after a moment of thought.

"Shaggy?"

"Yes. I couldn't leave him here alone all day."

"Fine," he said, straightening from his slouching position on the arm of the couch. "We'll make a day of it, then. We'll leave early . . . say about seven?"

She smiled at him and wrinkled her nose. "It's just impossible to say no to you, isn't it?"

He rose to his feet and towered over her, both hands

jammed into his pockets. Humor danced in his eyes. "I'm glad you're beginning to realize that."

He was preparing to go, and she actually felt a bit disappointed. *Couldn't he stay for a bit longer? Just to talk? They hadn't even watched any TV at all. And, it wasn't so very late. Only eleven o'clock.*

She looked up, and met his gaze. "Are you leaving?"

Surprise flickered in Sean's eyes, but he concealed it quickly, without her being any the wiser. *So, she wants me to stay.*

Happiness tightened the muscles in his neck, and he cleared his throat to cautiously say, "Well, I was going to stay a bit longer, but you seemed to be getting tired, and I didn't want to overstay my welcome."

"Oh, don't worry about that," she said. "I've decided that I like you, so you can stay until you absolutely have to go."

He sat again, but not before picking up the remote and depressing the MUTE button. "I'd better be on my best behavior, then—before you decide not to like me again."

Racquel beamed at him and thought how very lucky she was to have found this kind of male friend, for the second time in her life.

Eight

Sean left an hour later, and Racquel went off to bed feeling happier than she'd felt in a long while. She slept soundly, with the dog lying in his basket at the foot of the bed, and awoke to the ringing of the alarm clock at just before six the next morning. She lay in bed for a few long minutes, watching the fine drizzle come down. The droplets pooled, then trickled down the glass in long, narrow streaks. Such a very gray morning might have made her feel a bit glum only days before, but today she felt buoyed with energy. She didn't care to examine too closely her reasons for feeling so. What did it really matter that she was looking forward to this little outing with Sean KirPatrick? She didn't need to feel guilty about that. She had told Ralph not long ago that she was not interested in men any longer, just in her career, and that was still true. It wasn't as though she had any romantic intentions toward the doctor. She didn't. She just needed a friend. That was all. Just a friend.

She peeled back the warm blankets, exposing a length of soft, golden thigh. The air was chilly, and it took her more than a moment to get completely out of bed. Once she was out and moving around, she warmed up quickly. With the dog following her every step, she bustled about the room, first making the bed and then neatly stacking the doggy toys in the basket and pushing the entire ensemble out of sight beneath the bed. She spent the next little while thoughtfully selecting her clothing—a burgundy sweater, blue jeans, fashionable ankle boots, and a blue, lightweight water-resistant jacket, just in case it continued to rain throughout the day.

She was bathed and ready by the time the rugged black Range Rover pulled to a stop at the gate. Sean was out of the vehicle and ringing the bell before she could make it to the living room. She turned off the alarm, and opened the door.

"Good morning," she said, giving him a wide smile of welcome. "Come in." She stood back to let him enter.

"All set?" He looked at her with a smile of his own. *Lord, but she was beautiful. If only she knew how hard it had been for him to leave her last night. It had taken every ounce of willpower he possessed not to pull her into his arms at the front door and hold her as he'd longed to do for so many years, and damn the deal he'd made with her father to hell.*

"I think so. I'll go get the dog. He's eating in the kitchen. Nothing can tear him away from his food when he's in the middle of it."

Sean nodded. *And, nothing will tear you away from me again. Ever.*

She was back in less than a minute.

Sean whistled to Shaggy, and his ears perked up immediately. "Where did you find him?"

Racquel gave the dog a tickle behind the ears. "The pound. I saved him from certain death. He was just about to be put down when I got there. So, he's completely in love with me now."

"I don't blame him."

Racquel met the dark gaze for a moment. "Are you flirting with me?"

He gave her the kind of smile that made her feel like a giddy teenager. "I know you don't want me to, so I'll say no."

She laughed, despite herself. "I don't know what to make of you. Really."

He linked his arm with hers in a way that seemed completely natural. "I packed us a picnic basket," he said. "Actually, my housekeeper did."

"Oh," Racquel said, and she wrinkled her nose. "I should've done that."

He closed the door behind them, and removed the key from her grasp. "Don't worry, I've taken care of everything. All you have to do is just enjoy yourself."

She turned glowing eyes to him as he helped her into the front seat of the Rover. "Thank you," she said, and for the life of her she could not think of a word more to say. He ran an index finger down the soft curve of her cheek.

"You're welcome." He smiled. *Sweet Racquel. I'll never let anyone hurt you again.*

With the dog sitting on the backseat and hanging his huge head out of the window, they set off. The 405 Freeway was heavily congested, as was normal for this time of the day. Cars pressed in on the Range Rover from every direction. Sean drove with the skill and ease of a native Californian, paying little attention to the bleating horns and impatient gestures.

Racquel cracked her window a bit. The drizzle had faded away, and watery sunshine was beginning to seep through the clouds. She turned in her seat to offer the dog a biscuit.

"Is it always this crowded on the freeway at this time of the day?"

Sean glanced into his rearview mirror, and changed lanes. "Uh huh. Especially around rush hour. It eases off for an hour or two after that, but it's usually very busy on this freeway all the time."

"Incredible," Racquel said, and reached into the large bag at her feet. "Did you have breakfast?"

He gave her a sidelong glance. "No. I thought we'd stop somewhere along the way and have something."

"Well, I brought sandwiches. I have spicy cheese. Turkey. Roast beef. Would you like one?"

"I thought you hadn't prepared anything."

"It's just a few sandwiches to nibble on. Not a whole picnic basket."

A smile flickered at the corners of his lips. It was so obvious that she was a country girl. "I'd love a roast beef, but I don't think I should drive and eat in this traffic. It might not be safe."

"Maybe I can hold the sandwich while you eat," she said after a minute.

"Would you?" He turned soulful eyes in her direction.

She reached into the bag again and removed a large ziplock sack. "I usually cut the edges off. I hope you don't mind."

"Whatever you do is fine with me."

She tried not to look directly at him for several minutes after that. She bent her head and spent a good while looking aimlessly into the bag of sandwiches. When she was certain that she was once again in full control of her nerves, she lifted out a large roast beef sandwich and said with a flicker of humor in her voice, "Be careful you don't bite my hand off."

He seized the opportunity to wrap his fingers around the tender flesh of her wrist, under the pretext of holding her hand steady, then bit into the soft bread. His lips touched the tips of her fingers, and the simple feel of his flesh against hers sent such a jolt of electricity through her that Racquel very nearly dropped the sandwich in his lap. Before she could even take a breath to steel herself he was biting again, and gently holding her wrist, even briefly massaging the inner side of it with his thumb.

"Look," she said breathlessly, "I don't think this is going to work."

His tongue flickered out to touch a finger, and there was definitely no concealing the shudder that raced through her, then. She jerked back, looking at him with eyes that had suddenly gone wild and hunted.

Sean cursed himself for his lack of caution. She'd started opening up to him. Why had he allowed his emotions to so completely take control of his actions?

"I'm sorry, Kelli."

Racquel was so overwhelmed by what had just transpired, that she failed to realize that he had just called her by the pet name that only one other living soul had ever used.

She shook her head. "Not your fault. You were bound to find out sooner or later." Her hands were knotted in her lap to hide the trembling.

Sean longed to comfort her, but he knew instinctively that she would not welcome it. Instead he asked in a gentle tone, "Find out what?" She obviously felt that she was the keeper of some deep dark secret.

"That I . . . I don't like being touched."

His brows crinkled. She had seemed fine last night when she had lain against him. He had massaged her neck, spent glorious minutes running his fingers down her arms.

"I don't understand," he said.

She gave a sharp laugh. "It's a pity you're not a

psychologist. Maybe you could've helped me figure it out."

Sean took a moment to speak, and when he did he was careful with his words. "Are you afraid of being touched in an intimate way?"

She darted a quick glance at him, and he could clearly see the embarrassment in her. "Yes . . . I think that's it. I . . . I don't know why."

He longed to say, *Hush, babe. It's OK. Whatever has happened to you is past. Dead and buried forever. Now let me help you deal with the present. Take my hand. Lean on me, and I'll help you through it.*

Instead, he gripped the wheel and tried to think of words he could say—safe, soothing words that would not scare her or make her feel threatened in any way. He took her mind away from the situation at hand by pointing out sights along the way. When he was sure that she was calm again, he tuned the radio to a mellow, easy listening station.

Halfway to San Diego, Racquel ventured a glance in his direction. He had spoken quite kindly to her following her involuntary panic attack, but she felt certain that he must now be regretting the fact that he would be faced with several hours more of her company. Her throat was sore from worrying, and if there was anything at all that she could have said or done to take away what had happened before, to reestablish the easy camaraderie, she would have done it. She did so want to be his friend. Regardless of what had happened before with Ralph, she had a very solid feeling about Sean KirPatrick. The kind intent in his eyes could not be feigned. She was certain of that.

He turned to look at her at that very moment, and Racquel ventured a little apologetic smile.

"We're almost there," he said. "I thought we might go to Sea World first, then spend the rest of the day on the beach somewhere—maybe in one of the coves. I brought some poles, and baskets for crabbing."

She blinked at him, wondering whether he was angry. "Sounds great."

"You OK?" It was the most natural thing in the world to want to reach out and touch her, but he was worried that if he did he might throw her into another panic.

She nodded. "You mad at me?" she asked like a child who feared a rebuke.

"No. Why would I be? If I'm mad at anyone at all . . . it's myself."

"Oh, don't be," she said, and in her desire to make the point her hand came out to grip his thigh. "It was all me, all my fault, something I couldn't control. It's happened many times before. You weren't to know. Any normal woman would be happy that you were paying any attention to her."

He looked down briefly at the hand on his thigh. "Don't think any more about it, OK? Let's agree to just have fun today. Deal?" *God knows he had a lot more self-control than he'd originally thought.*

She agreed immediately. "All right." And she was happy again, looking out the window at the buildings on the outskirts of San Diego.

"Everything looks so clean now," she said. "And the traffic isn't so bad anymore."

"You're going to love San Diego. Remember how you always—" He stopped himself in the middle of what he had been about to say. It was so hard not to lapse and naturally reminisce when she was seated right there beside him, but he didn't want to tell her who he was just yet. If she hadn't remembered him by now, he would just let the memory come back naturally.

He slanted a look in her direction. There was a frown of puzzlement on her face.

"Why did you say—remember?"

His hands tightened on the wheel. "Don't you feel as though you know me? I feel that with you." *That was as close as he would willingly come to telling her.*

She was silent for a long while, and he tried to read her face but couldn't. "I don't believe in past lives or any of that stuff . . . do you?"

"I don't actively believe it, but who's to say if it's true or not?"

"Well, it seems incompatible with the beliefs of Christianity."

"You're a Christian, then?" He knew she'd been born a Catholic. She'd shown him many pictures of her christening.

"I used to be Catholic, but I'm not anymore. I kind of fell out of step with the church . . . so I'm not sure what I am right now."

Maybe he wasn't so surprised about that. She had always shown a strong rebellious streak as a child. There had been a willingness in her to absolutely think for herself. He was glad to see that had not changed.

"You still believe in God, though?"

"Oh, yes." She seemed genuinely shocked by the suggestion. "Of course I do. I'm just not sure which denomination to follow."

"I'm in the same transition right now. Maybe you can help me decide."

She darted a quick look at him to see if he was joking, but he seemed sincere enough. "If you think I might be able to help. Sure."

He smiled at her. "This might be quite a project, you know. It usually takes me a very long time to decide on the least little thing. Are you sure you're up for it?"

"I dunno. We'll have to see."

She was back to joking with him, and he was glad of it.

They were off the freeway now, and driving down past several very ritzy looking hotels.

"Sea World's just a few minutes away. Would you like to stop at the Hyatt first? Maybe tidy up a bit? I called ahead before we left this morning. Got us two rooms, just in case."

A smile twisted the corners of her mouth. He was the soul of discretion, but she had no pressing need to make a bathroom stop.

"I'm fine," she said. "But if you want to, go right ahead."

He gave her a quick wink. "Well, we're all ready to have fun, then."

The next several hours passed so quickly that Racquel found herself wishing that they had decided to spend more than just one day in San Diego. There was so much to see and do, and so many wonderful things to eat.

They left the dog in the car, with all the windows slightly cracked. Sean had found a shady tree to park beneath, and had left a bowl of water on the floor in the back. Then he had taken her by the hand and steered her away from the car, promising all the while that the dog would be fine.

"We'll come back in an hour to check on him," he assured her. "Don't worry, he'll be OK."

Once the worry over the well-being of the animal had subsided, Racquel threw herself into the spirit of the park. They bought double-decker ice cream cones and wandered from exhibit to exhibit, holding hands. It seemed perfectly natural and comfortable to walk with him in this manner now, so she did not pull away from him when he linked his fingers with hers. They were just friends, after all. She waited in line for fish to feed the dolphins, and was amazed by the slick feel of their skin and the great intelligence so very apparent in their eyes.

At one point, she stumbled backward when one of them surprised her by sliding directly onto one of the sloping sides of the enclosure. Sean, who was standing immediately behind, caught and steadied her with an arm. She turned, and in a moment of madness gave him a quick kiss on the cheek which startled him so terribly that he very nearly let go of her. His heart thundered against her back, and he was certain that she could probably feel the beat of it straight through to her skin. It took every ounce of self-control he possessed not to turn her fully into his arms and kiss her right there in front of everyone. Somehow he made his hands release her, and she went back to feeding the dolphins.

They visited the sharks next and stood in the water tunnel looking up through the glass at the tiger sharks and the strangely misshapen hammerheads. Then, it was on to the bird exhibit. During the show, as exotic birds of every type swooped and danced to the direction of their trainers, Sean was able to join hands with her again. She held his willingly enough, and even gave his fingers a little squeeze from time to time. It was the happiest Sean had been in years. Sitting there with her in the afternoon sun, he felt as though he had everything in the world that he needed.

Nine

The hours passed very quickly, and it was early evening before Racquel realized it. Sean had gone back to the car more than once to make certain the dog was all right, and each time when he returned Racquel had looked at him with worried eyes.

"You sure he's not dehydrated, or anything like that?"

"I took him out for a minute to use the grass. He's made quite a mess of the backseat area, but other than that, he's fine."

"Oh," Racquel said, "I'm sorry. I'll clean it up as soon as we leave here."

Sean gave the tip of her nose a playful tap with his index finger. "You'll do no such thing, young lady. It's all taken care of."

They stayed to see the orca show, and finally left when the lights of the park began coming on.

Racquel pulled out a mirror and looked at the skin of her face as soon as she was comfortably seated in the passenger seat. She was sunburnt. There was no doubt about it. She opened up her bag and rooted about for several minutes. She finally straightened with a large bottle of cold cream in her hands, and began struggling to remove the tight cover.

Sean said, "Sunburn?"

She nodded. "Just a little. It's not really that bad, though."

He opened up the glove compartment and removed a small leather case. "I've got something a little better. It's just short of prescription strength. It'll soothe your skin within seconds. Here, let me," he said, as she reached for the tube of ointment. "I'm a doctor, remember?"

She relaxed under his hand as his fingers moved in circles across the skin of her face. It was so easy to forget that he was more than just a very nice man. She didn't think of him as a doctor at all, now. Not at all. He was just Sean to her. Just Sean.

She closed her eyes, and allowed him to have his way with her face. His fingers were pure magic, and he was right about the ointment working wonders. Her skin had a wonderfully supple feeling now, and the burning had disappeared completely.

"Feeling better?" His fingers had stopped moving.

Her eyes sprang open. She hadn't wanted him to stop. "Much. You have beautiful hands."

And you have beautiful lips. His eyes stared into hers, dark and seductive. "Do you want to drive back to LA tonight . . . or stay over at the hotel?"

"Let's go back to the hotel," she said. "You must be tired. It's incredible how very quickly the day went by, isn't it? We didn't even have a chance to have our picnic . . . or do any crabbing, like you wanted to."

He rested an arm along the steering wheel. "Well that's not a problem . . . we can have the food in the basket tonight, go crabbing tomorrow, and drive back to LA in the afternoon."

"Hmm," Racquel said. "But we can't miss Morganna's barbecue, though. She'd never forgive me."

"We won't," he said, starting the engine. "We'll be

back in LA long before eight o'clock tomorrow. And there'll be more than enough time for you to freshen up, maybe even take a nap if you like."

At the hotel, they were checked in quickly. The two rooms Sean mentioned turned out to be ocean view suites. Racquel went immediately to the window to pull back a section of drapery. They were quite high up, but the ocean seemed almost touchably close. The rippling blue waters, almost silver in certain parts because of the setting sun, was nothing short of breathtaking.

Sean came to stand beside her. "So . . . ," he said after a long moment of just looking, "what do you think?"

She turned, eyes glowing. "Wow. It's beautiful. So perfect. Almost hard to believe that it's actually real."

"There're going to be fireworks at about eight. We should have our dinner out on the verandah then."

Racquel nodded. "This has been a wonderful day. Thank you for being so . . . such a very good friend."

"You had a good time, then?"

"I've never had a better time, and that's the truth." She stood looking at him for long moments, as though trying to decide on the appropriate course of action. Then she said, "Can I give you a hug? Would you mind?"

Sean laughed. *Would he mind?* "I won't push you away."

She went to him, intending to give nothing more than a quick embrace, but his arms wrapped around her like twin bands of steel, and he pulled her to him and held on for a lot longer than she had envisioned. Strangely, she experienced no need to struggle. In fact, she felt safe there, with his arms about her—safer than she'd ever felt before.

She rested her head on his chest, and a hand came

up to gently stroke her hair. He was so warm, and solid, so well-suited to her physically. They almost seemed to fit together, like two pieces of some inscrutable cosmic puzzle.

She raised her head to look at him. His eyes were deep and dark, and very gentle. She sensed a hesitancy in him, and knew instinctively what it was. It was completely natural, in this moment, to want more than she was giving. She raised herself onto her toes, and without saying a word he lowered his lips to hers. He kissed her, slowly, slowly, holding her as though she were the most precious cargo in the world. Her hands went around his back, and she felt more than heard him moan.

He deepened the kiss with subtle movements of his head.

For Sean, time had gone away. It had no meaning anymore. All that mattered was here and now, and holding her this way. When she attempted to move away from him, he shifted her mouth back, with the muttered protest, "Not yet." *He'd waited so long for this. Almost an entire lifetime.*

Racquel's hands slid softly across the muscles of his back. She had never known that the simple act of kissing another human being could be so very, very enjoyable. It had never been so with Ralph. In fact, she had no real memory of kissing him at all. She just remembered the times with him in bed, and how rough and ugly he had been when she had not responded to his liking. She remembered very well being slapped across the face and called, of all things, a frigid whore. He had called her that so frequently during their time together that, maybe on some level, she had actually come to believe it. But Sean was different. There was

no violence in him. He did not force her to do anything—not anything at all.

"Racquel—" His voice echoed through her mind like
a whisper from the past. "You're not afraid of me, are
you?"

She pressed a dewy, soft kiss to the corner of his
mouth. "No." It was true. She no longer felt any fear
at all around him.

He intercepted another of her kisses with the full
blunt of his mouth, and took a moment to savor the
softness of the petal-shaped lips before continuing. "Do
you think that at some point in time—not right away,
I understand that—do you think you might be able to
let me into your life? Just a little?"

Racquel's eyes cracked open. She knew exactly what
he was asking of her, and she wasn't certain that she
could give it. She had promised herself, promised
Ralph, that she would not get involved with another
man. She still had quite a lot of healing to do. There
were parts of her that were broken, that might take her
years to discover, and still years more to correct.

"I . . . don't know."

He kissed the fine lines of her cheekbones. "Let me
help you try."

She rested her head against him again, and seemed
to take strength from the simple rise and fall of his
chest. It would be so nice if she could just let go, say
yes to him, but she was afraid—afraid of what Ralph
might do if he ever found out. He would attempt to
hurt Sean. She was sure of it.

"Can't we just be . . . friends? For a while, at
least?"

He took her chin between thumb and forefinger, tilt-
ing her face toward his. "Who is it that hurt you so
badly, Kelli?"

Everything in Racquel came to a slow, tumbling halt. *Kelli? No one had called her that since Stephen. God, in addition to everything else that was wrong with her, she was now beginning to lose her mind, as well. She just had to get a grip on things. Every man who was kind to her was not Stephen Parker.* Kelli *was* a common nickname for Racquel.

She realized that he was waiting for her reply, so she forced herself to say, "My ex-husband. He used to—" She found that she could not finish. Somehow, she could not bear the thought of him turning away from her once he knew her shame.

Sean's fingers traced her collarbone and found the small dip. He gently massaged the area. "Did he do this?"

She nodded and looked away from him, not daring to see the expression in his eyes. She was saddened by the thought that now he would no longer wish to be friendly with her. He would retreat from her. Gently, of course, because he was such a kind man. How could he behave any differently? After all, who would really want to be around someone like her? She steeled herself to meet his gaze, and what she saw threw her into an immediate state of confusion. Tears. There were tears in his eyes.

"Sean?" She was panicked. What was the matter? Why was he crying?

He took her hand and pressed a kiss to the center of her palm. "Where is he now?"

"My ex?"

He could barely bring himself to nod.

"As far as I know, Ralph Penniman is in Idaho."

So, it was Penniman that she had married. He remembered the lout. The boy had always shown a remarkable affinity for cruelty, and it would appear that the man had not turned out much different. How could his sweet Racquel have made such a very obvious mistake in judgment? Choosing someone with considerably more brawn than intelligence made no sense whatsoever. Her father must have forced the union on her. He had always been one to put personal gain above such relatively minor considerations as happiness. And, he had admired the Penniman farm.

Sean pulled her down to sit with him on the sofa. When she was comfortable, he took both of her hands in his.

"I want you to understand one thing," he said. "Whatever your ex-husband did to you was not your fault. You were not to blame for it. Do you believe me?"

She blinked rapidly, as though holding back tears of her own. Her throat was dry, and it was hard to swallow. "I know that makes sense. It wasn't me, it was him. He hurt me."

Lord Almighty, if he ever got his hands on Ralph Penniman he would not be responsible for his actions.

"Let's go eat," he said. He knew that just telling her that she was not to blame would not be sufficient. It would take more than that to convince her, a lot more. But he would be there, and they had all the time in the world now.

Late evening meandered into night, and they sat out on the verandah watching the night sky and enjoying the breeze as it drifted off the ocean. Sean reclined on a lounger, hands linked behind his head. Racquel sat in a straight-backed chair, her legs propped on the edge of a circular glass table. It was such a long time since she had done this with anyone. Sitting beneath the night sky, enjoying the immensity of space, was a pleasure she had not indulged in since early childhood.

"Look, a shooting star," she said suddenly, pointing to an arching shower of lights.

Sean shielded his eyes with a hand. "Might be the fireworks display starting up."

Racquel got up and went to the rail. She followed the curve of light through the night sky. She turned back to him, her eyes glowing like those of a child's at Christmas.

"Come on, quick—make a wish, Sean."

He stood and came to her. "I wish—"

She cut him off. "Don't tell me. If you do, it won't come true."

He quirked an eyebrow at her. "My wish has already come true, so I'll give this one to you."

She closed her eyes, and her lips moved wordlessly.

Sean wondered what it was that she had wished for. Wealth? If that was her desire, he could give her that. Happiness? He could give her that too, if only she would let him. What else would a woman like Racquel Ward wish for?

He put his arms around her, bent his head, and kissed her on the side of the neck. At almost that very moment, a burst of red light exploded in the night sky. Then there was green. Blue. Yellow. White. Wonderful expanding balls of light, falling, dancing, intertwining. The sky was suddenly a live thing, a dark entity that somehow tantalized. And, from the streets below, horns sounded in acknowledgment of the spectacle.

When it was over, they both stood silent, each filled with a measure of contentment that neither had experienced since childhood.

Racquel finally spoke: "Does this happen every night?"

He pushed aside a silky curtain of hair, and pressed his cheek to hers. "No. Just on some weekends. There's jazz, too, at many of the hotels—mostly during the summer, though."

She drew in a breath, and let it out. "God, this must be a great place to live. Right on the ocean . . . and it's so clean and quiet. Not like LA." She shifted a bit to give him a puzzled look. "Why do you live there, anyway? In LA, I mean."

He played with the lobe of her ear. "I guess I was waiting for . . . someone."

Ten

The remainder of the evening went by so very quickly that before Racquel fully realized it it was almost midnight. It was incredible how very much she seemed to have in common with Sean KirPatrick. They liked a lot of the same things, had similar interests. They had fallen into an easy conversation, and had talked about every subject under the sun. Music. Politics. Science. Even sports. He was easy to talk to, and seemed genuinely interested in her opinion on things.

At one point in the evening she had come close to telling him of some of the very peculiar occurrences at the cottage, but things had been going so well that she hadn't wanted to spoil the relaxed mood with any mention of that bit of unpleasantness. There would be time enough later—if things continued in the same vein, there was every chance that she and Sean KirPatrick would become very good friends, and maybe even more than that.

When she began to yawn at a few minutes before twelve, Sean reluctantly came to his feet.

"I guess I should let you sleep. It has been a long day."

It suddenly occurred to Racquel that she had not brought a change of clothing with her.

"Sean," she said, "did you bring extra clothes with you?"

"A couple T-shirts. Why?"

She wrinkled her nose. "Could I borrow one, do you think?"

He gave her a wink. "Be back in a second."

He returned with an oversize Lakers T-shirt. "How's this?"

She took it from him and held it under her chin. "Perfect." When he continued to stand there, she said, "Would you like to stay in this room? There are two beds."

Sean gave the suggestion a moment's consideration. *Did she imagine he was made of steel? Or did she really have no idea of how very desirable she was?*

"No . . . no, I don't think I'd better do that. I . . . snore. Wouldn't want to keep you awake." He didn't, but it was the first available excuse that his mind had seized upon. "I'll see you in the morning. Seven OK?"

"Seven's fine." She nodded, wondering why it was that he suddenly appeared uncomfortable. She walked with him to the door, and wished that there was something that she could say to make him stay at least a bit longer. Could it be that she had only known him for mere days? It seemed completely impossible. They were so much in synch.

At the door, she asked again. "Sure you don't want to stay? It seems silly. We're both adults. Able to control our baser desires."

He looked down at her, humor dancing for a brief instant in his eyes. "Don't be too sure of that."

She was still thinking over that particular comment as she slid beneath the covers and drifted into contented sleep.

* * *

They spent most of the morning of the following day walking the beach. With pants legs rolled up, crabbing baskets in hand, and the dog chasing seagulls up and down the sand, they walked for what seemed miles. At some point in the day, before the sun was very hot, they located a quiet little cove and proceeded to search some of the shallow puddles for crabs.

"You know what just occurred to me," Racquel said after several dips of her basket into a deep pool. "What're we going to do with the things if we catch any?"

Sean plunged his basket down deep, then lifted, letting the water seep through the weave. "Eat them of course, my girl."

Racquel sat back on her heels, and allowed the basket to sink again. "I am not eating any of those horrible little things, Sean KirPatrick."

He laughed. "Yes you will, after I'm finished with them. Ever had sweet and sour crab salad?"

Racquel wrinkled her nose. "Sounds terrible."

He smiled. She had said the very thing about pickled pepper shrimp when he had introduced her to the taste of it so many years before.

He held out a hand. "Come on. There're no crabs here."

They continued up the beach, stopping every so often to explore a pool. At about two o'clock, Sean shielded his eyes against the sun to look at his watch.

"We'll have to come back here one of these weekends."

Racquel was in the middle of unearthing a particularly large and undamaged shell from the sand. She looked up at him from her squatting position. "Do we have to go?"

He sat in the sand beside her and leaned back on his

elbows. "Uh huh. You don't want to miss Morganna's barbecue, remember?"

She trailed a clump of sand through her fingers. "I wish we could stay longer." She didn't want to return to reality so soon. Reality meant going back to the cottage. Being alone. Being without him.

He wrapped long fingers about her wrist, and pulled her to lie beside him. "We can come back if you like . . . and stay longer, too. Maybe a week next time? Or two?"

She touched the side of his face and ran a finger slowly to the curve of his mouth. "Really?"

He pressed the softness of her palm to the flat of his face. "Really. Any time you like."

She traced the outline of his lips. "Isn't it funny how we just seem to get along?"

He kissed the inner flesh of her wrist. "Do you think we're soul mates? Somehow fated to be together through all eternity?"

She chuckled and pushed at his shoulder. "Ah, you're making fun now."

"You don't believe in any of that stuff, do you, Miss Practical?"

She pushed a swatch of hair behind an ear. "Are you saying I'm not a romantic?"

"I dunno. Are you?"

A smile flickered somewhere deep in her eyes. "I used to be."

Was it when we were together as children? Was that when?

The urge to ask was strong, but he held back the words. It was important to him now that she come to love the man he had become. He didn't want any of those feelings to be confused with what they might have shared in childhood. He had been her friend then, but his intentions now were distinctly different.

He came slowly to his feet and extended a hand to help her up. They stood for a while, looking at the ocean as it curled its offering of foam across the grainy sand.

Racquel sighed. "One of these days, when I have enough money . . . maybe I'll buy a house here. Somewhere right on the beach."

He looked down at her. "You like the ocean that much?"

"I love it. Always have. The sound of the waves. The salt in the air."

He took her by the hand again, and they began to walk back toward the car. "We'll have to come again soon, then. Take a look at some houses. Prime beachfront property, only."

Racquel laughed up at him. "I can't afford that right now. Not unless I sell the house back in Idaho, and maybe not even then. Besides, I have to stay in LA, for my acting."

"Hmm," he said, and he opened the front door to the Range Rover and guided her in. She turned in her seat to watch as he calmed the excited dog down sufficiently and got him into the backseat.

"He's really taken to you," she said. "I guess that must be a good sign."

Sean came around, got into the driver's seat, and closed the door. "Still don't trust me?"

"Oh, no," she said immediately. "I mean, I don't know you very well, but I think you're . . . you're OK." She had been about to say something much stronger, but had managed to restrain herself just in time. It wouldn't do at all for him to know how very taken with him she was at the moment.

He started the engine, and turned to smile in her direction. "Well, that's a start. The dog likes me, and you, Ms. Ward, think I'm OK."

She grinned at him. "You must be really popular with your female patients."

He slanted a look at her. "Oh, yeah? And why's that?"

"You're too, too charming. Good-looking, too. I bet you anything that you have tons of women chasing after you all the time."

He laughed. "Never the right ones, though."

They continued their banter back and forth, and the miles back to LA just melted away. It was a few minutes before five o'clock when he pulled the Range Rover to a stop before the little cottage. Racquel took a breath.

"Well," she said, turning in her seat to face him. "Here we are."

"Yes," Sean said, and he rested an arm on the steering wheel. "Are you going to be my date tonight at the barbecue?"

She nodded, and a playful expression danced in her eyes. "I would've been a little upset if you'd shown up with someone else."

He smiled. "Would you?"

She leaned forward to press a kiss to the side of his face. "I would. Very much."

His fingers came up to shift her face slightly, and his lips pressed warmly against hers for a moment. "You don't have to worry about that. I'm yours."

She pulled away from him, trying to hide her pleasure at his words with brisk activity. "Come on, Shag. Time to get out. We're home."

Sean walked around to the back door to let the big dog out. For the next several minutes, the animal pranced about the yard, barking loudly.

Sean walked her to the front door and stood waiting while she got out her key, opened the door, and fiddled around with the burglar alarm. When she was through, he whistled for the dog and slapped it on the rump as it went tearing through the front door of the house.

"Would you like me to come in and take a look around the place just to make sure everything's secure?"

He seemed not to want to leave her, and the very idea of that made Racquel happy. "Yes, thank you. That's . . . that's very thoughtful."

He entered, and for the next several minutes went from room to room, checking in closets, under beds, and other possible hiding places. When he was through, he returned to her. "No one but you, me, and the dog."

Racquel flopped onto the sofa. "I guess that burglar alarm really works."

Sean came to sit beside her. "I've been wondering about that. You recently installed that, didn't you?"

"Yes," Racquel said, and the memory of the music box came back to her. "I've had a couple of problems since I moved in here. Someone broke in here a few days ago."

Sean straightened, his face suddenly gone serious. "Someone broke in here? When? Was anything taken? Were you here?"

Racquel told him about the music box, but decided not to get him worked up about the voice on the phone. It had probably just been a prankster, anyway.

"I don't know if you should stay here alone," Sean said. "A woman obviously on her own is often a target for many of the predators out there."

Racquel gave his hand a tiny squeeze. "I'm not on my own, really. I've got the dog and the alarm system. And Morganna's just a few houses up the street. What can happen?"

Sean rubbed the back of his neck. "I don't know, but if someone is watching this house for some reason—"

"It was just a one time only kind of crime," she assured him. "These types of criminals strike once, and keep moving."

Sean shook his head. "But, he didn't take anything. He left you . . . a . . . a gift of some sort. That means he's no ordinary criminal, that he's singled you out for some reason. I don't like the sound of it at all."

Racquel sighed. She shouldn't have told him. The very same thoughts had occurred to her, too, but she had been trying to push them all to the back of her mind, hoping that somehow whoever it was would just go away and leave her to live in peace.

"Well . . . right now there's nothing else I can do. I've spoken to the local police department, and they agree that nothing else can be done until there's something more for them to go on."

"You can come and stay with me. I've a big house. A housekeeper. You could have your own room. No one would be able to bother you there."

"Oh, I . . . I couldn't live with you," she said, "it wouldn't be right."

Sean took her hand in his. "We wouldn't be living together. Not in that sense. The house is so big that many days, if . . . if you wanted it, you wouldn't even have to see me at all."

Racquel shook her head. "I don't know. All my things are here. I think we may be overreacting a little."

Sean stood, hands in pockets. "Well, I'll leave you to think it over. I'm going to get on home so that I can take a shower." He looked around the small room. "Lock every window and door when I leave, OK? Don't take any chances at all."

At the door, he said, "I'll be back for you at about a quarter to eight." He pressed a quick kiss to her mouth. "I'll wait here while you lock the door." He stood and waited until he heard the lock turn before he walked back to the Rover, opened the door, waved a hand out the window, and drove away.

Once he was gone, Racquel rested her back against the flat of the wooden door and closed her eyes. What a man. She was going to have to seriously rethink her position on not getting involved with anyone. Sean Kirpatrick was a rare find. Men like him definitely did not come along every day.

She went slowly up the stairs, still thinking of him. In her bedroom, she hunted quickly through the closet for clothes to wear that evening. She thought of wearing one of the light cotton dresses she and Morganna had picked up on Rodeo Drive. There was one, a little black sleeveless number that fell just above the knee and was deeply scooped in the back. With just the right heels, her hair held back in a tight ponytail, and a pair of dangling silver earrings, the right blend of casual sophistication might be achieved.

She spread the clothing out on the bed, then went to check the answering machine. Morganna had left her three messages. The final one asked that she call as soon as she got back in.

Racquel picked up the phone and dialed. A female voice with a slight Spanish accent answered, and Racquel said, "Is Morganna in?"

The woman, who turned out to be quite friendly and informative, told Racquel that Mrs. O'Bannon had run out to the grocery store, but would be back within the hour. Racquel thanked the woman, left her name and number, and went to take a long, hot shower. She stood under the showerhead, letting the force of the water beat against her scalp. Then she washed her hair, shaved her legs, and stepped from the shower cubicle to skillfully wrap her head and body in thick towels.

She was just bending over to dry her legs when the phone rang. She picked up her watch and took a glance at the face of it. Morganna was probably back from the supermarket. She walked across to the bed and lifted the handset.

"Hello?" she said, and her voice was bright and cheerful.

There was a pause, then, "You've been a bad girl, Racquel."

The sound of the man's voice was so unexpected that Racquel stood for several startled seconds with the receiver pressed against her ear, completely numbed into silence.

"I warned you that I'd be watching, didn't I?"

Her lips felt suddenly like stiff rubber. "Who . . . who are you?"

"You went away with that doctor. Spent the night with him. I don't like that. I don't like that at all."

"What . . . what do you want with me?" she screamed into the phone. "Why can't you just leave me alone?"

The voice continued in a strange monotone, almost as though she had not spoken. "I want you to stay away from that doctor, Racquel. If you don't, I'll make you sorry. Very sorry. Do you understand me? Stay away from him. I won't tell you again."

She dropped the receiver and stood looking down at where it lay on the floor, her eyes wild. Who was doing this? Why was he tormenting her in this fashion? What did he want?

She went quickly to the bedroom door, slammed and locked it. Suddenly the day had gone cold, and she was trembling. She walked to the bed on shaky legs and sat. From where the phone lay on the floor, the endless beeping of the dial tone gave a surrealistic feel to the entire situation. She sat until she could bear the sound no longer. Almost as soon as she replaced the receiver, the phone rang again. She stood with cold fingertips pressed to her lips, waiting for that voice to come over the answering machine. Even though she was petrified, her brain was still working. If the man did speak, she would have hard evidence of this harassment. It would be something definite to take to the police.

The answering machine beeped, and Morganna's bright voice came on:

"OK, Racquel . . . where are you? You'd better be at the barbecue tonight. I've got someone I want you to meet."

Racquel reached for the phone. "Morganna. Thank God."

Her friend's voice was immediately concerned.

"What's the matter? Had a fight with Sean so soon?"

Racquel took a steadying breath. "No. That's not it." And in one continuous gush she told her the entire story—everything that had happened since she moved into the cottage.

Morganna was silent for a minute after she was through. Then she said, "It's your ex-husband. You have to go to the police and let them know that he's been harassing you."

Racquel shook her head. "It's not him. I know his voice. There's no way he could disguise it in this way, either. This voice was deeper, raspier . . . you know? It sounded a bit as if the man had some sort of breathing problem, like, like—"

"Asthma?" Morganna asked.

"Could be," Racquel said. "It sounded as though he

was struggling for breath. I noticed it more this time than last."

"You mean he was breathing heavily?"

"Yes."

"Change your number right away to an unlisted one. You may have nothing more than one of those neighborhood perverts on the line. They usually prey on single women. Most of them are harmless, but you never can tell."

"But he . . . he must've been watching me. 'Cause he knew about Sean."

"Hmm." Morganna agreed, "Yeah, that's strange. Listen, do you want to come over early? Before everyone else gets here?"

"Sean's picking me up just before eight. I guess I could call him. Maybe I should, since—"

"Don't let that guy spook you," Morganna said. "Don't call it off with Sean . . . tell him about everything. Promise me you will."

"I promise," Racquel said, but she was not at all certain that she would.

"See you tonight, then?"

"OK."

"Don't worry, kiddo. This guy's probably one of these Hollywood weirdos. You're just not accustomed to them since you're from farm country in Idaho." Morganna made a feeble attempt to joke her out of the numb state she was in, and Racquel responded with a weak laugh.

"Yeah, maybe that's it," she said. But in her heart she knew that it was something else entirely. Something deeper, much darker. Something dangerous.

Eleven

Sean arrived at just before eight, as he had promised. He was dressed in a silver-gray cotton shirt buttoned down at the neck, and matching charcoal-gray slacks. Racquel was momentarily taken aback by the seamless male beauty of him. He stood looking down at her, his dark eyes gleaming in the light cast from one of the small, overhead lights above the front door.

"Wow," he said, "you look gorgeous."

Racquel gave him a tentative smile. She had settled on the little black dress with the scooped back, and clog-heeled, strappy sandals. Her hair was swept into a ponytail of cascading ringlets and secured with a lacquered bamboo clasp. She had applied very little makeup. A simple dusting of her lips with an orange bronze color, a black kohl pencil skillfully applied to her eyebrows, and the merest suggestion of rouge on her cheekbones. Although she had little awareness of the matter, she could very easily have stepped right onto the front cover of any of a variety of high fashion magazines.

Sean extended his arm. "My chariot awaits." He had driven his Jaguar this time.

Racquel closed and locked the door, then accepted his arm. It was a wonderfully balmy night, with an unseasonable Santa Ana wind stirring the treetops. A long line of cars was already winding its way up the hill to Morganna's house. Sean looked down at her shoes.

"I don't think we'd better walk. The hill might be a bit too steep for those shoes."

Racquel wrinkled her nose at him. "Yeah . . . I might turn my ankle. I guess they weren't a very smart choice." She was trying desperately not to think of the voice on the phone, and the implicit threat of violence in the man's tone.

"They were the perfect choice. Come on, we'll drive up there. If there's nowhere to park on the street, we'll just have to ditch the car in the middle of her lawn."

Racquel chuckled. "You're a crazy guy."

"Thank you," Sean said, and guided her into the front seat of the car. He walked quickly to the driver's side and climbed in. Before starting the engine he leaned toward her with a quizzical look.

"Do you have a kiss for the crazy man . . . before we go?"

Racquel took a surreptitious glance around to see if there was anyone watching. Then she leaned across to place a lightning kiss on his lips. When she drew back there was a smile lurking about his lips.

"Is that all I get?"

She grinned at him. Already her spirits were beginning to lift.

"For now."

He turned in his seat to start the car. "Heartless girl."

She laughed outright, then. Oh, what fun he was. She almost wished that she could spend all her available free time with him.

"Sean—" she began.

He turned to look at her. "Umm?"

The words were there, but she hesitated. She would tell him later about the caller, and about everything else. Tonight, she wanted to just have fun. She wanted to mingle with Morganna's friends, and completely forget the ominous feeling of foreboding that was beginning to nag at her.

The house at the top of the hill was completely ablaze with lights. There were colorful Japanese lanterns strung out front, and fairy lights blinked on and off in the surrounding trees and bushes. Cars of every size and description lined both sides of the street, and there were two men dressed in red coats standing in the middle of the road, directing traffic. "Well," Sean said, rolling down the window. "This is going to be much easier than I'd thought. She's hired a valet parking service."

Racquel waited by the side of the road while Sean spoke briefly to the parking attendant.

"What'd you say to him?" she asked when he came back over to her.

"Just asked him to find a good spot for the car . . . and gave him a little incentive to do so."

Racquel quirked an eyebrow at him. "Is that how business is done in Hollywood?"

"Hollywood, as well as in most big cities." He offered her his arm again, and they proceeded up the long stretch of cobblestone pathway. The sounds of a party well in progress greeted them as they approached the front door.

Racquel glanced at her watch. "We're not late, are we?"

Sean pressed the bell. "No. Right on time. I've heard that Morganna's parties are always an event, so it could be that a few people got here a bit early. She always invites the best of the Hollywood 'A' list. You can expect to run into movie stars, musicians, studio heads— just about anybody who's doing something newsworthy in town."

Racquel gave her dress a look. "Do you think I'm dressed all right? I mean, I had no idea it was going to be something like this."

"You look beautiful," Sean said, and leaned on the bell again. After the second ring, the door was thrown back. Morganna stood on the threshold, smiling warmly. She was dressed in a svelte, turquoise-blue dress, with matching slip-on, high-heeled sandals. Her hair was immaculately styled, and fell in soft curls about her ears.

"You're here," she said, and enveloped Racquel in a huge hug. "Come in . . . come in. We're just getting started." She waved a hand toward a large group of people who were milling about with drinks in their hands. "Do you mind if I steal Racquel for a minute, Sean? You'll find hors d'oeuvres and drinks over there."

With that, she wrapped a hand through the crook of Racquel's arm and pulled her away. In the kitchen, she closed the door and then said, "So, did you tell him?"

Racquel went to the window and looked out on the massive backyard. "You didn't tell me it was going to be this big. I thought there'd be maybe ten people at most. Looks like you've got about a hundred out there right now."

"Well," she said, momentarily distracted, "I didn't really intend it to be this big, but I kept inviting people, and they kept saying yes."

Racquel turned from the window with a smile. "So . . . you really know all those people out there, huh?"

Morganna nodded. "Most of them. Charley invited a few cronies from Warners . . . and they may have invited a few of their own friends. You know, producers, maybe a couple stars—who knows? People come to these things mostly to drink booze and network. Lots of deals are made at events like this." She took Racquel's arm again. "Let me introduce you around. I want a few people from the studio to get a good look at you."

The spacious living room was even more crowded now, and for a moment a feeling of panic overtook Racquel. What if she made an absolute fool of herself in front of all these people? What would she say to them? They all appeared to be so very urbane and sophisticated, so well in tune with the Hollywood jet set.

Morganna was pulling her along, weaving her way confidently through the crush of people. "There's Rod," she said, and waved at a tall, lanky man dressed in black leather and shades. Racquel was barely able to get a look at the man before Morganna was yanking her along to someplace else.

Above the noise of multiple voices, she asked, "That wasn't who I think it was, was it?"

Morganna nodded. "Yeah. I'd heard he was in town. He's probably doing a gig at the Bowl. Oh, *there* he is. Come on. You have to meet this guy."

A fine sheen of perspiration now dotted Racquel's brow, and she fanned herself with her free hand.

"Here. Wipe your face with this." A square of tissue was pressed into her hand. "This guy," Morganna whispered, "is looking for a new face to star in his next movie. If you impress him, he may just cast you on the spot. I've seen him do it before."

Racquel carefully blotted her face, and prepared herself mentally. "Do I look OK?" she asked Morganna in a low voice.

"Perfect. Come on."

They approached two men who were standing out on the wraparound verandah. Racquel made eye contact with the tall man who was facing her, and smiled. The shorter, more rotund man, who was standing with his back to them, turned to see who his companion had just smiled at. Racquel felt everything in her come to an icy, slithering halt. There was no mistaking the bulging gut, the florid, jowly face, the horrible soft mouth. *Armand Jacques.*

Her heart lurched in her chest, then commenced an awful pounding. He was smiling at her in the same lascivious manner she remembered. Her throat tightened up, and she tried to bring her distress to the attention of Morganna, but her friend was still pulling her along. Before she could even think to do anything else, she was standing directly before him.

"This is the young lady I wanted you to meet, Armand," Morganna was saying, pushing Racquel's icy cold hand into the grasp of the producer's meaty paw.

The soft hand folded around hers, and an involuntary shudder raced through Racquel. His eyes squinted at her from behind his black-rimmed glasses.

"So, this is the one," he said.

Racquel pulled her hand from his. "Mr. Jacques and I have met," she said coldly.

Armand Jacques gave her a genuinely blank look. "We have?" Then he laughed. "Oh, yes. You were at Ron's house for that post-premiere party last week. Nice to see you again."

Racquel swallowed, and forced herself to be calm. Could it be that he had actually forgotten his attempted assault on her? Could he really not remember the face of the woman whose career he had threatened to ruin even before it had gotten a chance to get started? Or was the blank lack of recognition in his eyes just a very deliberate pretense?

Morganna flashed a quick look in her direction. "Racquel's pretty hot property, Armand. I've been talking to a couple of people at Warners about her. She just has that sex symbol, leading lady quality, doesn't she?"

Racquel's hands were bunched at her sides as the producer looked her over. "Have you signed with Warners yet?" he asked.

Seeing him again in the light of day made her so furious that the simple act of carrying on a conversation was too much for her. Without any thought to the consequences of her actions, Racquel turned abruptly and walked away from him. She pushed her way through the crowd until the front door was in sight. She wouldn't stay, couldn't stay, in the same room as Jacques, not without hurling a drink in his face, or bashing him over the head with the largest vase in the room. The bastard. The slimy bastard. He didn't even remember her.

The front door opened, and two more people came in. From somewhere behind, she could hear someone calling out to her. Before she could make it to the door, she felt a hand on her arm.

"Where're you going? What happened?" It was Morganna.

Racquel shook her head. "I can't stay."

"Why not? He liked you."

"A little too much, I think. I've met him before."

Morganna blinked at her. "In Idaho?"

"Right here. In LA. He tried to attack me."

There was bald disbelief on Morganna's face. "He what?" She took Racquel by the arm and pulled her away from the front door. "Come on, let's go upstairs. We can talk there."

There was another sitting room on the second floor of the house. It was a sprawling, very well-furnished and decorated room that ran the entire length of the house. Racquel sank into the first available chair, and Morganna came to sit beside her. "Would you like something to drink? You look ill."

Racquel took a deep breath. "No. I'll be fine. Really. It was just the shock of seeing him again."

"Tell me," Morganna said, and Racquel proceeded to do just that. When she was through. Morganna sat back.

"My God," she said, "I don't believe it. I mean, I'd heard rumors about him, but I never thought any of it was true. I always knew that he maybe drank a little too much."

"Well, he was probably drunk that night. Maybe that's why he doesn't remember me."

"We're just gonna have to turn him down, then."

Racquel frowned. "What do you mean?"

"He told me after you'd walked away that he thought you might be right for the part in his movie. I didn't know about any of this other stuff, so I told him if the terms were agreeable, you might consider it."

"Oh, God," Racquel said, and buried her face in her hands. "This can't be happening."

"I have an idea," Morganna said. "We'll play him off against Warners."

"What?"

"We'll use his offer to get an even better one from Warner Brothers." She leaned forward. "OK, here's what we'll do . . ."

* * *

Sean found them huddled together on the sofa, talking when he entered the room. He was carrying a plate stacked with savory pastries, sandwiches, and barbecue.

"I've been looking all over for you two," he said with a smile. "I brought you some food," and his gaze rested for a second on Racquel's lips.

He came to sit on the long sofa, and Morganna rose to her feet. "We'll talk more later," she said to Racquel. "I'm going to go down and get the music started. Come down when you're ready." With that, she was gone.

Sean rested the plate on the center table, which sat directly before the chair. "What's wrong?" he asked.

Racquel looked at him, and wondered how it was that he was so very perceptive. "It's a long story," she said.

He stretched a hand out to capture one of hers. "Come here." She sidled closer, and he put an arm about her. "Do you want to go?" he asked softly.

Racquel nodded. "It's . . . it's a nice party, but I don't really feel much like staying now."

He stroked the side of her face with a finger. "Me neither. Let's go."

It took a bit of doing to get out of the house. There were people sitting on the stairs, and an ever increasing crowd milling about before the front door. Sean took Racquel by the elbow and maneuvered her through the crush of people. When they were finally outside, Racquel took a grateful breath of fresh air.

"My God," she said, "it's just wall-to-wall people in there." She opened up her clutch bag and removed a delicately embroidered handkerchief. "We really should have let Morganna know we were leaving."

Sean took a glance back at the house. "She'll understand. You can give her a call once you get back home."

"OK," Racquel agreed. "Did you see Charley in there?"

Sean nodded. "He was out in the backyard barbecuing the meat. He asked for you."

"I like him," Racquel said. "They're both nice."

Sean looked down at her. "You're nice, too."

Racquel blinked. "Me? Nice?"

He touched the tip of her nose with a finger. "Yes . . . you . . . nice."

She beamed at him and settled herself comfortably in the passenger seat of the car. Sean went around to the driver's side and got in.

"Do you want to go straight home, or would you like to go for a drive?"

"A drive? Where?"

He shrugged. "Anywhere you like."

She looked at her dress. "Should I change first?"

He laughed. "Jeans and a T-shirt?"

"That's it," she said, giving him a cheeky grin. "Maybe we can go see a movie, or just sit and talk somewhere—"

He started the engine. "OK. I'm game. We'll do both."

Back at the house, Racquel darted up the stairs and slid quickly out of the dress. She pulled on a well-worn pair of jeans and a maroon sweatshirt. In less than ten minutes, she was trotting back downstairs to the living room with Shaggy at her heels.

"I think I'll leave him out in the yard until we get back. We shouldn't be gone that long, right?"

Sean's eyes flickered over her trim form. "Couple hours at most."

"OK, then," she said, her eyes sparkling. "Let's go."

For the remainder of the night, she did her best to forget about Armand Jacques—and the faceless man who continued to harass her on the phone.

Twelve

The morning rain came down in a fine, soporific drizzle. The sky was a dirty metal-gray, and a blustery, northeasterly wind skidded across windshields, flattening the puddling raindrops and making the morning commute tough going.

The Monday morning rush-hour traffic was always a challenge, but this morning Sean KirPatrick found himself on the freeway stuck in a mile-long, slow-moving queue of cars. Every so often a car would pull off to the side, drive the shoulder, then slip back into the stack of vehicles ahead of him. Ordinarily, indulging in behavior such as this would not have been a viable option for Sean, but this morning, he considered it for a second. He was in danger of being late for his first consultation. Admittedly, it was only a nose job and a breast reconstruction, but it was important to him that he never keep any of his patients waiting. It was a courtesy which he afforded everyone, clients and friends alike. And, the only reason he wasn't at the clinic at this very moment was because he had overslept—something that had never happened before.

He checked his watch again, picked up the car phone, and hit the quick dial button. The crisply efficient voice of the head nurse answered after the first ring.

"Nurse Brown—good morning. Is Mrs. Friedman there yet?"

Holly Brown checked the patient log. "No, Doctor, not yet. Will you be late?"

Sean scanned the cars ahead of him. "There's a very good chance that I might be. I'm stuck on the freeway. If she gets there before I do, extend my apologies and keep her entertained, will you?"

Holly Brown chuckled. "I'll do my best, Doctor Kir-Patrick."

Sean hung up and went back to doing battle with the rain and the traffic. For the first time in his entire professional life he wished that he might have been able to take the day off. He had not been able to sleep well the night before for worrying about Racquel Ward. He had not mentioned any of his suspicions to her, but it was his belief that someone had been on her property on more than one occasion in the last several weeks. On Sunday evening he had taken a casual look around the yard, and had found an empty box of cigarettes with fresh ashes, and—most disturbing—a large, sharp-bladed kitchen knife stuck into the ground beneath one of the orange trees. He had gone back to his car, and returned with two ziplock bags. The knife had gone into one, and the cigarette ash into the other. He had made a late-night call to Henry Yau in LAPD forensics. Yau was a good man, well known for his technical expertise in difficult criminal investigations. If there was any information to be had from the knife or the ashes, Sean was convinced Yau would find it.

He had not been able to do too much more looking around after that—because Racquel had come out of the house in search of him. He had not wanted to worry her with something that might not even be important—but he had made up his mind to watch her carefully.

He was even considering hiring a private investigator to keep an eye on her house.

A car horn blared loudly from behind, and Sean inched the sleek nose of the Jaguar forward, paying little attention to the demeanor of the motorist. California drivers were notoriously rude and impatient in the rain.

The sound of sirens came suddenly out of the slushing quiet, and a black-and-white unit with flashing red and blue lights zipped by on the shoulder of the road, only to be followed by a second and third car just minutes later. A frown rippled the smooth skin of Sean's forehead, and for no clearly discernible reason he reached for his car phone again. He dialed her number with the handset tucked beneath his chin, and waited with uncharacteristic impatience as the ringing continued. He listened to her voice on the answering machine, and forced himself to be calm. She was still asleep, that was all. It was still very early in the morning, not even eight o'clock yet. Or, she could even have gone for a run. She was very conscientious about her exercise program. There was no need to panic just because she didn't answer. No need at all.

Half an hour later, as he was finally exiting the freeway, Sean dialed Racquel's number yet again. A fine sheen of perspiration had broken out on his forehead, and he wiped the moisture away with an impatient hand. He left a message this time, asking her to ring him at the office as soon as she got his call. He tried to keep the note of urgency from his voice, but the unexplainably crushing worry he felt made his voice seem clipped, almost brusque.

Walking into the office fifteen minutes later, he greeted the bright good mornings of his staff with a brief nod. Holly Brown straightened her white tunic before collecting the first patient file and following him back into his consulting rooms. Usually, she made light chitchat with him before launching into the business of the day, but she sensed something different about him this morning, and wisely decided to focus her attention on the morning roster.

"Mrs. Friedman has just arrived, Doctor," she said. "She's in examination room A." Sean accepted the file, scanned it quickly, then said, "If someone by the name of Racquel Ward calls while I'm in consultation, please come and get me right away."

Nurse Brown nodded, and a pleased smile came and went in her eyes. So, Doctor KirPatrick was in love at last. She'd been wondering when it would happen. Racquel Ward, whoever she was, was a very lucky young lady, indeed. She had seen scores of beautiful young women come and go during the five years that she had worked at the KirPatrick Surgery. The women, without exception, had come to adore the handsome young doctor in very short order, but there had always been a distinct lack of reciprocation on his part. The office staff had, unbeknownst to the doctor, often indulged in friendly wagers on the possible longevity of one female companion or another. This time, her money would be on Racquel Ward. There had been something different in the doctor's eye, and in his manner, when he had mentioned her name.

Holly Brown went back to her other duties presently, and Sean walked briskly down the whitewashed corridor, knocked on the door marked with a large A, then entered.

Gloria Friedman was seated in one of the comfortable, soft-backed chairs, her legs elegantly crossed at the ankles. She was one of the wealthiest widows in Beverly Hills, and took much delight in letting everyone know how very much she suffered because of it. She gave Sean a peevish look.

"Doctor KirPatrick. I can always count on you not to keep me waiting. Everyone else takes such advantage of me because I am a lonely old woman."

Sean gave the widow a charming smile, and before long she was sufficiently calm and ready for the preliminary examination.

A half hour later, a nurse's aide was helping the woman back into her clothing, and confirming an appointment for reconstructive breast surgery. Sean had managed, quite successfully, to talk her out of having any cosmetic nasal reconstruction done.

His next appointment was with a well-known actress—a routine face-lift consultation. He spent several minutes answering the standard questions about scarring and subsequent sagging of the skin and several minutes more in the actual examination of her face. His fingers were light and skilled as he turned the face from side to side. Near the tail end of his examination, Holly Brown pushed at the door and entered. "That call you were expecting has come in, Doctor KirPatrick."

Sean stood back with a reassuring smile. "Well, I don't anticipate any problems here," he said. "Nurse Brown will schedule you for surgery this week." With a few additional words of reassurance, he left the actress in the capable hands of his nurse.

In his office, he glanced at his watch before telling the receptionist to send the call through. He had exactly ten minutes before his schedule of afternoon appointments would begin.

"Kelli," he said, picking up the phone after the very first ring. "Are you—" He paused to collect his thoughts. Why shouldn't she be all right? He was allowing the irrational fear he felt for her safety to addle his brain. "I mean, how are you?"

Racquel looked down at the dog lying beside her. His right paw was heavily bandaged, and he rested rather mournfully, head between his legs.

"I'm great," she said, "but Shag had a small accident."

Sean's heartbeat quickened. "Accident?"

She nodded, even though he couldn't see her. "I'm not sure what happened. I let him out early this morning, and he was running about in the backyard, barking—you know, the way he usually does—then he suddenly cried out, and started the most terrible yelping. I took him to the vet. Seems his paw's broken, poor thing."

"Where was he playing?" Sean asked, and tried to keep any note of concern from his voice.

"In the backyard. You know, close to that clump of orange and lemon trees?"

Sean gave a noncommittal grunt. He knew very well which clump of trees she was referring to.

"Listen Racquel—" he began, but she interrupted him before he could finish.

"Thanks for the roses," she said.

Sean blinked. "Roses?"

"You sent me an entire basket of bloodred roses this morning, didn't you? I thought maybe that was why—" She paused, too. "You didn't send them?"

Sean rubbed a hand across his jaw. "I would like to say I did, but no, I didn't send them."

A frown creased the skin between her brows. "Well, maybe it was someone else." Someone like Armand Jacques. But, why would he? It didn't make sense, somehow.

"Kelli," Sean said, "there's something I want to talk

to you about, but I have another patient appointment in a couple of minutes. I'll call you back at around two o'clock. Will you be at home?" He was tempted to tell her to lock the doors and windows and not venture from the house. Even after he had hung up he sat for a full minute wondering if it would not be better to err on the side of caution, and be wrong.

Racquel hung up after assuring him that she would be at home, and continued listening to the messages on the answering system. Sean's message had been the very first, and she had stopped the play of the tape and called him as soon as she had listened to his message. She had thought he sounded anxious, and had assumed that he might have been waiting to hear from her about the roses.

The final message on the system had her sitting right on the edge of the bed, and gripping at the bedclothes. She pressed the repeat button, listened to the entire message again, then picked up the phone and dialed Morganna. As soon as her friend came on the line, she was babbling happily.

"Oh, my God, Morganna . . . I can't believe it. I just can't believe it. What did you do? Who'd you call?"

Morganna grinned at the receiver in her hand. "So, Warners called, did they? I thought they might. It's a game they play, you know—anything Jacques wants, they also want."

"But . . . a movie contract? Without seeing a screen test, an audition tape? How? I mean, it can't be. It must be a joke. You're playing a joke on me, right? You got one of your friends to call?"

Morganna gave an indignant cluck of her tongue. "Joke? Don't be silly, kiddo. I never joke when it comes to big money. Don't call them back yet. Let them stew for a bit. They already know that I'm work-

ing as your agent. I'm seeing a seven-figure deal
here . . . and of course I get ten percent."

Racquel nodded stiffly. Ten percent, fifteen percent . . .
who cared? What mattered was that she was just about
to be signed by one of the largest movie studios in the
world. The very thought of it was enough to make her
drop the phone and begin shrieking at the top of her
lungs. It was a miracle. Just too unbelievable to be true.

"What if . . . what if they—they don't like me? You
know after—after I sign? I mean, what if they think I
can't act? Do I get fired?" She picked up the phone
again with trembling hands.

Morganna chuckled. "That's what contracts are for,
kid. You sign, they sign, and if they try to back out of
the deal, we sue them."

Racquel took a large breath. "Incredible. I had no
idea you were so tough."

"That's the way the game is played. Don't worry,
you'll learn it. Listen, I've got to run, but I'll call you
back later, OK? And congratulations. Enjoy it."

Racquel sat on the corner of the bed for a long time
after that, listening to the message over and over again.
Then she picked up the phone and called her aunt in
New York. She had to tell someone. She had to tell
everyone. Anyone at all who would listen. She was so
very happy that she could almost pick up the phone
and call her ex-husband in Idaho, but not even the
promise of a movie contract was sufficient enticement
to make her behave in such a foolhardy manner. It was
highly unlikely that Ralph would even be happy for her.
Besides, in very short order, he would know exactly
where she was. After more than a month spent bliss-
fully without him, she wasn't at all anxious to have
him dogging her footsteps again.

Her chat with her aunt Ada, who was getting on in

age, was brief. Racquel spent a bit of time inquiring after her health, and reassuring her that she was fine living all alone in the wilds of LA. Then, she explained what it meant to have a movie contract, and how much money she was likely to make. She rang off after a while, and went outside to collect the mail. Although it was a very wet and murky day, there was a deep, satisfied happiness in her. Her life's ambition was about to come true. She was actually on her way to becoming a real actress—a genuine Hollywood star, with a dressing room on a studio lot somewhere—her name on the door, flowers, and seltzer bottles filled with the purest water on a little table arranged just for her. It was going to be wonderful. Life was really beginning to go her way. Finally, finally, things were coming together.

She knew no one other than Sean and Morganna well enough to call, so for most of the afternoon she contented herself with the knowledge that she would soon be speaking to Sean again.

At a few minutes after two the phone rang and Racquel, who had been right in the middle of preparing a huge batch of butter sponge batter, quickly ran the cold water tap on her hands, and went to answer the phone.

"Sean," she said, after hearing his voice. "Never in a million years will you be able to guess what's happened."

Sean's heart contracted, and a feeling of near panic overtook him.

"What? What's happened now?"

She appeared momentarily startled by his response. "Oh . . . it's nothing negative. It's just one of the best things in the world that could ever happen to me."

Sean relaxed visibly. "You got a part?" he asked, a smile creeping into his voice.

"More than that," she said. "I've gotten a contract.

A contract from Warner Brothers. Can you believe it? They want to create a couple of projects around me, they said. Isn't that incredible?"

Sean laughed. "Finally, after all these years. You're really going to become an actress. I'm so happy for you, Kelli. Listen," he said, "we have to celebrate. I want you to come over to the house tonight. I'll cook you dinner and we'll talk about some things—things I should've told you long ago. I should be there by about six. All right?"

"Sounds great," Racquel said. "I was just preparing a butter sponge. I'll bring that for dessert. You like sponge cake, don't you?" she asked, a hint of hesitancy suddenly in her voice.

"I love it," he said. *And I love you.* The words were there, but he knew that he could not say them to her. Not now. Not so very soon. She didn't love him. She hardly even knew him. At least she was no longer afraid of him. And he liked to think that she trusted him a little.

"Bring Shaggy, if you don't want to leave him alone."

"I will," she said, and went happily back to mixing the batter, after hanging up the phone.

By late afternoon there were three freshly baked cakes sitting atop the center island in the kitchen. Racquel spent several more minutes icing them with a specially prepared, cream-colored butter frosting, and carefully added a ring of silver balls to the face and base of each cake. When she was through, she stood back to take a look at her handiwork. After a moment of consideration, she decided that the only thing needed now was a slight grating of milk chocolate. She did this with quick hands, dusting the top and sides of each cake with slivers of chocolate gratings. Two of the cakes were placed on cakestands, and covered, while the remaining was shoved back into the oven.

By five-thirty, Racquel was making her way down the path to the little Volkswagen. In her hands, she carried two cakes. She opened the passenger door, settled them both very carefully in the seat, then turned and whistled for Shaggy.

"Sit right here until I get back," she said. The dog gave a thump of his tail in response. She climbed in behind the wheel and carefully pulled into the street. As soon as she was safely on the road the dog stood up, balancing itself on three legs, and began to bark. Racquel wound the window down, and shoved her head out.

"Ssh," she said, "I'll be back for you in a minute." The dog flopped down onto his paws again, and stared after the retreating car with mournful eyes.

Racquel drove the short distance up the hill to Morganna's house. She was in and out of the car quickly, balancing the cake and stepping with great care around huge puddles of rainwater. At the door, she leaned forward and pressed the buzzer with her forehead. When the door opened, she smiled at the housekeeper.

"Is Morganna at home?"

The woman returned her smile, and told her that Morganna had gone out for a little while. Racquel handed over the cake. "Tell her that I stopped by," she said, "and that I'll give her a call later on tonight."

She was in her little car, and driving back down the hill in less than five minutes. At her gateway, she stood on the brake, and was forced to pump it more than once in order to bring the car to a complete stop. She unfastened her seatbelt, and shifted the cake to sit between her legs. Then she leaned across to open the passenger door and whistled for the dog. He came immediately, his limping gait causing him to take a lot longer than usual. She put her fingers under his collar, and helped him into the passenger seat. Once he was comfortably settled, she released the brake and continued down the hill.

Sean got home at a few minutes after six o'clock. His housekeeper, Mrs. Robards, a stout, middle-aged woman with merry eyes, met him at the door.

"Good evening, doctor," she said pleasantly, and took his coat across to the finely carved stand in the nicely polished foyer.

"Has Miss Ward arrived yet?" he asked once he was inside and the door was closed.

"Not yet. Are you certain you don't need me to stay and cook dinner for you tonight?"

Sean gave his watch a quick glance. "No, Mrs. Robards. It's going to rain again this evening, by the looks of the sky. You go on home, take an early night. I'll be fine. I promise." He smiled reassuringly at her while his mind went on to something else entirely. There just might be enough time to grab a quick shower, a change of clothing, and a shave. Also, he wanted to spend some more time carefully thinking about what it was he wanted to say to Racquel. He had firmly decided to give up the silly memory game he had been playing, and let her know exactly who he was. He also wanted to broach the subject of her living with him, once again. This time, he intended to be a little more persuasive.

"Maybe I might help you prepare the roast, Doctor KirPatrick?" Mrs. Robards pressed. Sean gave his housekeeper a speculative look. He was very sure that the only reason she was so intent on delaying her departure was to have a look at the young lady with whom he would be having dinner. For some reason, still decidedly unclear to him, most of the women in his employ appeared to take an enormous amount of interest in his love life.

He was a reasonable man, though, and tonight, a happy one. And he did want them all to see Racquel. Why not? He was proud of her.

"Just the seasoning, then, Mrs. Robards . . . and maybe if you have the time, the potatoes?"

He went off to take a shower, amused by the look of genuine pleasure that flashed across his house-keeper's face.

Thirteen

Racquel shifted gears as the car coasted down the steep hill. The road was still very slick from the day-long rain, and the runoff from a broken drainage pipe streamed down one side of the street. At the light, she stopped to adjust the positioning of the cake stand in her lap, then continued on down the hill. Ahead of her, the rush-hour traffic was beginning to thicken, and she gave her watch a quick glance, then stepped on the gas. If she got caught in the stream of cars exiting the freeway at the next major intersection, it would be at least an hour before she made it to Sean's house.

Beside her, the dog raised its massive head to give her arm a soft nuzzle. Racquel took her eyes from the road for a second, and reached across to stroke the hairy head. In that split second, a tractor trailer making a right turn onto the intersecting street began its laborious maneuver, cutting across one of the oncoming lanes of traffic.

Racquel shifted her eyes back to the road, and her heart lurched. The tractor trailer was slanted across the road, completely blocking her lane of traffic. On instinct, she wrenched hard at the steering wheel and swung out into the oncoming traffic lane. What happened next seemed to unravel in a peculiar sort of slow motion. First there was the sight of a car approaching at a rapid pace in the oncoming lane and her foot pumping anxiously at the brakes, then a certain realization that she was going to collide head-on with it. Then there were the sounds of screeching brakes, horns blowing, glass breaking, people shouting. At some point before she lost consciousness, she realized that her forehead had hit something very cold and very hard.

Her cheekbones shattered as she was catapulted through the tiny windshield and out onto the hood of the car. The driver of the tractor trailer, who had been largely responsible for the pileup, was the first one out of his vehicle. He ran across to the tiny Volkswagen, which was now wedged beneath the trailer portion of his truck.

"Oh my God," he said, and his voice took on a note of near hysteria. "She's under the truck. She's wedged under the truck!"

In less than five minutes, there were several police cars at the busy intersection. Sergeant Dickerson, who had been witness to many an accident in his long career with the LAPD, found himself hoping, as he directed traffic away from the scene, that the girl wedged beneath the tractor trailer was dead. He watched as the jaws of life cut through the side of the truck, and slowly, piece by piece, removed the tangled wreckage of the little car. The girl was lying faceup, in a strangely twisted position on the hood of the car. Her lower legs still dangled in the body of the little car, and one of her arms lay across her body and was turned at a peculiar angle.

His eyes flickered quickly over the bloody body. Then he turned back to manage the gathering crowd of onlookers. He figured that the girl was dead. And, a good thing too, for, as far as he could tell, her body had been very badly mangled, and she no longer possessed any semblance of a face.

At five minutes before seven, Sean removed the roast from the oven, tested the tenderness of the meat with the tip of a cooking fork, then shoved the transparent dish back into the oven. Mrs. Robards, who had managed to talk the doctor into a grand dinner, was busy over the candied yams.

"Well," she said, looking up from her busy ministrations, "we've got everything prepared now. The potato salad's cooling in the fridge, and the beans are nicely steamed—"

Sean's attention had been caught by the sight of a car pulling up before the gateway. He wiped his hands on a dishtowel and went to the window. A slight frown creased the skin between his eyebrows. Morganna.

The housekeeper noticed the car, too, and asked when the doorbell rang, "Do you want me to get that?"

Sean shook his head. "No. You finish up here. I'll take care of it." Morganna had quite probably dropped by for a social visit, not knowing that he intended spending a very intimate evening with Racquel.

He opened the front door after the second ring of the bell and prepared to politely explain things to her. The expression on Morganna's face caused a prickle of cold fear to skitter across his skin. He stood in the middle of the doorway, a hand resting on the doorjamb. His eyes flickered over her face, taking in the trembling of the mouth and the gathering of tears in her eyes.

"Where is she?" he asked. The question was rapped out almost viciously. Morganna took a breath, and tried to control the tremor in her voice.

"She's had an accident," she managed after a momentary struggle. "She's at Cedars Sinai."

Sean swallowed away the dryness at the back of his throat. "How bad?" he said.

Morganna blinked two bloodshot eyes at him, and said, "Bad. Very bad. She . . . she may not make it." Then she burst into a spate of uncontrolled sobbing.

Sean turned away from the doorway. "Mrs. Robards," he bellowed. "Get my bag, please. And put in a call to Nurse Brown. Tell her to meet me at Cedars."

The housekeeper, well-trained to assist the doctor in cases of emergency, asked no questions about the large meal sitting at the ready in the kitchen. She returned with the doctor's medical bag in very short order and walked with him out to his car, all the while taking rapid-fire orders.

"Leave your car here," Sean said to Morganna. "You can pick it up later. You're going to ride with me. I need to know more about Racquel—her condition, and what happened exactly. OK? And don't worry," he said to the still sniffling woman, "she's not going to go . . . away. I won't let her." He was completely professional now, his voice as calm and reassuring as it would be during one of his more taxing surgical procedures.

At the hospital, they were quickly shown to the intensive care unit. The attending physician, Doctor Van Cooten, was well acquainted with Sean and his particular set of skills. He took Sean aside and spoke to him in a low professional tone.

"She's still in a coma," he said. "Severe head trauma. Broken bones. If she makes it through the night, though—and that's a big if—she's going to need your help."

Sean listened with little visible emotion to the medical description of Racquel's injuries. At the end of it all he said, "I'll sit with her through the night, doctor. I've asked one of my nurses to meet me here. I hope you don't mind."

Doctor Van Cooten walked with Sean into the tiny, curtained off ICU room. "At times like these, all feelings of professional territoriality should be suspended. Sit with her, Doctor KirPatrick. Who knows, a familiar voice may help her."

Tears prickled at the backs of Sean's eyes as he stood over the bed, looking down at the body lying so still, hooked up to a network of tubes and monitors. The entire head region was bandaged, leaving slits for her eyes, nose, and lips. One arm was also bandaged and in a sling, while the other lay limply at her side, very badly lacerated and covered with purple bruises.

Doctor Van Cooten came to stand at his side. "We had to shave her head, of course. Her scalp was very badly torn."

Sean pulled a chair close to the bed, and sat. He picked up the bruised hand with great care, and gently stroked the fingers. Doctor Van Cooten, after checking on the vital signs of his patient, left the room. It was not often that he allowed himself to become personally attached to a patient, but the severity of this particular case made him feel an automatic sympathy for the terribly disfigured young woman clinging to life in the narrow bed. If she made it, she would require major reconstructive surgery on her face. He had heard, as had most others in the medical community, of the almost magical skill of Sean KirPatrick's fingers, but in this case he had to wonder if even KirPatrick would be able to restore the girl's face to any semblance of normalcy.

Morganna crept noiselessly into the room shortly after Doctor Van Cooten's departure, and sat at the other side of the bed. She covered her mouth with a hand, and sat for long minutes nibbling on a thumbnail.

"Do you think we should let that ex-husband of hers know what's happened?" she finally asked. "Just, just in case? I don't think she has any other family."

Sean looked up at her with cold eyes. "Ralph Penniman is not her family. I am."

Morganna was shocked into silence by the vehemence of his response.

Several minutes passed before Sean was able to lift his head again and say, "I'm sorry. I didn't mean to snap at you."

Morganna nodded. "I understand." And she did. As incredible as it seemed, and after such a very short acquaintance, too, Sean KirPatrick appeared to be in love with Racquel Ward.

"We'll talk to her," Morganna said, after a moment spent studying Sean's face. "I've read of many accounts where people in comas have responded favorably to—to the voices of people they care for."

Sean nodded, and continued to stroke the back of the bruised hand. "You talk . . . I can't right now."

Fourteen

Ralph Penniman got out of his battered jalopy and stood for a long while looking up at the wonderfully constructed edifice—Cedars Sinai Hospital. The cool morning breeze whipped around the edges of his raised collar, and he took a moment to fasten the buttoning at the neck and draw the string tight about his face. Then, with head bent against the wind, he walked purposefully toward the entrance of the hospital. Under one arm, he carried a bunch of long-stemmed roses.

Sean had stepped out of the room to have a word with Doctor Van Cooten, so when Racquel's eyes flicked open for the first time since the accident of the previous day, the man seated at her bedside, with a look of grave concern on his face, was Ralph Penniman.

Racquel struggled with the heavy weight pressing at her eyelids, and tried to focus on the hulking form at her bedside. After a moment, she gave up and closed her eyes. She tried to move her lips, but the slightest twitch caused terrible pains to radiate out toward the dome of her skull.

The shape at her bedside reached out to give one of her hands a pat. "You're fine," the voice said. "You're going to be fine."

Racquel struggled to open her eyes again, and managed it after a few tries. She knew that voice. She forced her lips to respond to her, and groaned with the pain of it.

"What . . . what happened?" she asked.

The voice responded in a soft tone. "You had a very bad accident. But, you're going to be OK. Go back to sleep now. I'm right here."

Racquel's eyes sagged shut again. The effort had taken everything out of her, and she drifted once again into blissful unconsciousness.

Sean returned to the ICU with Nurse Holly Brown at his side. He entered the room, and came to an abrupt halt. "What are you doing in here?" he asked the man who now sat in the very chair he had just passed the night in.

Ralph Penniman turned, and his eyes flickered over the tall man standing at the door. "Are you her doctor?" he asked.

Sean took a step toward the bed. "I'm going to have to ask you to leave," he said. "No one is allowed in this room."

Ralph Penniman stood, slowly. "Not even her husband?"

Sean's eyes narrowed to slits. "Penniman?" he said.

The other man gave him a sharp look. "So, she's told you about me."

"She's also told me that you're her ex-husband, and I'm relatively certain that she would not want you here. So, as I said, I'm going to have to ask you to leave."

Ralph Penniman grinned. "Until she tells me so herself, I aim to stay. I have every right to be here. She is in a coma, after all—one which she may never come out of—and I—"

Sean cut him off before he could finish. "I will call security if I have to, Penniman."

Ralph Penniman ambled slowly forward. He was not averse to brawling in a hospital room. Most men, sensing this complete lack of restraint in him, would naturally back down and let him have his way, but Sean KirPatrick stood his ground, and Penniman paused a few feet away to glare dully at the doctor. He was not accustomed to being defied, but he sensed something dangerous about the man standing before him. He blinked a couple of times, and wondered if he should chance it. "I'll be back," he finally said, and ambled slowly through the doorway.

When he was gone, Sean took several even breaths to calm himself. It had been all he could do not to go at the other man. It had been years since he had felt such all-encompassing rage. Just a few more minutes in Penniman's presence, and he would have forgotten that he was a doctor of medical science.

Holly Brown stepped around Sean and went briskly to Racquel's bedside. She spent a minute replacing the IV bag and rearranging the bedclothes. When she was through, she looked up at the doctor. She had never seen him quite so riled up before.

"Our patient is resting comfortably," she said. "This young lady is a fighter, Doctor. I'm certain that once she's aware of the extent of her injuries she'll take the news well. She'll get used to it . . . eventually."

Sean came over to the bed and sat in the chair once again. "There will be nothing for her to get used to," he said. "I'm going to repair her face." He steepled his fingers beneath his chin. "I spent all of last night thinking about it. There'll be many operations required, of course—given the extent of her injuries." He sat back and closed his eyes, and Nurse Brown felt a crushing wave of sympathy for him. What a very terrible thing to have happened, and to such an undeserving couple.

She struggled for something appropriate to say. There were dark shadows under his eyes, and she was sure that he had eaten nothing in hours.

"Shall I get some food from the cafeteria for you, Doctor?"

Sean opened his eyes. "No. Nothing, nurse, but you get something. I'm going to stay here with her."

After a momentary hesitation, Nurse Brown went away, and Sean bent over the bed and began speaking in a low voice. He talked about anything that came to mind—a funny movie he'd seen, their trip to San Diego, childhood memories.

When Morganna returned at midday, she found him in exactly the same position as when she'd left in the early hours of the morning. She placed the large, brown paper bag in her hands on the bedside table before saying, "How is she?"

Sean's dark eyes flickered over her, and Morganna saw the signs of weariness in them. "Her vital signs are stronger than they were last night," he said.

Morganna reached into the paper bag and removed a round container. "I've brought soup. And don't tell me," she said as Sean was about to interrupt, "that you're not hungry. You probably haven't had a thing to eat since yesterday. If you get sick, too, we'll all be in trouble. Besides, Racquel would want you to eat. Starving yourself won't help her get better any faster."

A tired smile twitched at the corners of Sean's lips. "You're an amazing woman, Morganna O'Bannon," he said. "What kind of soup do you have there?"

"Creamy chicken noodle. I made it myself. Many people swear by it, by the way." She handed him a large Tupperware container with a red lid. "There's a spoon taped to the underside."

Sean accepted the offering, settled back in the chair, and began to eat. Morganna made light conversation while somehow managing to keep a close eye on the soup in Sean's hand.

"Eat all of it," she said at one point when Sean was about to put the container down. Sean gave a hoarse chuckle. "Is this what poor Charley has to put up with all the time?"

Morganna winked. "That's right, buddy."

Racquel opened her eyes again sometime near mid-afternoon. This time it was a lot easier for her to focus. She blinked a couple of times and managed a barely audible, "Thirsty . . ."

Sean, who had closed his eyes for a second, jack-knifed into a sitting position. His heart pounded at his rib cage, and for a second he was certain that he had merely imagined the sound of her voice. He leaned forward. "Kelli?"

The barely visible lips behind the bandages moved. "Sean . . . you're . . . here. Why?"

A feeling of such profound relief swept over him that all he could do was hold her hand and silently thank the God who had saved her life, over and over again.

"I . . . hurt all over," she said. "And . . . my throat is sore."

There was a dry sob in his voice when he spoke. "I'll get you some water."

He returned with Nurse Brown and Doctor Van Cooten in tow. Holly Brown fed Racquel a small quantity of water through a soft straw while the two doctors had a hushed conversation in the corner of the room.

Doctor Van Cooten came to stand at her bedside. Racquel struggled to focus on him. She was beginning to realize that this was not some strange and disorienting dream. She was not in her bedroom at home, apparently.

"Am I . . . at your house . . . Sean?" she asked in a croaky whisper. She hadn't realized that he had such a large staff, and a butler, too. Why was the butler standing by her bed, and looking down at her with such a kind smile? And who was the nice woman in the white dress? It was all a little too confusing.

"I'm glad to see that you're back with us," Doctor Van Cooten said.

Racquel closed her eyes again. She didn't feel very much like talking with the butler right now. She hoped he wouldn't mind if she went to sleep again. She felt so tired. "Maybe . . . later," she said, and drifted off again.

For the next several hours, Racquel faded in and out of consciousness. Nurse Brown was constantly at her side, adjusting the dosage of Demerol, sponging her lips with water. At some point during the early evening, Sean went off to the attached bathroom and had a shave. He returned to find that his patient was wide awake, and for the first time was looking about her with bright, aware eyes.

He sat in the chair next to the bed, and Racquel made a supreme effort to turn her head in his direction. "Try not to move too much," he said, and he leaned forward, his dark eyes filled with kindness.

"I . . . had an accident?" she asked with great difficulty.

Sean nodded, and reached out to hold her hand. "Your car . . . collided with one of those big trucks."

"Oh," she managed. "The dog? He was with me. He's . . . OK?"

Sean gave her hand a squeeze. "By some miracle, he came out of it without any injuries. Morganna has him."

"Good," she said, and her eyes fluttered closed, then open again. "Why . . . do you look so . . . worried? Am I dying?"

Sean swallowed hard before answering. "No, babe, you're not dying. I left you once before—through no fault of mine—but I promise you we're never going to be separated again. OK?"

"OK," she muttered, although she had not really understood what he'd said. Her eyelids sagged shut again.

Doctor Van Cooten checked on his patient again at ten o'clock. "She's doing surprisingly well," he said to Sean. "Maybe you should go home and get some rest now. Come back in the morning. I'll be sure to call you if there's any change."

Sean massaged one of his temples. "Thank you, Doctor, but I think I'll stay." As tempting as a few hours of sleep sounded, he knew that he could not leave her. As irrational and unscientific as it sounded, he felt strongly that she was relying on him for strength. "I can't leave her," he said.

Doctor Van Cooten nodded. "I'll have a bed set up in here for you, then. You have to get some rest."

Fifteen

It was an entire week after the accident before Racquel was told the full extent of her injuries. With Nurse Brown standing at the bedside, Sean told her without too much preamble how much her face had been damaged. When he was through, the only sound that could be heard was that of her very labored breathing. Sean motioned to the nurse to leave the room, and once they were alone he sat on the edge of the bed and gently turned her head so that she could look directly at him.

"Did you understand what I said, Kelli?"

Her lips trembled before she managed to say, "Yes. You said that I don't have a face anymore."

Sean took a breath, and chose his words carefully. "That's not exactly true. You still have a face. It's just very badly sliced up. You went right through the windshield, and a lot of glass was embedded in the skin."

A tear slipped out of an eye, and soaked into the bandages. "Why didn't I die, then?" she asked. "I would've preferred it. I have nothing and no one, after all. And now you tell me that I'll have to spend the rest of my life as some . . . some sort of twisted freak?"

"You have me," Sean said, and intertwined his fingers with her undamaged hand. "You always have me."

She ripped the hand away from him. "I don't want your pity."

Sean took a breath, and let it out slowly. He was relatively sure that unless he found the right words, she would refuse to allow him to operate on her face. She would consider the many expensive operations required nothing more than an attempt at charity on his part.

He shifted his position on the bed, and went to great pains not to touch her. "Your face can be repaired," he said.

She focused on him for a minute. "Repaired?"

He nodded. "Yes. By reconstructive surgery."

"You mean that you can give me a new face? No scarring anywhere?"

He chose his words with care. "It may take several operations, of course. And I can't guarantee that there will be absolutely no scarring. There are only a few surgeons in the world who can effectively perform the particular kind of reconstructive surgery that you will need. I'm one of them."

She closed her eyes. "I don't have a lot of money. How much will all this cost?"

He gave her the figure, and she turned her head away. "Not even if I sold my house in Idaho could I raise that sort of money."

Sean's brow furrowed. "Is there anyone you might ask? Morganna, maybe?"

Racquel shifted her head back to look at him. "Morganna? I couldn't ask her to lend me that much money. Even if she had it to lend, how could I ask her?"

Sean straightened from the bed and went to stand at the window. There was another way, but to get her to accept his offer he would have to bring Ralph Penniman back into the picture. The man had visited the hospital every single day since she had been admitted, and had been turned away each time. Today, when he arrived, orders would be given to let him through.

He turned back to face her, hands in pockets, a frown creasing the skin between his eyes.

"I have to go in to the clinic for a little while this afternoon. I'll ask Nurse Brown to sit with you until I get back."

Racquel moved her broken arm with great difficulty, and attempted to shift her position in bed.

"Sean," she said, and there was a trace of regret in her eyes, "thank you for all that you've done for me. I know I've been terrible these last few days. It's just that my . . . my whole life's destroyed now. My face was all that I had . . . can you understand that? I've lost my contract opportunity with Warner Brothers. No studio in the world will sign me now. Not with scars."

Sean came to stand by the bed. He looked down at her. "You have a lot more than just a face to offer, Racquel. Why do you underrate yourself in this way?"

Another tear seeped onto the bandages. "There's nothing else. There's nothing else that I do well. Nothing."

"You cook well."

Racquel managed a hoarse croak of laughter. "Are you suggesting that I become a chef?"

"If you like."

"I *don't* like. I don't want to do anything but act. Do you understand? Nothing else. What would you do if you could no longer practice as a surgeon?"

Sean sat on the edge of the bed again. "I'd do something else."

Racquel stared fixedly at the ceiling. "Very easy for you to say, since you're not in this situation. Only if you lost your hands would you understand what I mean."

"I understand now."

She closed her eyes and said mournfully, "You don't. Nobody does. How can anyone understand this? My arm's broken, my face is gone, I have a six-inch gash across my midriff. I'm bruised all over. It hurts to even breathe. How can you tell me that you understand? I should've died. I wish I'd died."

"Why would you want to hurt me like that?"

Her eyes blinked open again. "Hurt you? Why would that hurt you at all?"

He leaned forward, and the light in his eyes halted the stream of words on her lips. "Because I care about you. I care what happens to you. When you hurt, I hurt. Can you understand that?"

His words shocked her into complete silence, and she could only stare at him.

Sean stood. "I'll ask the nurse to come in and sit with you. Would you like me to bring you anything?"

Racquel moved her head from side to side. "No. Nothing." She was beginning to feel very ashamed of herself.

"I'll be back at six, then." And with that, he was gone from the room.

Nurse Holly Brown came in shortly afterward with a tray. "You'll soon be off this liquid diet," she said, smiling brightly. She stacked the pillows behind Racquel's back, and very skillfully, causing the minimum of pain, helped her to an elevated position.

Racquel sipped slowly at the straw, while the nurse dabbed at the corners of her mouth.

"Doctor KirPatrick is a very nice man, don't you think?" Nurse Brown said conversationally.

Racquel took another sip of the liquid, struggled to swallow, then said, "Very nice."

"He was very worried about you."

Racquel released the straw, and eased slowly back onto the pillows. "He worries about everyone, I think. You, me—everyone. He would probably do the same for you if you were sick and in the hospital."

"Hmm," the nurse said, and she settled back in her chair. She didn't feel that it was her place to point out that which was so painfully obvious to everyone else. Her patient would come to terms with the knowledge in her own time. She suspected that Racquel Ward was afraid of being loved by anyone, and was therefore doing her best to keep that particular emotion at bay.

"Have you worked for him for a while?" Racquel asked after a good stretch of silence.

Holly Brown nodded. "Oh, yes. It's been five or so years now."

"So you've seen him on his good days and bad days . . . right?"

The nurse smiled. "Well, I can't really say that I've ever seen him have a bad day. He has the sweetest temperament of any man I've ever met."

Racquel said nothing for a bit. Then, after thinking on the information the nurse had just given her, she was about to go on to even deeper probing when a shadow loomed in the doorway.

The nurse looked up. "Oh," she said, "you seem to have a visitor."

Racquel turned slowly toward the doorway, and her heart stopped cold. Ralph. How had he found her?

Nurse Brown was getting up from her chair and excusing herself before Racquel could properly object. Ralph came slowly into the room, a lopsided smile twisting his mouth. He pulled at the chair by the bed with a foot, turned it around, and sat.

"Surprised to see me?" he asked.

Racquel swallowed, and the pulling of her throat

muscles caused intense pain to radiate through her face. "What are you doing here?" she managed after the quick burst of agony had died down. More importantly, how had he found her?

"I've been here from the very first day . . . but your doctor friend wouldn't let me in." The sound of her breathing was harsh and shallow in the small room.

"What do you want?" she said.

He leaned forward, his grin widening. "They tell me you need a new face."

"Yes," Racquel said in a dull monotone.

He reached out a hand as if to touch her, and Racquel shrank into the pillows. The big hand came to rest on the bed just beside her uninjured arm.

"Not so pretty anymore underneath those bandages, are you?"

Racquel remained silent.

"Oh, come now," he said, "let's not fight. I'll admit you had some fun with me, telling me all those lies about going to New York. Did you really think I wouldn't find you?"

"I want you to leave," she said, and her voice croaked harshly.

He continued as though she had not spoken. "I'm willing to forgive you, though. I'll even pay for the fancy operation on your face. But"——he laughed softly—"for a price."

"Price?" Racquel said. "What do you mean, for a price? Do you want the house in Idaho? Is that it?"

He pressed her hand. "Oh, what I want is of far more importance to me than a musty old house. I'll pay the money for your operation, yes, but, only if you agree to come back to me. Return with me to Idaho, and you can have your face back. What do you say? A pretty fair trade, isn't it?"

"I want you to leave now," Racquel said softly. "Please."

Ralph stood, and Racquel turned frightened eyes away from his. In the brief instant that their eyes had met, a striking clarity had come over her. There was something very wrong with him. It wasn't just cruelty, as she had thought before. It was something much darker. Much harder to define.

"You will never be free of me," he said staring down at her, his eyes beginning to bulge. "Never."

When Sean returned later that evening, he found her lying in bed staring at the TV set mounted above the bed.

"I brought you some ice cream," he said, resting the bag in his hands on the bedside table. She turned her head slowly to look at him, and he was shaken by the hollowness in her eyes.

"My ex-husband Ralph Penniman is here—in LA. He visited me this afternoon."

"Oh, yes?" Sean focused on the contents of the bag, reaching in to remove a covered container of machine-twirled strawberry soft serve. "And did he have anything interesting to say?"

"He offered to pay for the operation on my face," she said, and her tongue darted out to wet her lips.

Sean experienced a strong need to go to her and hold her in his arms, but he forced a blandness he didn't feel into his voice. "So, we can go ahead, then?"

"No. I turned him down."

Sean's eyes flashed across to meet hers, and he held her gaze for several moments.

"You turned him down? Why?"

"His . . . terms were a little too high. I couldn't accept what he proposed."

"Remarriage," Sean said flatly.

Racquel shifted in the bed so that she might easily look at him. "Why do you say that?"

Sean shrugged. "Just a guess. I couldn't think of any other reason why you would turn him down."

"Well," Racquel said after a long moment, "I suppose I'm gonna have to learn how to live with this face—the scars and everything. I didn't intend to marry again, anyway, so that part of it doesn't really matter."

Sean sat on the bed. "Are you cutting me out of your life, then? I thought you were beginning to like me a little . . . for a while there."

Racquel struggled into a sitting position against the pillows. "I don't understand why you would want to . . . to have anything to do with me. I've never really treated you as you should be treated. Still, you've been nothing but kind to me, and—" She began to sob, and the broken, hacking sound pierced Sean's resolve. He wrapped his arms gently about her and said softly, "Ssh, it's OK, Kelli, don't cry. Everything's going to be OK."

She shook her head against the solid warmth of his chest. "No, it's not. Everything's *not* going to be OK. I don't know what I'm going to do."

Sean stroked a gentle hand across her back. "There's another way you can have this operation done—if you agree to it."

She swallowed a hiccuping sob, then said in a voice that trembled, "Another way?"

Sean settled her back on the pillows, patted the tiny slit of exposed skin around her eyes with a square of Kleenex, then launched into the explanation in a very clear and dispassionate manner.

"A few of the cable stations have been after me for years. They've always wanted to film one of my more involved reconstructive procedures. Maybe do a sort of multi-part series, showing the patient before, during, and after the surgery. Until now, I've always refused. I considered it an invasion of privacy to a large degree. Also, I wasn't really interested in the fame and notoriety that could come from that sort of national exposure."

Racquel's attention was keenly focused on him. "You—you mean if I agree to . . . to having the procedure filmed, the money would be . . . would be put up by the cable station?"

"Well," Sean said, and he cleared his throat before continuing, "the specifics of it would have to be worked out with the station of course, but that's the general idea of it. The important thing is that it wouldn't cost you anything at all."

He could almost see the thoughts flashing through her mind, and he was ready for her next question even before she asked it.

"And will it cost you anything?"

Sean gave a very definitive shake of his head. "Nothing at all, providing an appropriate arrangement can be reached with the cable station."

She was silent for such a long time after that that Sean was unsure if she was still awake. He leaned forward. "Racquel?"

Her eyes flicked back open, and there was a strange light lurking in the depths of them. "I'll do it," she said. "I don't really have any other choice."

Sixteen

Things swept ahead in a whirlwind of activity after that. Rapid plans were made, and a date was set for the first reconstructive operation. Sean spent many hours going over exactly what was to be done. He was very clear, and explained each procedure in simple language. Racquel mostly listened as he told her of the need to rebuild her cheekbones, of the skin grafts required, and the X-ray therapy.

At the end of the second week following the accident, she was moved from the ICU into a spacious private room, and was tended skillfully by Nurse Brown, whose ebullient cheer was exactly what she needed. Each day, the nurse bustled in brightly with news of one kind or another, and before Racquel realized it she was smiling and exchanging humorous anecdotes with the woman. The nurse was full of information concerning the goings-on in the hospital, and possessed a sharp eye and a live-wire wit. Racquel found herself warming to the woman, and gradually accepting the fact that at least for now, she was going to be an invalid.

Morganna was also a regular visitor. She came to call each afternoon, and sat at Racquel's bedside, often for several hours. Sometimes she brought the latest editions of the scandal sheets with her, and spent time ferreting out and reading aloud the juiciest goings-on of the stars.

Within days of her removal from intensive care, Racquel was able to sit up in bed with only minimal soreness around her rib cage area. Nurse Brown was a great help with the daily hygienic considerations, carefully sponging her still very bruised body with ample quantities of nicely scented water, and gently replacing dressings as needed.

Sean was happy to see, when he came to visit on Friday evening of that week, that Racquel's spirits were much improved. She even appeared glad to see him when he came to sit on her bed and lifted one of her hands to take a professional look at the bruising.

"Well? Will I live?" she asked after his gaze had run the entire length of her arm.

He grinned at her in a way he had not done since her accident. "You're too stubborn to do anything else, I think."

Racquel's gaze drifted over the harsh planes and angles of his face, and for the first time since her ordeal had begun she noticed how very tired he appeared.

"Are you eating . . . well?" she asked.

Sean's eyes flickered. "Yes. Of course." She could not know that he hadn't been able to eat a proper meal since he'd learned of her accident. He also had not yet managed to sleep through the night without awakening bathed in a sheen of perspiration, with distorted images of her twisted body dancing before his eyes.

"You've lost weight," she said, and lifted a hand to touch the side of his jaw.

He took the hand in his, and met her eyes with his. "Don't worry about me, Kelli. I'll be fine. I want you to concentrate on getting better. OK?"

She nodded. "Sean?"

His eyes sought hers again. "Yes?"

"There's something I've been wanting to tell you for days, now."

Sean's brow furrowed. "Are you in pain? Doctor Van Cooten recommended that your dosage of Demerol be re—"

"No, nothing like that. It's about the accident."

She had his full attention. "What about it?"

"I don't think it was . . . I mean, I think my brakes were tampered with." She told him about the veiled threat the man on the phone had made just days before the accident.

Sean's expression hardened. He'd had his own suspicions, but had decided not to raise them until she was better able to deal with the possible implications.

"Your ex-husband," he said, "do you think he might be capable of something like this?"

Racquel turned away to look out the window. "He's always been vindictive, but I never thought he'd try to kill me. It's only God's mercy that I wasn't killed in that crash. Besides, the man on the phone had a different voice—more nasal. It wasn't Ralph. I'm sure of that."

"Hmm," Sean said. He was unconvinced. After running into Ralph Penniman again, he was almost certain that this was the very thing that he would be inclined to do.

Sean gave her hand a reassuring squeeze. "Well, we'll have to let the police know. Penniman is in LA, so that definitely makes everything seem very suspicious. Did he threaten you in any way during his visit last week?"

Racquel blinked, and did her best to keep the tremor from her voice. "Not directly. He just said that I'd never be free of him—or something like that."

Sean stood and went to the window. He was convinced that there was a connection between the kitchen knife in the backyard, the cigarette ash, the menacing phone calls, and Penniman's sudden appearance in Los Angeles, but to prove it without fingerprints, without hard evidence, would be difficult. Even an expert like Henry Yau at the LAPD's forensics lab had been unable to come up with something tangible.

He turned back. "Kelli, remember the clinic up in the mountains—the one I told you about a while ago?"

She nodded. "Up at Mammoth Lakes, you mean?"

"I want to take you there after the first operation," he said. "The mountain air will do you a lot of good. And if Penniman is stalking you, you'll be much safer there."

A hint of fear shone brightly in her eyes. "You think whoever it is will . . . will try again?"

Sean did not want to scare her unnecessarily, but the truth had to be faced. He tried to soften his words as much as possible. "There's a chance of that. If it is Penniman, he may just have intended to scare you a little—not kill you."

"Scare me into going back to him?"

Sean considered that possibility. "Could be," he said. Another idea occurred to him. "Your parents . . . when did they die?"

Racquel swallowed. She hadn't really thought about the entire circumstances surrounding their deaths in a long while.

"About . . . five years ago. Before my marriage to Ralph. They . . . went to Las Vegas for the weekend, and I guess they rented a car while they were there, and . . . and they were involved in a pileup on one of the highways. My dad was killed right away. My mom lingered for a few days . . . but . . ."

Sean held her gaze. "I'm sorry," he said. He had

never cared much for either of her parents, but that was neither here nor there. Their deaths must have affected her terribly.

Racquel shrugged. "The last five years haven't been the best. My parents died. I married a man that I should never have, and suffered terribly because of it. And now, just when things were beginning to improve . . . this happens."

Sean moved to stand by the bed. He wondered if telling her who he was would make a difference in the way she felt about him—about things in general.

"Kelli," he began slowly, "did you have many friends growing up in Idaho?"

Surprise came and went in her eyes. "Many friends? No, not that many."

"Did you have any special friends?"

"Well, not . . . not really. My parents didn't really encourage me to socialize. There were girls I knew at school. And of course there was Stephen."

A smile curled the corners of Sean's lips. So, she hadn't forgotten him, after all. It pleased him immensely that after all this time she still remembered the boy he had been.

"Would you . . . do you think you might recognize Stephen if you saw him again?"

Racquel's jaw dropped. "You're not—you're not suggesting that it's Stephen who's—who's behind all this?" It was inconceivable that Stephen would return in adulthood, to victimize her in such a manner.

"No," Sean said hastily. "What I meant was . . . if he was standing right before you, would you . . . would you know him?"

Nurse Brown poked her head through the door at almost that very moment with a cheerful call of: "Dinner." Racquel gave Sean a hurried look before saying,

"I hope it's not that meat loaf and mashed potato dinner I've had for the past two nights."

Holly Brown wheeled the trolley in. "Tonight," she said smiling, "you get roast chicken breast with brown gravy. Rice. String beans. Lemonade. And for dessert"—she removed a covered silver dome—"Jell-O."

"Well," Racquel said, adjusting herself against the pillows. "At least it's a change."

Holly Brown positioned the tray across the bed and snapped it into place. "I'll come back when you're finished." She shot a lightning glance at Sean. It was her fondest wish to find a man like the doctor. Kind, patient, loving. She wondered whether Racquel Ward realized how very fortunate she was.

Sean exchanged a brief nod with her. "Thank you, nurse."

Racquel bit into a tender slice of chicken, chewed, and swallowed before saying, "Why were you asking me all those questions about Stephen, about recognizing him? I'm sure he'd be no threat to me at all. He was one of the nicest boys . . . a very close friend."

Sean pulled up a chair and sat. There was no time like the present, and he would get no better opportunity to tell her who he was. She might even be more inclined to trust him if she knew. His fingers steepled beneath his chin. Then he took a breath and plunged in. "That boy you remember grew up."

Racquel carefully speared a forkful of string beans. "Yes," she agreed. "He would be about . . . thirty-three or so now . . . I think." She chewed the very bland beans without much enthusiasm. "I can't help wondering what happened to him, though. He was special." She gave a fractured chuckle. "You know, we even promised to marry each other once we were old enough. Can you believe it?"

Sean picked up the extra napkin on her tray, and twirled it between his fingers. "You didn't keep your promise."

She looked up. "Well," she said after a moment of staring at him, "that was a long time ago. Besides, he went away and didn't even write."

The twirling of the napkin stopped, and midnight black eyes met hers. "That's not true. I wrote you lots of letters—every week for years."

Racquel paused, and a piece of string bean fell from her fork back onto the plate.

"What?"

"I wrote you letters every week for five years, but you never answered. You just sent them back."

Racquel put the fork back onto her plate. Suddenly, the food had no taste.

"What . . . what do you mean?" she finally managed. "What letters? How could you write me any letters when we just met a short while ago?"

Sean leaned forward in the chair. "Look at these eyes, Kelli. Don't you know them?"

Racquel blinked owlishly at him. "What you're doing is very cruel, Sean—very cruel. And not funny at all."

"Have you forgotten all those plans we made so many years ago? We used to sit out under that big oak tree each night once your folks had gone to bed, and count the stars. I taught you to ride your first horse—a fat chestnut mare. What was her name?"

Racquel had forgotten all about the food. "Sally," she said in a voice that was barely above a whisper. "Fat Sally."

Sean nodded. "I never forgot you, Kel . . . never. Not in all these years."

A tear rolled down and soaked into the bandages. "It can't be. It can't be you. Your name is different."

"I decided to use my middle name after college. And since I was adopted, Parker became KirPatrick."

Racquel pressed both hands to her lips, and her eyes slid over his face. "But you can't be—you look so different. Stephen had . . . had really big teeth—"

Sean laughed. "I got braces, and I guess eventually I grew into them."

"Let me . . . I mean, can I see your—" she said a bit wildly. "Stephen had a large—"

"Scar?" Sean asked, and he ran a finger down his shirt, crossing his breastbone and pausing at a spot along his side.

Racquel gave a numb nod. A feeling of unreality was beginning to settle over her. How could Sean and Stephen be one and the same? That they should find each other after all this time in such a very unlikely way just wasn't possible. Things like this only happened in movies, not in real life. Not to real people.

Sean pulled his tie, and unbuttoned the first few buttons on his shirt. Racquel's eyes followed the progress of his fingers with hungry curiosity. He pulled back the shirt, and Racquel found her eyes lingering on the hard washboard stomach before sliding slowly around to the raised, four-pronged welt on his side.

"Oh, my God," she said, and for the life of her couldn't think of anything else to say. Sean rebuttoned the shirt and said, with a slight smile playing around his mouth, "I don't want anyone walking in here and getting the wrong idea." The sound of his voice penetrated the haze, and Racquel met his eyes almost hesitantly.

"Why didn't you tell me before? Did you . . . did you recognize me from the start? Or did you figure it out, somehow?" Now everything made sense. His relentless pursuit of her. The strange, knowing way that he looked at her sometimes. And, now that she really thought about it, there had always been something about his eyes that seemed so very familiar.

Sean leaned forward. "I knew you right away. Right from that very first day that you came jogging by my house. I didn't tell you because . . . well, I had my reasons. So, what do you think? Did I grow up to your liking?"

Racquel felt the sudden urge to laugh. What a very strange situation. Never in a million years had she ever thought that she might see him again. Stephen. Her Stephen. Her eyes twinkled at him from behind the bandages. "You've grown up just fine. I just can't believe I didn't know you. I was so sure that I would. You always did want to become a doctor, but not a plastic surgeon. How did that happen?"

They settled into a long conversation that lasted until the end of visiting hours. When Sean rose to go, Racquel stopped him with a hand. "Can't you stay?" she asked. Suddenly, she was irrationally afraid—afraid that fate would engineer some other catastrophe in order to keep them apart.

Sean smiled down at her, his eyes magnetically black and very kind. "If you really want me to. I can go home, change my clothes, and come back later."

A sudden thought occurred to Racquel, and the possibility of it terrified her. Would whoever it was try to hurt Sean, too?

"Does . . . does your car have an alarm?" she asked.

Sean cocked an eyebrow at her. "An alarm? No, I've never installed one. Why?"

She rushed into the explanation without thinking too carefully about what it was that she wanted to say. "Your brakes—what if they try to hurt you, too?"

A lightning quick expression ran across Sean's face.

The thought had occurred to him, also. It pleased him that she cared about his well-being. No one else ever had.

He took her hand, and ran his thumb over the backs of her fingers. "I'll be OK. Don't worry. I'm going to be around, bugging you, for a very long while."

After he had left, Racquel sat up in bed and spent a good amount of time worrying about the problem at hand. She didn't have very much faith in his assurances. After all, her parents had been similarly convinced of their longevity, but where were they now?

Seventeen

On the morning of the first operation, Racquel was awoken just before seven. Nurse Brown bustled in briskly, throwing open window shutters, and making cheerful noises about the beauty of the day. Racquel watched her move about the room, plumping pillows and then making the preparations for her morning toilette. She shielded her eyes with her good hand and asked in a voice still very blurred by sleep, "Do I get to walk around by myself today?"

Holly Brown paused in her busy activities for a minute. "Doctor KirPatrick doesn't want you exerting yourself too much. Especially not right after the surgery. He'll explain."

Racquel's lips quirked in a brief smile. "He's going to see me before we go into surgery, then?"

Nurse Brown gave her a shocked look. "Yes. Of course he is. He sees all of his patients before. He'll be here in about an hour, so we have to get you all ready."

With very little else said, she drew the privacy screen about the bed and began undoing the ties on Racquel's gown. Her eyes ran over Racquel's body with professional thoroughness. The areas that had been bruised and torn just a few weeks before were now nicely scabbed and healing quite satisfactorily.

Racquel kept her eyes firmly closed as the nurse sponged and wiped her body. The sight of the scars on her chest, abdomen, and legs was enough to bring her to tears, and she couldn't bear to look. Even if Sean did manage to properly repair her face, her torso would still bear the ugly jagged signs of the accident.

Nurse Brown, who was well acquainted with dealing with the many psychological problems often caused by traumatic injury, said quite brightly, "It looks much worse than it really is. In a week or two, the scabs will fall away, and any remaining scarring can be corrected. Don't worry, Doctor KirPatrick is one of the best surgeons around. You're in good hands."

Racquel nodded. At least she knew that to be true. Maybe she was more vain about her appearance than she had originally thought. Since childhood, she had been aware that her looks were above average. In a way, she had come to take them for granted, never assuming that there might come a day when she would no longer have them. Sean believed that he could restore her face to some semblance of normalcy, but what if the end result was much less than what she had had before? What if she gained a face that was not even her own?

Nurse Brown gently poked her arms back through a fresh gown, and Racquel opened her eyes and tried very hard not to think too much about the long hours of surgery that stretched ahead of her. Sean had explained what was going to happen. Sometime before the surgery began, the bandages covering her face would be carefully peeled away. Then, the TV camera crew would begin filming. They would follow her gurney into the operating room, and continue filming while she slipped under anesthesia. Sean would then explain the extent of her injuries, and exactly what was going to be done.

Filming would continue throughout the entire procedure, and would only cease when she was again in her
hospital bed. It was all to be done seamlessly, creating
a minimum of inconvenience to her.

Racquel had asked Sean to ensure that she not be
shown any of the footage. Even though she was trying
her best to be strong, the unrecognizable sight of her
face—battered, horribly scarred, maybe even twisted—
was a little too much for her to endure. Sean had promised her that it would be so, and had gone about
making the appropriate arrangements. He had also
given orders for all of the mirrors to be removed from
the bedroom and bathroom of the private suite.

"Well," Nurse Brown said, straightening the bedsheets
and plumping the pillows at Racquel's back, "you're all
set." She gave her watch a quick glance. "The doctor
should be here any minute now." She gave Racquel's
hand a tiny squeeze of encouragement. "It'll be all right,"
she said. "Everything's going to be just fine."

"Hmm," Racquel said in response, and once the nurse
had left the room she stared fixedly out the window at
the rolling expanse of clear blue sky and powder-white
clouds, steeling herself. Whatever happened, whatever
the outcome of the operations, she would just have to
live with things, find some way to deal with the situation.
If she could no longer act, there was probably something
else she might do, behind the scenes. Direct maybe, even
write. Maybe she would try doing a screenplay about her
life. It was exactly the kind of script that Hollywood
would be interested in buying. She could just see the
promo for the movie as they promoted it on one of the
magazine talk shows: *Abused former actress loses her
face in car accident only days before signing mega-deal
with movie studio. Based on a true story. Tune in at
seven.*

Sean found her in exactly that position as he strode into the room only minutes later. She turned from the window at the sound of footsteps, and an involuntary smile softened her lips. He looked quite splendid, dressed in a white coat with a thick silver pen sticking out of his top pocket. His eyes regarded her warmly. "So . . . are we ready for the big day?"

Racquel swallowed away the dryness in her throat. The truth of it was that she was afraid—desperately afraid—of going under the knife, of being exposed on national TV, of possibly being told when it was all over that the operation had not been a success.

"Sean—" she began, "is there any chance that you might not be able to fix my face?"

He sat on the bed and took her hand, and the solid warmth of his hand bolstered her flagging spirits. "There are hardly ever any hundred percent guarantees with this particular procedure," he said, "but I can promise you that I'll do my very best for you." He rubbed a thumb across the back of her hand, and Racquel felt the sudden need to press a kiss to his cheek. She hesitated, knowing that in her current condition he might shudder at the very feel of her lips against his skin. So, instead, she just gripped his hand tightly and said, "Thank you," in a very small voice.

Several hours later, she was being wheeled back from surgery. Nurse Brown stood back as the camera crew followed the gurney to the room. A small frown creased her brow for a second, and she turned to the doctor, who was following a step or two behind.

"Is all this filming really necessary, Dr. KirPatrick?"

A smile flickered across Sean's lips. Nurse Brown was an untiring champion of the patient's right to privacy, so this entire production was obviously highly offensive to her. He'd been wondering when she would say something to him about it.

"It was the only way," he said, and walked quickly ahead to avoid the barrage of questions which he suspected were not too far off.

Racquel slept for hours, and was really not quite herself until early evening. She opened both eyes and, almost without thinking, raised a hand to her face.

"Don't touch the bandages," said a voice from a corner of the room.

Racquel blinked. "Sean . . . you're here." More and more, she was getting the urge to call him Stephen.

Sean came forward out of the shadows. "How do you feel?" he asked, and there was a smile in his voice.

Racquel struggled to sit up, and Sean reached a hand to help her. "I . . . I'm not sure," she said. "I don't really feel any different. Just a little sleepy, that's all."

"Good," he said, "you're not supposed to feel different." He sat on the edge of the bed. "The first procedure went very well—so well that I've arranged to have you moved to my clinic in the mountains tomorrow. We all agree that the change of scenery will help speed your recovery."

"Oh," Racquel said, and she tried to squelch the rising tide of happiness she felt. "But what about your patients at your clinic in LA? I mean . . . you can't just pick up and go . . . can you?"

Sean gave her hand a pat. "I've made arrangements. My consultations will be covered by another surgeon, and the actual surgeries will either be done up in the mountains at the clinic there, or in LA. I'll fly down if the patient can't come up. It's just an hour and a half flight."

Despite herself, Racquel's lips curved into an expansive smile. "You're a wonderful man, Sean KirPatrick, and I can't thank you nearly enough." Before she could prevent herself, she was leaning forward and pressing her lips to his cheek.

A spark of happiness came slowly to life in the depths of Sean's eyes. He had never been as worried about anyone or anything as he'd been about her in the last several weeks. Almost involuntarily, his hands came up to gently shift her chin, and his lips settled softly on hers.

Nurse Brown, who came walking through the doorway at precisely that moment, stopped abruptly and quietly crept from the room, a smile dancing around the corners of her lips.

A bolt of surprise shot through Racquel at the feel of his lips on hers. For the first few seconds of it, she couldn't quite believe that it was happening. Wasn't he repulsed by her appearance? How could he possibly want to kiss her at all? At best, she probably resembled something straight out of a horror movie with her bandaged face, scars, and broken bones.

The warm feel of him was simply divine, and after a very brief moment of misgivings, she yielded to him. He kissed her so very softly and with such infinite care that when he lifted his head to look at her it was all Racquel could do not to break down into floods of tears. Feelings of guilt and unworthiness twisted and writhed inside of her, throwing her into a state of utter confusion. Surely she didn't deserve such a man. Ralph had always said that she was a worthless tramp—not good for anything but a toss in bed.

Sean looked into the flashing dark eyes, and at that very moment the love he felt for her was so strong that hot, unintelligible words almost stumbled from his lips.

He forced himself to stand and walk across to the

window. He stood there silently for several minutes, engaged in a magnificent struggle with himself. If he told her of his feelings for her, would she see them as nothing but a string of pretty words, nicely wrapped up to disguise pity? Did it matter that she did not feel the same way for him? Was it too soon? She had told him any number of times that she had no intention of ever getting married again. What would she say if he told her that he had absolutely no intention of ever marrying anyone but her—that really, given his marked reluctance to commit to a serious relationship in the past, he had never at any time in his life really considered choosing anyone but her?

Racquel considered his long straight back from her position against the pillows. She knew that he was probably regretting his impulsive action, and was obviously trying to think of a way out of any embarrassing expectations that she might develop toward him.

She played with the hard, white plaster of the cast on her left arm and tried to think of something she might say to ease his mind. She wanted him to understand that she was not the foolishly romantic youngster that she had been. She believed that love did exist, but also that fate only gave it to some people to enjoy. She didn't want him to be afraid that she would suddenly declare that she was deeply in love with him. She really wanted him to understand that.

"Sean . . ." she said hesitantly, and waited until he turned to face her. "I—we—will always be good friends all our lives . . . and . . . and nothing will ever change that. I want you to know that."

He nodded at her, and an expression of sadness came and went in his eyes. "I know. You've told me . . . many times."

Racquel forced her lips into a smile, and tried to don

an attitude of cheer. "I'll be right there, dancing at your wedding, when you get married—to some lucky girl."

Sean regarded her in silence for a long moment, and for the life of her Racquel could not understand why he did not seem cheered by her little attempt at humor. Didn't he understand that she wasn't expecting any more amorous advances from him—that he was free to see other women, and he should not in any way feel honor bound to continually court her?

"I probably won't be getting married," he said finally, and turned back to stare out the window. His Jaguar was clearly visible just below, and his eyes followed the figure of a tall man in a long black coat as he walked rapidly away from the car.

The nurse returned at that moment, and this time she paused to knock on the door before entering. Both Sean and Racquel called, "Come in," and Holly Brown was left to speculate on what had transpired since her last visit, since neither doctor nor patient appeared particularly happy now.

Shortly after Racquel settled down to eat, Sean excused himself with the promise that he would be back soon. He walked briskly down the shiny corridor, stepped into an elevator, and rode it down to the ground level. The sun was just beginning to set, and the parking lot was cast in a dappled pattern of light and shadow. Sean cut across the lot, walking between cars while keeping an eye out for the man he had noticed from the room upstairs. When he reached his car, he walked around it. He very quickly determined that everything was as it should be, but as he was turning the key in the front door lock he noticed that there was a square of white paper stuck under a windshield wiper.

He stretched a hand around, yanked the paper out, and unfolded it. There were four typewritten words printed clearly on the sheet: *Stay Away From Her.* In reading them, Sean was swept with such a wave of fury that for a full minute he just stood completely immobile. Then he neatly folded the paper, slid it into his pocket, and climbed behind the wheel.

Preparations for Mammoth were begun very early the next day. Nurse Brown, along with two orderlies, assisted Racquel into a large, motorized wheelchair, and positioned a very comfortable pillow behind her.

"You won't need both hands to get about in this one," the nurse said, smiling. "The doctor was very insistent that you start doing things for yourself again."

Racquel returned the smile. She was feeling quite bright and optimistic this morning. "I've wanted to do things for myself for weeks now." She pressed a button, and the chair started slowly forward.

"Don't move around too much yet," Nurse Brown admonished with a shake of her head. "I have to show you how to properly use the chair first. We don't want you to have any more accidents."

Racquel brought the chair to a slow stop. "Yes ma'am," she said meekly, but the curling of her lips told the nurse that she wasn't nearly as contrite as she might appear.

"Sean promised that he would get my dog. Are we going to stop by Morganna's house on the way?"

Holly Brown paused in her neat packing of Racquel's bags. "No, I don't think so. We're going straight to the airport. Doctor KirPatrick is going to meet us there."

"Oh," Racquel said, and she worried about that for a bit. She hoped that Sean had not forgotten his promise to get the dog. She wouldn't feel right at all about leaving Shaggy with poor Morganna for another stretch of weeks. Besides, it would be nice to see that great furry face again.

The nurse zipped the final bag closed and declared to everyone in the room, "OK, that should do it. Let's go." With that, she was rolling Racquel out of the room, followed by the two orderlies and a bevy of baggage.

"I thought you wanted me to do this myself," Racquel said once they had gotten out of the room and were on the smooth stretch of corridor.

Holly Brown smiled. "Later. Once you're up in the mountains you'll have the full run of the doctor's property." She liked the enthusiasm of her patient. It boded very well for a speedy recovery.

On the ground floor, Racquel was wheeled out and lifted into the back of a very large ambulance. Nurse Brown climbed in first. Then the orderlies laid Racquel on one of the gurneys, got in, and closed the door behind them. She glanced around the interior, a bit overwhelmed by the whole production. She wasn't a critical care case, for heaven's sake. There was absolutely no reason, as far as she could see, to take such extreme precautionary measures.

"Doctor KirPatrick just wants us to be careful until after your face is fully healed," the nurse said.

Racquel nodded as though she understood and agreed with everything that was going on, but actually she was highly embarrassed that everyone was treating her as though she were made of precious Dresden china.

At the airport, she was removed from the ambulance on the gurney and whisked through an exit reserved primarily for VIPs. She had been a bit worried about appearing in public wrapped like an Egyptian mummy, but Sean had thought of everything. No one had seen her exit the ambulance, and before she knew what was happening she was being carried out onto the tarmac toward a waiting private jet.

As they approached, the stairs were lowered. Again, Nurse Brown went up ahead of everyone else, and at the top she paused to call out instructions to the two men beginning to mount the steps with the gurney. Racquel was settled comfortably on a reclining beige leather chair, and was able to inspect the cabin of the jet while the others scurried about. She had never been on a private jet. So, despite every attempt to keep a tight lid on the burgeoning tide of euphoria that she was beginning to feel, her eyes were positively sparkling when Sean came springing lightly up the steps with the huge dog at his side.

The pilot came out to greet him, and he exchanged a quick hello with the rest of his staff before going across to sit at Racquel's side. It soon became necessary for one of the orderlies to take hold of Shaggy, because on catching sight of Racquel, he became so very excited that Sean was concerned that he might somehow manage to tear the bandages from her face.

As soon as all was again calm, Sean was able to inquire, "Did everything go smoothly on your way over from the hospital?"

Racquel nodded. She was still a bit in awe. She'd had no idea at all that Sean was so very wealthy.

"Is the plane yours?" she asked as they began their slow taxi.

"Yes," he nodded. "It's a necessary expense. I often fly my patients back and forth between the two clinics. It would be a bit difficult to do that on a commercial jet."

"Wow," Racquel said, and the poetic justice of it all suddenly struck her. "Wouldn't it be great if all those people back in Idaho could see you now—all the ones who said that you wouldn't amount to anything?"

Sean laughed, and the husky male sound of him made an uncomfortably warm feeling settle somewhere in the pit of Racquel's stomach.

"Maybe one day soon, we should go back there," he said. "You and me."

Racquel shot an uncertain look in his direction. She wasn't at all sure if he was serious or not.

"Yeah, wouldn't that be fun?"

"Umm," Sean agreed, and reached out to hold her hand as they began their ascent.

As soon as they had leveled off, Sean removed his seatbelt, but when Racquel reached to do the same, his hand stilled hers.

"In case of sudden turbulence, I want you to keep it on. All right? It's not a very long flight."

Racquel grinned. "You think I might bash my face against the ceiling maybe?"

Sean took her joking comment quite seriously. "It's possible. At any rate, nothing else is going to happen to you while I'm around. You're completely safe with me. I promise you."

He turned to look directly at her, and Racquel was struck by the silky beauty of his coal black eyes. They were so warm and friendly, so full of vibrancy and life. Oh, if only she hadn't tried to turn him away before her accident. If only she had trusted her heart a little more, and not insisted that they be just friends.

"I don't know how to thank you enough, Sean," she said. "Everything you've done has been so selfless and . . . and I can't think of anything I can do for you in return."

He tightened his fingers around hers. "I want you to feel better again . . . on the outside, and in here." He touched a spot just above her heart. Hot tears clamored at the backs of her eyes, and she turned to look out the window so that he would not guess the depth of emotion lurking within her.

"Remember how we used to lie on our backs and look up at the sky when we were kids?"

"Umm," Sean said. "We used to pretend that we were responsible for creating each cloud that appeared above us. They seemed so very far away then, didn't they? Now, here we are, up among them."

Racquel nodded. "Life is incredible sometimes."

They lapsed into a companionable silence, one that was only broken by the soft clearing of Nurse Brown's throat. "Breakfast," she said.

There was a bit of activity while Racquel was shifted around in her seat and a movable table was rolled right before them.

"Are you going to eat the same thing I do today?" Racquel asked, a hint of mischief flickering in her voice.

Sean wrinkled his nose at her, much as *she* often did at him, and said, "From now on, whatever you eat I will eat, too."

Racquel laughed, and the pleasant sound of her voice ran through the cabin. "You don't have to be so self-sacrificing."

He raised an eyebrow at her. "Didn't you know how much I love baby food?"

Racquel giggled. "I am not having any of that . . . I promise you."

A smile twitched about his mouth. "Not even if I feed it to you on a spoon?"

She shook her head. "Nope. Not even then."

He lifted a hand and waved it about in the air. "Nurse. I think you'd better bring back the bacon and eggs. I don't think our patient is going to be cooperative."

Holly Brown came along with the cart, happy that her patient seemed so very relaxed. She fully admitted now that Doctor KirPatrick had been completely right. The change of environment, getting her away from the hospital and lying in bed all day, would be extremely good for her.

She laid the two trays down and whipped the covering linen off with a flourish.

"No baby food here," she said. The warm smells of buttered toast, thick sausages, eggs, and an assortment of other niceties immediately assailed their senses.

"Umm," Racquel said, "this looks good. Sure I won't damage anything in my face if I chew this?"

"Sure," Sean said, and for the next little while they both tucked into the meal.

Twenty minutes outside the Mammoth Lakes airport, the captain informed them of weather conditions. Racquel barely paid the announcement any attention at all. She was far too busy staring down at the snowcapped peaks of the huge, gray-black mountains. She turned slowly now, with lights dancing in her eyes. "I can't believe they're actually real. I've never seen anything like it. So people really live up here?"

"Uh huh," Sean said, and he leaned over her shoulder to indicate various points of interest as they began their rather steep descent between the mountains. There was a moment during their landing pattern when they came—it seemed to Racquel—dangerously close to the white slope of a nearby mountain, and involuntarily, her hand went out to grip Sean's.

"We're OK," he said, and took the opportunity to lift her hand to his lips.

The kiss was as sudden and no less startling than the unexpected bump the plane made as the wheels touched the black of the airport tarmac. Racquel let out a pent-up breath. She had enjoyed most of the flight, but for a few moments there, caught in the craggy teeth of a ring of snowcapped mountains, she hadn't been at all sure that they were going to make it.

Sean released his seatbelt as soon as they were at a standstill. He was about to rise when Racquel placed a hand over his.

"I don't want to go out on the gurney again. Can I walk?"

His eyes flickered over her. "One of the men can carry you down the stairs, and you can use the wheelchair on the ground. Your legs are still not fully healed, so I don't want you falling and hurting your face."

Racquel suppressed a sigh. It had been weeks since she had last used her legs. She was really beginning to feel like a complete cripple. Well, she would go along with things for now. It did make sense that she might not be exactly steady on her feet after such a long time.

The captain came out, introduced himself, and spent a bit of time talking to her while preparations were made for her on the ground. She learned that he'd been flying Sean around the country for the last several years, and it was clear to Racquel that the man regarded himself as a lot more than just an employee. She had noticed that very thing with Sean's entire staff. There was an easygoing yet somehow incredibly efficient manner in which they all seemed to conduct themselves. Her admiration for the man, who had more than fulfilled the promise she had seen in him as a boy, continued to grow in leaps and bounds.

Once everything was nicely situated on the ground, Sean came back to inquire, "Ready to go?" The captain relinquished the seat next to hers, shook hands with Sean, then disappeared back into the cockpit.

Racquel darted a glance behind Sean, then asked, "Are you going to carry me down?"

An unreadable look flickered across his face. "Unless you don't want me to."

"Oh . . . no. Of course I want you to." Actually, she could think of nothing she wanted more than to feel his arms about her.

He swept her from the chair with no further preamble, and in a couple of quick strides they were down the steps. The solid steel of his arms and the rhythmic thudding of his heart against her side was almost enough to make her forget the sharpness of the mid-morning air.

Instead of putting her in the wheelchair standing at the ready, he carried her all the way to one of two large vans parked on the tarmac. As soon as she was settled, they all piled in. In very short order they were off, driving along the very narrow and winding road which led to Highway I-395. Racquel was all agog. The mountains, which had seemed so pristinely perfect from the sky, were now all about her, and almost touchably close.

She sat back in her seat after a while to remark, "This is a beautiful place. Everything looks so unreal. Like something you'd see on a postcard."

Sean nodded. "Wait until you see the lakes."

Racquel's lips curved upward. "Lakes? Up here? You're kidding, right?"

"Nope," he said. "There're tons of lakes around here—in Mammoth itself, and also just outside the town."

Racquel took a deep contented breath. "Unbelievable."

Sean turned off at the exit. Then they began their steep climb into town. "There's lots of stuff to do here, if you choose to be active. Skiing and snowboarding during the winter, and fishing, hiking, camping, and hayrides during the summer. It's really a nice, quiet, little town. Close enough to LA to be convenient . . . but not too close for a lot of the traffic."

In a sudden burst of enthusiasm Racquel said, "We have to have Morganna and Charley up one of these weekends. It would be such fun to—" Then she realized that she had spoken as though she and Sean were a couple, and she very hastily tried to correct herself. "I . . . what I meant was—"

Sean cut her off smoothly. "We should have them up," he said. "Remember a while back I mentioned having a ski weekend?"

Racquel nodded, a bit shamefacedly. "You were really serious about that, then?"

Coal black eyes regarded her for a minute. "Of course I was serious, Kel. I don't play games with you. I never did. You should remember that about me."

"I keep forgetting who you're supposed to . . . I mean who you *are*."

He said nothing in response, and Racquel spent the next several minutes wondering if she had somehow managed to offend him. They turned off the main road after a while, and within a mile or so were pulling up to a pair of wrought-iron gates. The other van turned in behind them, and Sean waited until they were close enough before leaning out to press a button on the keypad.

"Doctor KirPatrick," he said, and in response, the huge gates slid open.

* * *

Racquel's first glimpse of the compound had her drawing a startled breath. It was gorgeous—a large, rambling, ultra-modern house set against the backdrop of shimmering pink and gold mountains. Rolling lawns that were somehow richly green despite the frigid cold. Neatly graveled pathways leading to and away from the building. Clusters of well-pruned bushes, and a delightful smattering of tall, leafy trees.

"Well, we're here," Sean said as soon as they had come to a complete stop. He gave Racquel an unreadable look. "What do you think?"

"Is this the clinic?" she asked, looking around and trying not to appear too impressed.

"Half and half. The top two floors are mine to live in. And the first floor and basement area are strictly for the clinic. Come on, I'll show you around."

While the luggage and other equipment were being unloaded from the two vans, Sean pushed Racquel from room to room in the huge house, pointing out the examination rooms, the surgery, the private elevator that ran between the floors. There were four nurses stationed on the first two floors, and one plastic surgery resident. Racquel met them all, and was quite overwhelmed by the genuine warmth of their greeting—so much so that she felt absolutely no embarrassment at all about appearing before complete strangers in her heavily bandaged condition.

With the round of introductions finished, Sean wheeled Racquel across to the smooth, oak-paneled elevator, rolled her in, and hit the button for the third floor.

The doors opened onto a tastefully decorated sitting room with soft comfortable chairs, a solid, big screen

TV set, and a very expansive wraparound bank of floor-to-ceiling glass windows. Sean pushed her out onto the carpeting, then inquired, "Do you feel like trying a few steps?"

Racquel was immediately enthused. "Yes," she said, and without further discussion slipped her feet from the footrests, pushed them aside, and stood up. A sensation much like lightning shot through her right side, tearing a hot path of pain from the sole of her foot all the way up to her hip joint. She gasped, and would have fallen if Sean's arms had not shot out to steady her.

"Easy," he said. "You put a little too much pressure on your legs, a little too soon. You have to let them get accustomed to your weight again."

Racquel shifted her weight from right foot to left, and took a more cautious step. Again, as her weight rested on her right leg there was horrible, almost unbearable, pain. She sagged back against Sean and moaned, "I can't walk. Oh, God, I can't walk."

Sean lifted her effortlessly into his arms, and murmured soothing words against her neck. She turned her head to look at him, and her eyes were almost wild with terror. "Tell me truthfully, Sean—and please don't spare me, because I have to know—am I . . . am I crippled? Did the doctors at Cedars tell you that there was a good chance that I might never walk again? Not without crutches . . . or a walker, or something?"

He stroked a hand across her back. "No. You're going to be fine. You'll be able to walk again, run again, do everything that you could do before the accident. You're not crippled. It's just that your legs are not completely healed yet. Tomorrow, I'll have Nurse Brown begin your program of physiotherapy. We'll start you out in the pool first—to ease the weight. Don't worry, you're going to be fine."

He spoke so softly and with such absolute conviction that Racquel found herself relaxing against him. She was beginning to understand that he would never lie to her. If he said she was not crippled, then she was definitely not crippled.

He put her in the wheelchair again, and Racquel bent her head by just a little, to avoid his eyes. His hand came out to tilt her head up.

"Don't be embarrassed with me, OK? There's nothing—absolutely nothing—that I won't understand. Trust me. Can you do that?"

She stared into the dark eyes, and was struck by the depth of warmth and integrity she saw there. "Yes. I think so." She meant it. She was really beginning to feel that she could trust him entirely. With her body, with her life—with her love?

She looked away from him again, and Sean said in a suspiciously cheerful voice, "Let me show you where your bedroom is. I had them prepare the one with the best view. I'm on this floor, too. Should you ever need me during the night, I'll be just a few steps away."

Eighteen

Life at the clinic over the next several weeks was seamlessly tailored to suit Racquel's every need. She awoke at just before seven every morning, had breakfast, and then began a rigorous day of physiotherapy for her legs and back. Sean had not told her that during her stay there she would be the only patient, resident or otherwise. It came as quite a shock when she realized that the entire staff's sole responsibility over the next months was to nurse her back to a situation of complete health.

One morning, after she'd been there for a little over two weeks, she was carefully getting out of bed, swinging her legs over the thick blankets to rest them on the carpeting, when the inner door to her bedroom swung open and Sean walked in. Her short nightdress was gathered high above her knees, exposing a substantial length of both thighs. She looked up with the words, "Good morning," on her lips, expecting to see Nurse Brown, but was frozen into silence by the sight of Sean standing there.

He appeared similarly startled, and for what seemed like several minutes they just stared at each other. Then Sean burst into speech. "I'm . . . sorry. I knocked at the outer door. I thought you would be up and dressed by now."

Racquel struggled to drag her nightgown back down over her thighs, thinking all the while what a silly situation it was, and that there was absolutely no reason why she should feel so uncomfortable just because he'd gotten a glimpse of her legs. He was a doctor, after all, and he surely would not be swayed by a simple pair of legs—and definitely not hers, since they were far less than perfect at the moment.

She looked up at him when he still continued to stand there without saying or doing a thing. "Could you help me up?"

He came forward, in what seemed to Racquel to be a very jerky manner, and when he was close enough, just about standing over her, she lifted her arms to wrap long fingers about his arms. Once she was on her feet, his arms slipped down to rest on the bones of her hips.

"Are you . . . eating well?" Again, Racquel was struck by the very hoarse and jerky manner in which he spoke.

She nodded, then asked, "Are you getting a cold?"

He cleared his throat. "No. It's just my . . . allergies acting up, I think."

She met his eyes for a minute. "But there're no flowers blooming up here. It's too cold. You must be coming down with something. Maybe you should go back to bed."

The dark eyes regarded her for what seemed an eternity. Then he said, "It's probably . . . the dust, then."

Racquel didn't bother to mention that there was most likely not a single speck of dust in the entire place, because in her estimation he really did not seem to be quite himself.

She moved away from him, taking slow, careful steps. The pain in her right side was almost completely gone now, and she could bend both knees without substantial difficulty. She made her way across to the windows and stood looking out at the silent beauty of the snow-covered mountains.

"I think I could live here forever," she said, turning to Sean, who had come to stand beside her.

"You like it up here, then?" He rested an arm above her head, and the faint scent of his warm, musky cologne wrapped itself around her. An involuntary shiver raced across her skin, and Sean's hand dropped to rub her arm.

"You're cold," he said. "You'd better go put on something a bit thicker. I'll wait. I want to have a look at your face. I'll put another log on the fire, OK?"

When she returned, dressed in a deep burgundy sweater and a matching pair of pants, Nurse Brown and another older nurse—whom Racquel felt compelled to address as *Mrs. Harlequin*—were both in the room.

Holly Brown gave her a huge smile. "You look wonderful today. And, I see those legs are getting much stronger now."

Racquel returned her smile, and said a chirpy, "Good morning," to Mrs. Harlequin. It was nice and warm now, and the flickering of the fireplace in the corner lent a certain cozy feel to the room.

Sean quirked an eyebrow at her. "Ready for me to have a look?"

Both nurses beamed, and Racquel truly felt as though they cared as much about the unveiling as she did.

"I'm ready," she said, and sat in a chair close to the window. Sean cut away the first bandage, unwrapped a length, then handed the swatch to one of the nurses at his side. He continued to follow this procedure until Racquel could actually feel the warmth of the room directly on her face.

"Close your eyes," he said to her after a bit, and she

did so without hesitation. His fingers on her face as he turned her head from side to side were cool and featherlight. After a short while, she heard him say to one of the nurses, "OK, replace the bandages. And prepare the surgery for tomorrow."

Then it was another long session of sitting completely still, and allowing fresh bandages to be applied. She steeled herself before she asked Sean, "Is it bad?"

He smiled at her, and she felt herself relax. He certainly would not be looking that happy if there was something seriously wrong.

"You are just amazing," he said. "You're a textbook case of how this sort of healing should proceed."

"You're going to operate again, then?"

He nodded. "This time I'll focus on doing the skin grafts I told you about. And, if everything goes well with that . . . I may not need to operate again."

Racquel gave him an expansive smile. "I can't thank you enough, Sean," she said. "I . . . I really can't think of anything—any way—that I can possibly repay you for all that you've done for me."

Sean waited until both nurses had disappeared from the room. "You can let me cook dinner for you tonight."

Racquel blinked at him. Since her arrival at the clinic, she had not spent even one evening in his company. She'd been aware that he was somewhere around, but it had puzzled her that he had not come anywhere near her bedroom suite, not even to talk for a while, before going off to bed.

"Of course, if you'd like," she managed after a stretch of confused silence.

He smiled at her. "OK, then. I'll knock on your door at about seven this evening?"

"OK."

He seemed to want to linger for a while longer, and Racquel asked, "What're you going to do today?"

He shrugged. "Catch up on some paperwork, maybe. Talk to the clinic in LA."

"You know," she said, standing to face him. "I think you might be a workaholic."

His brows lifted. "A workaholic?"

"Umm," she said. "You don't seem to do anything at all for fun. Only . . . only those couple of times before, when you were with me."

"Well—"

"I want you to take the day off. Absolutely no work. It's Sunday, after all."

A smile flickered about his lips. "There's nothing else for me to do today. Besides—"

"You could go skiing."

The dark eyes flickered over her. "Without you?"

She laughed. "Even if I wasn't all bandaged up I still couldn't go with you. I don't know how, remember?"

"That'll change," he said. "I'll teach you, as soon as you're well enough."

Racquel walked right up to him. "Listen, Stephen, Sean, we're not talking about me now. We're focusing on you for a change."

"OK," he said, and there was a definite grin on his face now. "You're the boss." Then, in a startling change of direction that had Racquel wondering just how it was they had gotten onto that subject in the first place, he said, "You know, you have very nice lips."

Her mouth hung open for a bit, then snapped closed. He had very nice lips, too, but this discussion was about learning how to let go of work, and have some fun. It was not about lips and arms, and long, muscular, hair-roughened legs, and definitely not about warm dreams of him, either, though God knows she'd had a few of those.

"Sean," she said, and there was a note of mock firmness in her voice. "You're not listening to me at all."

He lowered his head until his lips were a scant few inches away from hers. "I'm listening."

"Fun," she said.

"I love . . . your hands," he said in response.

Racquel giggled despite herself. "You know, you're very silly," she said. "I don't know what I'm going to do without you."

He slid a hand around her waist. "Why do you have to do without me?"

She was suddenly flustered. "I mean, once—once I'm all healed again, and you're . . . we're not together anymore."

An unreadable expression flickered in his eyes. "You mean to get rid of me, then?"

"No, of course not. Not ever. But, I mean, we're not kids anymore, and we do have to be practical about things. We can't expect to spend every hour of the day in each other's company. And, besides . . . you'll be wanting to get on with your life. You know—get a girlfriend, that sort of thing."

"Umm," he agreed. "I do need a girlfriend."

Racquel lowered her eyes, and tried to deal with the flare of jealousy that burst into life somewhere inside her. She knew it to be true. He was a healthy man, after all, and couldn't be expected to remain celibate for long stretches of time. Still, hearing him actually utter the words was painful, much more than she'd thought it would be.

He tipped her chin up. "I don't want us to be . . . friends anymore."

She stared up at him, completely bereft of speech.

Surely he could not be suggesting that their relationship become more professional than it currently was. She didn't think she could stand that.

"Well," he finally said when she still did not speak. "Aren't you going to say anything?"

Her words came out in a disjointed rush. "Yes, I understand how you must feel, what with the staff around all the time, and the nurses maybe drawing their own conclusions about things—our bedrooms being so close together, after all—and you being such a fine, upstanding doctor, with a completely stellar reputation to protect."

His forehead wrinkled. "What?"

"I understand why—why we can't be friends anymore." Her voice took on a quality that was nothing short of mournful.

Sean threw back his head and laughed, and Racquel stepped away from the arm that had been wound loosely about her waist until then. She didn't see anything even remotely amusing about the situation, and she was rapidly becoming very upset with him.

The arm sneaked around her from behind, to spin her about to face him. His eyes still sparkled with latent humor, and Racquel clenched her lips against the angry flood of words that threatened to spill over.

"I want," he began again, "you." Then, he repeated the words so that she could not possibly misunderstand him.

Her lips opened, but no sound came. Her mind was in a tailspin. What was he saying? How could he possibly want her the way a man wants a woman? She was hideous. Bald, faceless, and just hideous. It must be because he pitied her, and desired to help rebuild her crushed self-esteem. He was such a very kind man, after all. A magnanimous gesture was no less than she would expect of him.

"I thank you for that, but I just couldn't get involved with anyone right now. Not even you, Sean."

She felt the weight of his sigh against her neck. "Is it that you don't find me attractive? I know women have types that they go for. Am I not your type?"

Racquel swallowed in an awkward clenching movement of her throat. Of course he was her type. For heaven's sake, he was every normal woman's type. "No, that's not it."

"What, then? Chemistry? You think of me as a brother figure, or something like that?"

"No."

He tilted her chin so that he could look directly into her eyes. "A father figure?"

Racquel chuckled despite herself. A father figure, indeed. Was he completely out of his gourd? "No, I definitely don't see you as that."

His lips twisted. "If you tell me that you see me as a mother figure, I think I'll have to cry."

Racquel was laughing now. "There's no one else in the world who makes me feel the way you do. And that's the truth."

His eyes flickered over to her lips. "Does that feeling involve any of the more tender emotions?"

She tried to avoid his eyes, but he wouldn't let her. "Well?"

"I just don't want you to pity me, Sean. I couldn't stand it if you did."

He pulled her in closer, so that her chest was resting against the solid strength of his. "Why should I pity you?"

"Well, it's . . . it's obvious, isn't it? You may not even realize why you feel the way you think you do.

A girl without a face—how could you? I mean, it's . . . it's just not possible."

Again he sighed. "You're the one who has the problem with your face. I don't. And nobody else around here does. We've seen much worse, trust me, and I certainly know the difference between desire and pity."

"It's not possible," she repeated with a trace of stubbornness in her voice.

"OK," Sean said, deciding to try a new approach. "So . . . I guess you wouldn't mind too much if I started dating other women?"

Racquel croaked a harsh, "Yes," before she could even think of anything better to say.

"Yes, you mind, or yes, you don't mind?"

"Yes, I mind. I mean, I don't mind. Ah—" She pulled away from him. "You've got me all confused."

He grinned at her. "I'll accept that."

For the remainder of the day, while she went through her program of physiotherapy, Racquel was left to wonder at his meaning.

With the coming of evening the sky developed a tight, gray appearance, and an icy wind dipped the temperature to below freezing. Following true to form, Racquel saw to Shaggy's nighttime feeding, then went to prepare herself for dinner.

She soaked in the large, slate-gray tub for over half an hour, her casted arm resting on the ledge of the bath. Then, when the water finally began to cool, she rose to wrap herself in a thick length of toweling. She was never more aware than she was now of the little niceties in life. Being able to take a bath and dressing unassisted were things she had taken completely for granted all her life, but now she savored these things, was grateful for the use of her arms and legs. Being able to slide into a slinky pair of black pants and a matching turtleneck sweater with big droopy arms made her even more aware of how very fortunate she was.

She was in the middle of creaming her hands with smooth cocoa butter when a knock sounded on the door. She softened her lips with a coating of strawberry chapstick before walking through from her bedroom into the tiny sitting room area. At the door she said, "Sean?" and opened it when she heard his voice on the other side. Her heart tilted a little at the sight of him, and for a crazy moment she felt like walking into his arms and wrapping herself around him. Instead, she said, "You look . . . nice." Nice? He had never looked sexier. In his tapered gray slacks and thick navy sweater, he just oozed sensuality, and without even trying.

He smiled. "Thank you. You, on the other hand, look good enough to do just about anything at all." He looked her over in a manner that caused her heart to begin a heavy pounding in her chest.

She considered him from behind her bandages, not knowing quite how to respond to such blatant suggestiveness. Her ex-husband had never flirted with her at all, not even before they were married.

"Are you ready for me?" he asked when it became clear that she was not going to say anything in response.

She stepped back from the door. "Ah, yes . . . yes. Would you like to come in for a minute?"

He leaned on the frame of the door. "OK, but do I get a kiss first? It's been such a long while since you've—"

She took a breath and struggled hard to keep the

right note of firmness in her voice. "Sean, are you going to start all that again?"

He regarded her with eyes that were a little too innocent. "Start what?"

He wasn't going to unnerve her this time. "The—the whole routine—the desiring and the wanting and—and the—the—God knows what else."

His laughter echoed around the room. "Would you prefer it if I desired and wanted someone else?"

She sighed. She was getting absolutely nowhere at all with him. She was even beginning to think that the entire project might be hopeless. He was completely stubborn. And, now that she came to think about it, he'd always been stubborn—stubborn as a boy, and now, stubborn as a man. She wagged a finger at him. "You were never one to listen to reason, were you?"

He caught her hand about the wrist and gave a gentle tug, so that she was forced to step into his arms. Smoldering black eyes regarded her. "What were you saying?"

"I . . . what I'm trying to—" She swallowed, and attempted to get a grip on herself.

His lips twitched. "Are you trembling?"

"What?" A flood of embarrassment threatened to overcome her. "No, of course not. It's just my legs—they're not strong enough yet."

"Your legs . . ." He bent his head to slowly taste her bottom lip. "I'll have to ask the nurse to add daily massage to your physio . . . unless you'd like me to . . ."

A feeling of thick intoxication was beginning to take hold of her, and it was all that Racquel could do to even think straight. His lips were doing such strange things, such wonderful, warm things, and even though she knew his feelings were inspired by pity, oh how right it felt to be held just so by him—to have his lips on hers. His tongue—oh, the things he was doing with it, she could not even begin to articulate.

"Should I stop?" he rumbled huskily.

Racquel was able to rouse herself sufficiently to realize that her arms were somehow twined tightly about his neck. She attempted to drop them and step back, but the solid band of steel about her waist did not allow for much movement.

"I . . . don't know what happened," she said, and she really didn't. Never before in her life had she so completely lost control of herself—and over one little kiss, too. Lord in heaven, what would be next?

For some reason, he appeared to be enormously pleased with himself. His face was completely wreathed in smiles, and his eyes glowed with an expression that was difficult for her to interpret. "I'll explain that to you later. Now, it's time for dinner."

He wrapped her arm through his, and ushered her along the wide corridor. At the door to his suite, he stepped back with the gracious comment, "After you."

Racquel entered the nicely furnished sitting room area, very aware that Sean was no more than a half a step behind her. Her eyes ran over the deep comfortable chairs, the beautifully carved end tables, the wall paintings, and the expansive bank of windows at one end.

"Oh," she said, "it's exactly like mine . . . except bigger, and a different color scheme."

Sean came to stand beside her. "Uhm, we'll have to go house hunting later. When you feel up to it."

She flashed a quick, sidelong glance at him. House hunting? What in the name of heaven was he talking about?

He rested the flat of his palm against her back, and gently propelled her forward.

"There's a small dining room in this suite. Through here—" and he was pushing back another door to reveal a cozy room with a dark lacquer table, already set for two. At one of the placemats, there was a bunch of twelve, ruby-red, long-stemmed roses.

Racquel's eyes darted from him to the roses, then back to him. The trembling had started in her again. Sean went across to the flowers, selected one of them, then walked back to where she stood frozen.

"For you," he said, and looking up to meet his gaze she was shaken by the depth of emotion shining in his eyes.

Her fingers reached out blindly to clasp the green stem. "Thank you," she croaked. Then, there were silly tears swimming in her eyes. He had done so much for her, given so much, and she had not done a single thing for him in return. In her life with Ralph she had become so very used to suffering, so very used to doing without, that to be treated with tender kindness, with consideration, with love, was almost too much for her to comprehend.

Sean opened his arms to her, and this time she went willingly. She stood with her head bent against his chest for long minutes, unable to do much more than just sob brokenly. The strong arms about her held her close, rocking her softly, much as a parent would rock a child. She tried to explain herself, but words failed her, and Sean held her closer still, murmuring, "I know . . . I know."

She raised her head after a while to inquire, "Why didn't you come back for me, once we were all grown up? Why did you leave me all alone in Idaho?"

Sean sighed. "I should've come, anyway, but I thought you'd forgotten me."

"Because of the letters?"

"Uh-huh."

"I never got them. Not even one. My parents must've sent them back."

He nodded. "I know that now." He tipped her chin up. "Will you tell me what happened to you—in those years when you were married to Penniman?"

A shudder ran through her. "I . . . can't. It's too terrible. You'll probably hate me afterward."

He bent his head to kiss her lightly on the lips. "How could I hate you? I couldn't. Not now, not ever. Do you understand me?" He held her away from him. "Let's sit down to dinner, and we can tell each other all of the horrible things that we've been through in the past years. Remember how I would never tell you how I got that scar on my side?"

She nodded.

"Well, I'll even tell you that, now. Is that a fair exchange?"

He left her to think on that while he disappeared into the kitchenette. When he returned pushing a cart stacked with dishes she was seated at the table, cradling the bunch of roses. Sean's heart was almost stripped raw at the sight of her, and for a few seconds he didn't quite trust his voice.

Racquel rose from her chair at the table to help him unload, exclaiming over the salads and oven-warm bread, opening up steaming, glass-covered dishes to savor the delicious aroma of roast beef, lentils, creamy soup. There was even a crab salad, nicely displayed on square wheat crackers.

"Wow," she said. "Did you cook all of this?"

He smiled. "Don't compliment me until you've actually eaten some of it."

She chuckled. "Well, it certainly smells good."

They lapsed into dinner—eating, talking, and eating

some more. Dessert was thick, crusty slices of pumpkin pie topped off with scoops of vanilla ice cream. At the final piece, Racquel put her spoon down to say, "I can't eat a morsel more. That was probably the best meal I have ever had. You're a wonderful cook." He was a wonderful man, too, and she wished that she could have him forever. The thought rattled through her brain. *Forever.* How nice it would be to wake up every morning with the knowledge that he was right there at her side, how nice to go to bed wrapped in his arms, safe, loved. She had sworn never to marry again, but now she wasn't so sure of her feelings on the subject. She wasn't sure, at all.

Sean stood. "Let's go into the sitting room."

Racquel considered the table of empty and half-empty dishes. "Shouldn't we clear up first?"

Sean gave the suggestion no more than a moment's thought. "No. They'll take care of it tomorrow."

He stretched out a hand to capture hers, and Racquel decided in that moment that she would not resist him any longer. She would tell him of all the abuse that she had suffered at her ex-husband's hand, and she didn't even care any longer if her suspicions were true and his feelings for her were based on a mixture of compassion and pity. She was only flesh, after all.

Nineteen

Morganna called on the morning that the cast on her arm was scheduled to be removed. Racquel had risen especially early, unable to sleep past the coming of the dawn. She had bathed, dressed, and then gone to sit in a chair facing the windows. From her seat she watched the icy morning sky as it slowly shed its dark skin. The black faded softly away, leaving behind a silvery trail of gray that seemed to hang uncertainly for only moments before reinventing itself in acres of crystal-clear blue.

Across the valley, the tiny resort town came slowly back to life. Skiers clambered into their off-road trucks and headed out to test the recent fall of powder. Outside the gates of the KirPatrick clinic a car pulled up, and a man in a full-length coat got out. He raised a hand to protect his eyes against the bright morning sun. His breath came harsher than usual because of the altitude, and he was forced to make use of his inhaler on more than one occasion, just to get himself under control.

He stood for long moments looking at the sturdiness of the gate, the height of the fencing that ran the length of the property, the distance from the house to the roadway. Then he clambered back into the car, made a couple of quick notes on a pad, and drove off.

* * *

When the phone at her bedside began to ring at a few minutes after eight, Racquel rose quickly from her chair. Nurse Brown had promised to give her a wake-up call, and she couldn't wait to get the cast off and regain the full use of her arm.

She lifted the receiver. "Hello?"

Morganna's cheerful voice came back. "Great. I got you. Charley kept telling me that it was too early to call. He said you might still be asleep."

Racquel sank onto the side of the bed. "I've been up for hours," she said, and unconsciously wrinkled her nose. "I couldn't sleep."

"Hmm," Morganna said. "Are the bandages being removed today?"

Racquel lifted a hand to her face and lightly touched the cotton. "No, but the cast on my arm comes off. I have to wait until the end of the week for the bandages, and even then Sean might decide not to remove them completely. It depends on how well the grafts have healed."

Morganna made a clucking noise with her tongue. "Everything's going to be fine. Don't worry about it. Sean's an absolute genius with this sort of thing. Oh—" she said, "before I forget. One of your friends came round a few days ago, looking for you. I told—"

Racquel cut her off. "One of my friends? Who?"

"Well, he didn't leave his name. Said he wanted to surprise you. He's from Idaho, I think. A tall thin man with a scar under his neck."

"Tall thin man?" Racquel repeated, and a chill raced across her skin. Could this be the man who had been tormenting her since her arrival in Los Angeles? Could he be the one who had meddled with the brakes on her car?

"Did you . . . did you tell him where I was?"

There was a pause on the other end of the line. Then Morganna said, "He seemed so concerned about you when I told him about your accident. He said that he wanted to send you some flowers. So—"

"You gave him the address here," Racquel finished.

"Was that your ex-husband? I didn't even think about him. God . . . I really should've known that you wouldn't want to see him."

"No. My ex-husband has a hefty sort of build. You know—he's big-boned. Looks just like everyone's idea of a farmer."

Morganna laughed. "Thank God. I thought I'd really put my foot in it."

Racquel chewed on the back of a knuckle and tried to think of a way to soften her words. Morganna couldn't know that she was being stalked by a lunatic. She hadn't really shared much of the crazy instances with her. She had wanted to keep everything quiet. Stupidly, she had believed that whoever it was would eventually tire of the game, move on to more interesting prey, but she had been wrong, and she had very nearly lost her life because of it.

"That man," she began haltingly, "is quite probably the one who's . . . who was responsible for my accident."

Twenty

After she hung up, Racquel continued to sit on the side of the bed. She worried the corner of her lip. It was important that she remain calm about things. Even if Morganna's visitor and the persistent stalker were one and the same, what harm could he possibly do her here? She was surrounded at all times by people. And, of course, there was Sean. He would never let some maniac off the street break in and do her bodily harm. There was nothing, absolutely nothing, for her to get all worked up about. She would just let Sean know what Morganna had said about the man. Then she would try her level best to forget all about the entire sorry incident. It probably would not be worth the man's time, anyway, to drive all the way up to the mountains just to torment her. What was the point, after all? He'd had his fun with her in LA. Now, he would probably give up and leave her alone.

She reached for the phone again.

"Nurse Brown," she said after a minute, "is Doctor KirPatrick waiting for me in the clinic?"

She thanked the nurse after a moment of listening to her crisp voice. "I'll call his room extension, then."

Sean answered after the second ring. "I'll come over," he said, and in less than a minute there was a knocking at the door. Racquel called, "Come in," and turned to greet him with smiling eyes. "Today's the day, right?"

He returned her smile with one of his own. "For the arm, not the face."

She rose and went to him. "Can't I take a look under the bandages? Just a quick one?"

He tilted her chin up. "No. You're just going to have to wait. We don't want any problems with infection. You're going to get your face back, without any welts or visible scars, but you have to trust me. OK?"

She sighed. "OK. But I can't stand all this waiting. It's driving me crazy."

"Patience," he said, giving her an intent look, "is something else I could teach you a lot about." He was standing before her with both hands shoved into his pants pockets, and Racquel felt the sudden urge to hug him. In the past weeks they had become so very close, spending each evening together, sometimes talking, other times watching TV or just listening to music. It was becoming harder and harder to believe that there had ever been a time when they had not been exactly as they now were.

"After you take the cast off . . . could we go for a walk outside? There's something I want to talk to you about."

His brows quirked. "Something about us?"

She beamed. It pleased her immensely that he was being so very patient with her. She had come to a decision in the past week, one that scared her just a little. She had decided that once the bandages were removed she was going to gently suggest that they try living together. It wasn't something that she would have considered doing a few months ago, but a lot had changed since then, and somehow it didn't seem so very wrong now. Besides, Sean had hinted at it enough over the past weeks. She had not been ready to give him any sort of answer then. She would though, after the bandages were removed.

"Well, it involves us . . . maybe me, mostly."

"Hmm," he said, "we'd better get this arm taken care of right away, then."

Racquel walked with him to the elevator, and before long she was seated in one of the examination rooms, with the ever attentive Nurse Brown standing at the ready. The plaster was removed without much trouble, and for the first time in months she was able to move her fingers freely. She looked at Sean with bright eyes. "This is wonderful. I feel so . . . light."

On a sudden surge of feeling, she stood and threw her arms about him, suddenly not caring a jot what anyone might think. Sean's arms folded immediately about her, and Racquel noted absently that he seemed not to care who saw them, either. He moved his mouth close, and his breath brushed warmly against her ear.

"If you're this excited about your arm, I can't wait until we take the bandages off and take a look at your face. What will you do to me then?"

Racquel chuckled. Oh, it was so very wonderful being alive, being with him. "You'll just have to wait and see."

"Come on," he said, taking her by the hand. "Let's go take that walk." And, with the entire staff looking on, they walked hand in hand from the clinic.

Outside, the day was very bright, and it took a moment for Racquel to readjust adequately to the sharpness. She squinted up at Sean. "It's not so cold today. You can almost get away without wearing a sweater."

"Umm," he said, and wrapped her arm snugly through the nook of his. "I think we're going to have a warm spring. It should be a great summer, too." He looked down at her, and there was a smile in his eyes. "Remember how we used to dream of spending months of time together—doing whatever we felt like doing? Fishing . . . hiking . . ."

She nodded. "I remember." It was just unbelievable how he seemed to remember everything with such clarity. There were even some things that he recalled that she had somehow forgotten—like the time that she had fallen through the barn roof and landed on her back among five very startled cows. Sean had been certain that she had broken her spine, then, and had rushed off to the house for her father, making her swear that she would not move a single muscle before he returned. Her father, though, had blamed Sean for the entire episode, and had threatened to bar him from the farm if he continued to get his daughter involved in one scrape after another.

She looked up at him now with slightly regretful eyes. "Sometimes I was such a horrible little kid. I still don't understand why you continued to let me hang around you. I always got you into trouble with my dad. And you were always the innocent party."

He quirked an eyebrow. "I know. I still can't figure out why I like you, but,"—a trace of a smile played about his mouth—"payback day is coming."

She poked him in the side and giggled. "You're such an idiot."

He returned her smile, and a deep feeling in her heart came into full bloom. Was this the love that she had thought she might never feel? She was struck by the sudden and the absolute wonder of it. Love. What a curious emotion. It made her feel happy, and full of white light. She wanted to do everything for him, and she couldn't bear the thought of them ever being apart again. She looked up at him with bright eyes.

He said, "I want to show you something."

They had walked quite a distance from the house now, and were approaching the edge of the expansive property. Just ahead was a large leafy tree which Racquel had spied from her bedroom window. Sean motioned to a shady spot against the trunk.

"Let's stop here for a bit," he said. Once they were seated and leaning with their backs against the trunk of the tree, Sean pointed to the crest of a hill just visible in the distance. "See that?"

Racquel shaded her eyes against the sun. "The hill?"

He pulled her to sit closer to him. "It's a lot more than just a hill. It's prime real estate. What do you think of it?"

Racquel took another look. From all that distance away, it really didn't seem like very much at all. The only thing that she could make out was that it was huge, and it appeared to be completely without any type of human habitation.

"It's hard to say," she said after a moment of trying to decide what response to give. "It's . . . nice I suppose. Very big. If you lived up there, you'd have a bird's-eye view of everywhere else."

He nodded. "I'm thinking of buying it. Should make a really nice spot for a house."

"Umm," she agreed. "It should, at that. But you'll have to build a house, 'cause there's none there now. And it's also going to be kind of isolated, all the way up at the top."

He turned to give her a long look. "I won't be alone up there."

She smiled. "You won't?"

"I won't. Maybe I'll move my entire practice out of LA. Mammoth is a great place to raise kids."

Racquel's heart gave a tiny flutter. Kids . . . with him. What a wonderful thought. She had never wanted to, with Ralph. Bringing a child into the world was a special and important decision, not one to be made lightly—and definitely not one to be made if there was any chance at all that the child would be in any way abused.

"Are you planning on having a family, then?"

The dark eyes locked with hers. "Yes. I love kids."

"Hmm," she said, and decided not to question him further on it. She wouldn't, under any circumstances, willingly give birth to a brood of illegitimate children—that was one thing she would be firm on—and he had sworn that he had no intention of ever marrying.

Sean tilted her chin up with a finger. "You're very quiet all of a sudden. Have I scared you?"

She blinked. "No . . . no, I was just thinking."

"About what I just said about wanting kids?"

"Yes."

"You like them, don't you?"

She gave him a startled look. "Of course I like them . . . I love children."

Sean settled back against the tree. "Good. How many do you want to have?"

Her mouth worked silently for a minute. "I . . . I don't know. I've never really thought much about it at all." In fact, she had. She'd thought about it a lot lately.

He stroked a finger against the bandages on her face, pausing to remove a flyaway wisp of grass. "Does two sound about right? A boy and a girl?"

Racquel chuckled. "Gender preferences . . . that's not something you can control . . . if you go the natural way."

Black eyes turned to regard her intently. "I think we should do it the natural way, don't you?"

"Yes." A flood of blood rushed to pulse hotly just beneath the skin of her face. Why should the thought of such a thing throw her into a state of near confusion? She had been married before, after all, so she wasn't an innocent by any means. She hadn't liked sex at all with Ralph, but it might be different with Sean. In fact, she was willing to bet that everything would be different with him. He was such a very kind and understanding man. She forced herself to meet his gaze, even though a pulse was fluttering madly at the base of her neck.

"Sean—" she began tentatively, "I spoke to Morganna today."

"Umm," he said, and he pulled her to rest against his chest. "Once we take the bandages off your face, we have to invite Morganna and Charley up—maybe we'll throw a party, make a big thing of it."

Racquel nodded, then just blurted out what she intended to say, since she could think of no better way to do it. "I think the man who's been calling me on the phone all these months paid her a visit a few days ago."

Sean stiffened. "What do you mean, paid her a visit? Is he harassing *her* now?"

Racquel worried the corner of her lip. She hoped he wouldn't think her paranoid, but there was a deep sense of foreboding in her. She'd been trying to push the feeling away, to ignore it, but it kept coming back. She felt that something terrible was going to happen, and to her.

"I don't think he's interested in anyone but me. And"—her voice broke—"I can't think why. I mean . . . I don't even know who he is." She shook her head, before he could ask the question. "It's not Ralph. Morganna described him. She said he was tall and thin, and had some sort of scar underneath his neck."

A frown ran quickly across Sean's face. The man he had noticed walking away from his car in the hospital parking lot had been tall. Admittedly, he hadn't gotten a very good look at the man, because of the full-length coat, but it was certainly possible that he might also have possessed a thin build.

"Did she tell him where you were?"

Racquel nodded, but hastened to reassure him. "I don't think he'll come all this way, though. I mean, what's the point of it? Unless he's crazy or something. Besides, he would know that I couldn't be all alone up here . . ."

Sean shifted to wrap his arms more securely about her. He'd been rolling a thought around in his head for several weeks now, but he hadn't wanted to worry her with the possible implications of it. Now, he had no choice.

"Your parents' accident . . . was there ever an investigation?"

Racquel shifted to look at him. "Just the normal questions asked when that sort of thing happens. But nothing too much beyond that. You don't think that there was . . . I mean, that—" It was too horrible for her to even articulate. "But that couldn't be. That was years ago. Before I even got married. I mean, if there's someone out there who's trying to . . . wipe us all out, why wouldn't they have gotten me when I was still in Idaho? I mean, why wait years before starting up again?"

Sean's chest moved silently. He had no answer for her, but if there *was* no connection between her parents' death and what was now occurring, the only other possibility was that they were dealing with someone who was quite probably criminally insane. The thought of what that might mean scared him.

"I'm staying with you tonight," he said after a long period of silence. "The clinic is secure enough. But if someone's really determined to do you harm, I'm not going to take any chances."

She shivered, and although the sun was high in the sky she suddenly felt an iciness creep about her. She had never been a superstitious person, but she felt as though someone had just walked on her grave.

Sean felt the involuntary tremble race through her, and he bent his head to kiss the nape of her neck. "Don't worry, I won't let anything happen to you. We'll figure this thing out together. Maybe once he realizes that you're not alone any longer, he'll back off."

He didn't believe that for a second, but he hoped his voice had been convincing enough to make her believe it. He stood, and pulled her to her feet.

"Let's go back in," he said. He wanted to get her back indoors, where he was certain she would be safe. "Do you feel like watching a couple of videos?" His voice was deliberately cheerful, but he was afraid that she could see right through him.

"Sure." She looked at him with those gorgeous eyes, and he made a silent vow that as long as there was breath in his body he would let no harm come to her.

They walked slowly back, hand in hand, and from behind the fence a man watched their progress with a blend of anger and hatred in his eyes. He watched until they were no longer visible, then he said to the one beside him: "OK. I've seen enough. Go ahead . . . I don't care anymore."

* * *

Later that evening Racquel was getting herself ready for bed. It had always been part of her ritual to shower and cream her body, and even though her face was still swathed in bandages she did not vary from the comforting routine now. She was curled up in an armchair, flipping rather aimlessly through a magazine, when Sean entered. He carried a towel slung across his shoulder, and a pair of pajamas. Her face melted into a smile at the sight of him. God, it felt so very good to have him so close at hand. She almost felt as though nothing at all could possibly go wrong with him right there.

He came across to lean over her chair. "Will you come into the bathroom and wash my back for me?"

Racquel blinked at him. He always knew exactly what to say in order to startle her. "Wash . . . your back?"

He nodded. "There's always a spot, dead center, that I can never reach. Would you give me a hand with it?"

Unconsciously, she sucked in her bottom lip. She had never seen him without clothes, but it was silly to refuse him this on some spurious puritanical basis. They were both adults, after all, both well able to control themselves.

"All right." She stood gracefully. He had done so much for her in the past months, she could at the very least agree to wash his back.

"Is the bedroom door locked?" she asked once they were in the bathroom proper.

"Locked and double locked," he said, and proceeded to hang his towel and pajama bottoms from the hook on the door.

"Would you . . . would you rather that I wait outside

until you need me?" A sudden trembling had seized her at the thought of having him undress before her.

He turned the lock in the bathroom door and looked at her with very calm eyes.

"There's nothing to be afraid of, Kel, it's just me. And it's past time that you saw me like this, don't you think?"

She didn't know exactly how to answer. He was always so very direct with her. So much so that he hardly ever engaged in any form of preamble at all.

"Well, if you . . . if you want me to stay—"

He nodded. "I want you to."

He tugged his sweater off and let it fall to the floor. Racquel hastened to pick it up. She straightened and found him watching her.

"Want to come in with me?"

She clutched the sweater with fingers that were beginning to tremble a little. "No, I don't think . . . so. Maybe . . . later. I already took a shower."

His hands moved to loosen the buttons on his shirt. "OK . . . You'll just have to watch me, then." A sudden smile twisted his lips.

Racquel's breath quickened as the shirt fell to the floor, and he stood before her barechested. He was beautiful, and so very strong looking—the way his stomach muscles bunched in six little packets, the long arms, the broad chest, and slim waist. There was not an ounce of fat anywhere on him. She had never wanted to touch her ex-husband, but she did so want to run her fingers across the smooth expanse of Sean's chest.

She raised bashful eyes to his, and he returned her gaze without comment. Looking into the dark, silky depths of his eyes, she suddenly knew what he wanted of her. He wanted her to come to him, without fear, without coercion, to touch him, to kiss him, to hold him.

She moved to stand directly before him. His eyes coaxed her closer, and she went. With her hands resting against the flat of his chest, she offered her mouth to him. His arms wrapped warmly around her. She waited, almost impatiently, for the warm, wonderful feel of his lips on hers, but the kiss never came. Her eyes sprang back open to blink at him in a somewhat confused manner. He bent his head, then, not to kiss, but to brush his lips gently back and forth across the soft length of hers.

"You know I love you, Kel . . . don't you?"

A startled breath escaped her, and all she could manage to stammer was, "You do?"

He kissed her, then, pulling her close, deepening the kiss by small increments, softly demanding that she respond to him in kind. She stroked the smooth skin of his back, pausing to massage the area around his lower spine. He groaned in response, and she shifted her mouth to ask, "Did I hurt you?"

He turned his face into the smooth column of her neck, and after a few heated breaths, managed a very shaky, "No."

Racquel stroked the thick scar on his side, and she felt him tremble. He raised his head to look down at her, and the depth of emotion in his eyes humbled her. The thought ran through her head that he really must care for her—not just because she had been so seriously hurt and was, even now, still wrapped in bandages.

He stroked a finger across the curve of her ear. "I'd better go take a shower."

Racquel nodded. "OK. If you do, I'll . . . I'll wash your back for you."

He gave her a hooded look. "Somehow, I don't think that's such a good idea any longer."

Her eyes fixed on him, and she was immediately faced with the evidence of his discomfort.

"All right," she said softly, "I'll wait for you inside, then."

She sat in the chair in front of the window, staring out at the darkness, listening to the shower run and wondering why it was still so difficult for her to trust him with her love. Why could she not reciprocate in kind, with the actual words? Was she to be forever scarred by her past? Incapable of loving without fear?

When the bathroom door opened, she turned and watched him walk toward her. What a very fine specimen of manhood he was. He was wearing only his pajama bottoms, and for a moment an errant thought drifted through her head, and the words were on her lips before she could rethink them. "Aren't you going to be cold . . . dressed like that?"

He smiled, and a warm feeling curled about Racquel's heart. "Not if you agree to keep me warm."

She swallowed. *Did he mean to sleep in the same bed as she?* She had not really considered exactly where he would sleep, until now.

"We're going to share the same bed tonight, then?"

He went across to sit on the very item, and patted a spot beside him. "I'll sleep above the covers if you'll feel more comfortable that way. You didn't intend that I sleep on the floor, did you?"

She was horrified by the suggestion. "Oh, no . . . no, of course not. I just hadn't really thought much about where—" She suddenly felt quite foolish under the steady scrutiny of those wonderful black eyes.

"Come over here," he said, and reached to peel back the thick blankets. He shifted on the bed to make room for her, and she turned to give him a pensive look once she was properly settled.

His breath caressed the back of her neck. "Put your legs up."

Once her feet were up, Sean reached around her to tuck in the blankets. "Nice and snug," he said.

Racquel turned onto her side to face him, her head propped against her palm. "Are you going to sleep with me until this man is caught?"

He moved in closer, and Racquel's heartbeat quickened. "Is that all the time I get?"

She picked up on the teasing note in his voice. "You mean you're looking for more than that?"

He ran a finger down the smooth column of her neck. "A lot more."

"Hmm," she said, and settled down against the pillows. She felt safe with him there, and couldn't think of anything nicer than just lying there beside him.

"Sean . . . did you know that I had a crush on you when I was a kid?"

His brows flicked upward. "You did?"

She smiled. "I did. I used to follow you around, remember? I was always getting into things . . . always getting you in trouble."

He lay back, resting his head on the flat of his palms. "You were always such a cute little thing—long colt legs, gorgeous little face. I would've done anything for you." He turned onto his side. "What about now? Do you still have a crush on me?"

She touched his shoulder. "What would you say if I said I did?"

He bent toward her and, strangely, his eyes were completely serious. "I would say that . . . my prayers had been answered."

"Oh." She hadn't expected that, hadn't expected him

to say such a wonderful thing. She turned away so that he would not see the sudden tears that had welled in her eyes, but he turned her head back.

"Show me exactly where he hurt you, sweetheart."

Her throat clenched, and she croaked, "Exactly where?"

He nodded, and his eyes were serious again. "Let me see?"

After a brief hesitation, she touched the side of her jaw. "Here"—her hand drifted down to her collarbone—"and . . . here." Through the silk of her pajamas, she touched a spot just above her breastbone. "Here, too." Her hand continued to drift lower until it finally came to rest against her ribs. "Sometimes . . . here."

Sean took it all in, in complete silence. Then he moved to gently kiss the spot she had touched on the side of her jaw, went lower to press warm kisses against her collarbone. His fingers fiddled with the top button of her pajama blouse. Then his head dipped again, and his lips ran over the spot. Racquel's hand came up to stroke his hair as he drifted around to caress the side of her rib cage.

When he raised his head again to look at her, her lashes were thick with tears. He leaned forward, and his tongue captured a silver teardrop. "I love you Racquel, do you believe me?"

In the silence of the room, she could hear herself breathe. Yes, she believed him. She hadn't before. She had been a little too afraid to give her trust to anyone again. But she did believe him now. "Yes . . ." she said in a very watery manner, then again strongly, *"yes."*

"Do you love me?"

She'd been afraid of that question, and what it would

mean once she had answered it, but she did love him, and he deserved a fair answer. It was only right that he should know how very empty the future would be without him.

She cupped the side of his face. "I think that what I feel for you is . . . much deeper, much stronger than love. People fall in and out of love all the time. Sometimes I think that it's a state of convenience—something that people say and do, just to get what they think they want at the time. That's not how I feel about you, even though sometimes I can't think of the right way to show it. I don't know how to be consistently affectionate, like you. Something happened to me . . . along the way."

He turned his face into her palm, and his fingers interlocked with hers. "There're people who are just meant to be together through life, babe. You and I are two of the lucky ones. God brought us back together. There must be a reason for that. You're happy when you're with me, aren't you?"

She nodded. Her throat was so very tight at that moment that she was several measures beyond speech.

He rubbed a tear from the tip of her lashes. "And just seeing you every day makes my whole world just . . . I can't describe how good it feels, just knowing that you're close, that I can see you whenever—"

She stroked the flat of her hand down the length of his arm. "I . . . don't think I deserve you," she choked out.

He bent and took her lips in a soft kiss. "We deserve each other."

She came to settle against him, her head resting just under his chin, his arms wrapped snugly around her. Maybe they did deserve each other. Maybe, finally, things would be right for them.

Gently, gently, as his heart thudded beneath her ear,

she fell into soft sleep. Sean lay awake for hours, just holding her, turning over in his mind exactly how he would ask her to be his wife, thinking of ways around possible objections that she might have. The promise he had made to her father was no longer important. No longer valid.

Gradually he, too, was overcome by sleep, and his head came to lie just above hers on the pillows.

Twenty-one

It was just after 2:00 A.M., and Racquel came abruptly awake. The terror of the nightmare that had held her in its grip was so real that it took a few moments for her to remember exactly where she was, to understand that she was in no immediate danger. In her dream, she was being chased by her ex-husband through a swampy marsh. There was thick, treacherous mud on the ground making it hard for her to run, and there were trees everywhere, the spindly branches tearing at her clothes, her face, her arms. And all the while she could hear him behind her, his footsteps pounding, getting closer, closer, closer. He was screaming at her, telling her that he loved her, but she could clearly see the gleaming blade of the knife which he held in his hand. She had known then that he meant to kill her with it, that he would catch her and slice her neck open if she didn't run. *Run. Run.*

Her heart was still pounding, and the bitter taste of fear was still in her mouth. It took a moment for her breathing to slow, and she turned to look at Sean, wondering if her thrashing about had disturbed him. He was still asleep, peacefully so, one arm thrown above his head, the other curled about her.

She lifted his arm gently, not wanting to wake him,

and padded on silent feet to the bathroom. When she returned, she walked across to the window, drawn by the majestic beauty of the towering mountains. In the moonlight, they appeared almost surreal, floating on a swirling bed of white mist, their peaks a wonderful blend of pink, gold, and some other color which Racquel could not define. She stood there for long minutes, taking quiet strength from the night. It was terrible that she had let Ralph Penniman torment her for such a long while. Even now, when she was free of him, he still had the power to invade her dreams and snatch away her peace of mind, but she was determined to beat the fear that she still had of him. She would not stay up for the remainder of the night, fearing sleep and the twisted images it might bring. She would turn right around, go back to bed, lie close to Sean, and sleep peacefully.

With that intention firmly in her mind, she turned away from the window. Then on a moment's pause, she turned back. From the corner of her eye, she had seen a flicker of orange. She peered out into the night, her eyes scouring the jutting piece of building. Then she saw it again, and her heart thudded heavily in her chest. Fire. The house was on fire.

She ran to the bed, sliding on the oval bedroom rug, and tearing at Sean's shoulder. She shook him violently. "Fire!" she screamed. "Wake up . . . Fire!"

Sean came out of sleep with amazing mental quickness. "Where?" he asked. "Where's the fire?"

Racquel pressed a trembling hand to her lips. "I think it's the clinic, but I can't be sure." Sean was out of bed, and pulling on his clothes. "Get dressed," he said quickly. "Grab a couple sweaters, your coat, and make sure you put on socks and boots."

Racquel followed his instructions almost blindly,

rushing about the room, opening drawers, pulling out items of apparel. In less than five minutes, she was ready. Sean was on the phone, barking orders into the mouthpiece. Then he grabbed hold of her hand and hustled her from the room and down the stairs to the ground floor. The nurses were already assembled at the bottom of the staircase, and Sean herded them all outside with the command, "Don't worry about trying to save any equipment. Everyone out—out into the courtyard." He took a quick glance around to be sure everyone was there. Then he wrapped an arm about Racquel, who was shaking terribly, and hustled her through the door and into the frigid night air.

Outside, the wail of approaching fire engines rent the night, destroying the usual quiet. Everyone stood back, watching in horrified fascination as flames billowed out of the clinic windows, consuming the wood and plaster like a hungry demon.

Sean held Racquel before him, wrapping his thick coat about her shoulders and running his hands down the length of her arms. He spoke softly into her ear, hoping to calm her.

"It's OK . . . you're safe. It's OK." She turned to him to cuddle into the warmth of his embrace. The fear that had been with her while she slept was with her again, and there was no way for her to control it. They were going to get her, whoever it was. They wouldn't stop until they got her. This fire was no accident. It had been set. She was sure of it.

She raised her head suddenly to cry out, "Sean . . . the dog . . . he's still inside!" She moved as if to dash back into the building, but Sean grabbed her by the shoulders. "Stay," he said. "The firemen will get him. He's not in the part of the house that's on fire. He'll be all right."

She began to sob. "He's going to die . . . I'm going to die. Nothing's going to stop until . . . until I'm dead."

Sean hushed her, rocking her gently back and forth. "No," he said, "I won't let him. I won't let anything happen to you. I promise you that. I promise you that."

The property was swarming with firemen now, some pulling hoses, others issuing curt orders to the group of people who stood about staring at the flames in dazed fascination. Sean spoke to one of the officers about Shaggy, telling him exactly where in the building the animal was being housed, and before long the man returned with the dog at his heels. Only then could Sean lead Racquel across to a vehicle and guide her into the front seat of the car. He herded the dog into the back, closed the door securely behind him, then went to finish his conversation with the fire captain. He returned a few minutes later to open the driver's door and slide behind the wheel.

"Everyone's going to have to stay at a motel tonight. They're going to check the entire place out. I told them what we suspect."

Racquel turned frightened eyes in his direction. "I can't believe this is happening . . ."

Sean started the engine and shifted the car smoothly into gear. "Let's just wait and see. It might not be arson."

Racquel shifted her eyes to the dark roadway and made no response. Somehow, she knew without question what the investigators would find. The fire had been set. There was a madman out there who was determined to kill her, and he would not be satisfied until he did just that.

Sean lifted her cold hand into his lap and massaged her fingers. "Tell me about your parents' accident," he said. "Everything that you can remember about it. Everything."

In the minutes that it took to drive from the house to the motel, Racquel recounted the events surrounding her parents' accident. Sean listened, largely without comment, only stopping her here and there to clarify a point.

At the motel, there was no question about whether or not they would be sharing the same room, and before long Sean was closing the door to the suite, deadbolting and sliding the golden link chain across the door.

Racquel looked at him with eyes that were unnaturally bright. "I'm so sorry about the clinic, Sean . . . all your equipment. Everything must be destroyed."

He came to sit beside her on the bed. "At least you're safe, hmm? Besides, insurance will take care of most of the damage."

She bent her face against her hand. "God, it's so unbelievable . . . everything that's been happening these last months. It's like something out of a bad dream."

"Get under the covers while I make you some hot chocolate. There's an idea I want to discuss with you. Instead of running from this man, whoever he is, we're going to go on the offensive. We're going to get the bastard."

Twenty-two

It was not until several days later, as Racquel sat in the only examination room that had been undamaged by the fire, that she finally made up her mind that Sean was right. It was past time that she stop running. She realized now that for as long as she continued to run the man would give chase. So, they would turn the tables on him. It was now her turn to chase.

She smiled at Nurse Brown as the woman wheeled a trolley filled with utensils into the room.

"Well . . . this is it, I guess. Do or die, this is what my face will look like for the rest of my life."

Nurse Brown gave her shoulder an encouraging little pat. "Remember, nothing is absolutely final. Doctor KirPatrick will operate again if necessary. But let's see first. OK?"

Racquel nodded. Despite every effort to the contrary, she was as nervous as a gadfly, and she felt as though a herd of cattle was doing a merry jig in her stomach.

She understood how very superficial this line of thinking was, but still, she did not want to spend the remainder of her life hiding her face behind huge diaphanous scarves. She did not want to be a twisted freak. She didn't mind at all if she was not a stunning beauty, but she did desire a face that would at the very least, not frighten animals and children.

She swallowed audibly when the door behind her opened and Sean walked in. He looked as calm as he usually did. There was not an ounce of worry in him, at least not as far as she could tell. He had a word with the nurse, then came over to her smiling.

"You look as happy as a condemned prisoner going to the electric chair."

She managed a weak chuckle. "Are you going to take everything off now?"

He nodded. "Everything."

"Will you let me look . . . no matter what?"

"If you like." He picked up a pair of scissors with long narrow pincers and inserted the instrument under the first bandage. He pulled up and away from the face, cutting skillfully and unraveling the lengthy maze of wrappings. He handed the gauze back to the nurse, who disposed of the cotton with equal dexterity and speed. His hands moved about her face, gently probing, touching, then unraveling some more.

Racquel sat completely still throughout the entire process, hardly daring to even breathe. She closed her eyes and said a couple of fervent prayers. *All I ask for is a normal face, God, just a normal face.*

When all the bandaging was gone and she could feel the puff of the heater on her face, she reopened her eyes. Her gaze shot immediately to Nurse Brown, who was obviously doing her valiant best not to give vent to a spate of tears. Then her eyes returned to Sean. His face was as unreadable as ever, and Racquel gritted her teeth. It was bad—maybe worse than she had been able to imagine.

"Can I . . . see?" she croaked.

Sean helped her down from the chair, and she walked

on shaky legs to a large mirror which they had wheeled in for this very purpose.

She lifted a hand to run her fingers over the short growth of hair atop her head. Then, slowly, wonderingly, her hand drifted down over her face. It was incredible. Incredible. After what had been described to her—the extent of the damage to her face—it wasn't possible, surely? There was nary a scar or a raised welt of skin anywhere at all. The skin was as smooth and unblemished as a baby's bottom. He had rebuilt her face exactly. The cheekbones that had been so shattered by the windshield were there again. Maybe they were a smidgen higher than they had been before, but that only added somehow to her overall beauty.

From some distant point she heard the sound of someone sobbing, and slowly, as she came back to herself, she realized that the noises were coming from her. Sean came to hold her, and she grabbed hold of him and held on for dear life.

"Thank you," she said over and over again, "thank you."

The nurse left the room to speak to the camera crew waiting just behind the door.

"Give her a few minutes," she said, and then went off to the bathroom to have a good cry of her own.

Sean bent his head to press a kiss to the soft mass of hair. "You like it, then?"

Racquel raised eyes swimming with tears. "Like . . . like it?" she stammered. "You're a genius . . . a saint. How can I ever repay you? What can I ever give you to express how much . . . how very much—"

Sean tilted her face up, and wiped the tears away with the blunt of his thumb. "You can marry me."

Racquel's mouth worked, but no sound came. After

several seconds of groping for words, she managed, "Marry?"

He kissed her softly on the lips. "Marry. What do you say?"

Her head was spinning with the wonder of it, the absolute magic of it. Marry Sean? What could possibly be better? To live for the rest of her life with such a man would truly be a blessing from none other than God.

"Yes," she said, and she was throwing her arms about his neck, and peppering his face with abundant kisses. "Yes . . . yes . . . yes."

He held her close. "I can't believe that you're mine, finally. After all these years of wanting you, loving you."

Racquel's eyes were diamond-bright. "I thought you wanted me to live with you. Not marry you."

He pinched the tip of her nose. "Don't you know that I've loved you since you were a child? How could I not want us to spend the rest of our lives together? I've never wanted anyone else. Never considered taking anyone else as my wife—my mate."

Racquel swallowed the lump in her throat. "Sean," she said, and she lifted a hand to touch his face, "my love. I should've waited for you. I should've—"

He hushed her with the words, "You've got me now, babe. Forever. And if there's anything on the other side of eternity, you'll have me then, too."

The camera crew found them wrapped tightly in each other's arms, and after a few minutes of rolling tape the man holding the camera turned off his equipment and motioned to the others to leave the room.

Later that evening, Racquel washed her face carefully with special soap. It was wonderful to be able to touch her skin again, to do everything unassisted. What a blessing it was to have two good arms, good legs, a face . . . Sean. She had completely gotten over thinking of him as Stephen now. He was just Sean—kind Sean, beautiful Sean, the man she would willingly spend several lifetimes with, if that were at all possible.

The sound of the outer door closing had her turning from her ablutions. She pressed her face into a soft towel and poked her head around the bathroom door to smile at him.

"I'll be out in a minute," she said.

Sean came to stand in the doorway. "I love to see you so happy."

She finished patting her face dry and then went to wrap her arms about his waist. Between kisses, she said, "And I love you."

He pulled her in close to inquire, "Are you sure you really love me? Or is it just gratitude you feel for me . . . because of your face?"

Racquel gave him a poke in the stomach. "Gratitude, my eye. I was getting ready to tell you that I'd live with you—in sin, mind you. I was actually willing to go against my very beliefs, just to be able to have you with me every single day. You've shown me so much in these last few months . . . opened my eyes to so many things. . . ."

He ran the back of his index finger down her cheek, and there was a flame burning in the depths of his black eyes. "Come to bed. There's something else I want to show you."

Twenty-three

"Are you certain this will work?" Racquel gave the note pinned to the face of the front door a doubtful look. "I mean, isn't it a little too obvious?"

Sean pressed the thumbtack into the hard wood until the head was a barely discernible bump on the surface of the paper. "Sometimes obvious is best. Besides, whoever it is, won't be expecting you to go on the offensive. He'll just think that you're running scared . . . going back home to Idaho to get away from him. If I'm right, and I know I am, he's going to follow you back there."

"But . . . I mean, what if, what if you're wrong, and he doesn't? What then?"

"We'll just have to come on back, and think of something else. Maybe hire someone to protect you. But, I want to get this thing settled now, so that we can get on with our lives. This is the only way to draw him out into the open."

Racquel chewed on the corner of her lip. She was still very nervous about her role in the entire thing. Being used as bait to trap the stalker was definitely not her idea of a fun time. What if the plan didn't work, or something went horribly wrong?

"Sean?" She hesitated a bit, her eyes bright with the beginnings of fear. "Wouldn't it be a better idea to get the police involved somehow? I mean, wouldn't that way be much safer? What if you get hurt doing this? I would never forgive myself if something happened to you."

Sean pulled her into his arms and tilted her head up. "Nothing's going to happen to me . . . or you, I promise. I've hired two private investigators—big guys—and they'll be staking out the roads leading to the farmhouse. Anything going or coming, they'll be able to see. No one will be able to get onto the property undetected. Once he's in the house, we'll grab him."

"We'll tell Morganna what we're doing, then?"

"Uh-huh, just in case he happens to check with her again. She'll be able to confirm that you've gone back to Idaho."

Racquel rested her head against his chest. "I wish this was all over with, already. Why can't we do the same thing here? I mean, trap him here?"

Sean massaged the back of her neck. "We need more space to play with, as well as unequivocal proof that this guy not only followed you from Idaho to LA, but that he also followed you back there."

She nodded. She had to be strong. For once in her adult life, she just had to be strong. She would make Sean proud of her, even if she had to put on an Oscar-winning performance.

"OK," she said, and with just the barest hint of a tremor in her voice, she managed: "I'm ready to go."

Later that evening, as Sean and Racquel were headed toward Idaho, safely buckled into the soft, leather seats of the KirPatrick jet, two men stood on the winding, gravel-strewn pathway leading to the old Ward farmhouse.

"This is going to be much easier than we thought,"

the taller of the two said. "Putting that listening device in his car was a great idea."

The other man, with the burnt-berry eyes, rubbed a hand across the back of his neck and said in a voice that was more than a little tired, "Yeah, but I'll be glad when it's all over with. You made sure the box is lined with velvet, right? Soft purple velvet?"

The taller man nodded. "Purple velvet, just as you said, though I don't see that the color of it makes a whole lot of difference. She's not going to survive for very long in there . . . especially not once we put all that dirt on top of it."

The other man said nothing. He simply turned and walked across to the long, black car parked on the side of the road, opened the driver's door, and climbed in. Just behind his seat, lying on the floor of the car, was a smooth silver coffin.

He leaned back against the headrest, and his lips moved in a silent whisper: "Now . . . all we have to do is wait."

Racquel was snuggled warmly against Sean's side, more asleep than awake, when the captain advised them to prepare for landing. The airport landing lights twinkled up at them from out of the darkness, and before too long the landing gear ground out of the belly of the plane and the sleek aircraft went into its final descent.

Sean rubbed a hand along Racquel's arm. "Time to wake up, babe. We're here."

Racquel opened eyes that were flushed with the slightest tinge of pink. "It's a good thing I didn't manage to rent the house out. This plan would never have been possible otherwise." She raised a hand to stifle a yawn. "I'm so tired."

Sean pressed a warm kiss to her lips. "You'll be able to sleep soon—nothing's going to happen tonight—nothing's going to happen for at least a few days, maybe even weeks. It'll take him a while to realize that we're not up at Mammoth, and once he does he'll head straight to your cottage in the Hollywood Hills."

Racquel stroked a soft hand across his face. "Oh . . . I hope this works."

Sean turned his lips into her palm. "It will. It will. The PIs are already stationed on the property, so there's absolutely nothing to worry about. OK?"

She smiled, and the love she felt for him shone softly in her eyes.

Twenty-four

The long, black car pulled carefully off the gravel road at the sound of the approaching vehicle. The man sitting in the passenger seat reached for the glove compartment and yanked it open. From within, he removed a dangerous-looking little gun. The man at the wheel said, "Make sure you don't miss."

The other gave him a sanguine look. "What about the doctor?"

A look of hatred twisted the face of the one behind the wheel. "No. It won't be anything this quick for him. I've got something else entirely planned for him."

The rental car rounded the final bend, and Racquel straightened up in her seat. She had never thought that she'd ever feel even vaguely excited about coming home, but with Sean at her side everything seemed different.

"Do you remember anything?" she asked, and there was a happy note in her voice.

Sean's brow wrinkled. "What happened to all of the barns? And the trees?"

Racquel turned to look out the window. "Everything ran to ruin in the last few years of my parents' life. My dad turned to drink . . . in a major way. The farm started losing money. He fell into debt, and had to sell the animals off. Then there was a fire in the main barn, and that spread to the others. Then the trees . . . most of them seemed to just wither up and die. We had a lot of really bad luck in the last years before—"

A popping noise from the side of the car halted the words in her throat.

"What?" She was barely able to utter the word before she was thrown heavily against Sean's shoulder as the car lurched crazily from side to side. Crushing memories of her own accident just months before swept over her in such an unrelenting tide that it was all she could do to hold back the strangled cry that welled up in her throat.

She turned and instinctively clutched at Sean's shoulder as he turned the wheels of the car into the skid and rode out the tremors of the vehicle.

When the car came to a shuddering halt on the lip of the road, Sean turned to gather her into his arms. "We're OK," he muttered against her temple. "We're OK. It's just a blowout. Just a blowout."

Racquel's face was buried against his side. In her mind, she had seen visions of her face going through the windshield again. She saw the glass tearing at her skin, ripping away at the beautiful work which Sean had so painstakingly done. Her breath came in broken little pants, and it was only because she had made herself the promise to be strong that she did not give vent to the hot tears pressing at the backs of her eyes.

"We're . . . we're OK?" she finally managed.

Sean gave her a reassuring little squeeze. "Don't worry, the men are out there somewhere. I'll just get out and take a look at the tire. We can probably just walk the rest of the way to the house, anyway. But don't move until I tell you to, all right?"

She nodded. "OK."

Sean climbed from the car, pulled the collar of his

coat up about his ears, and walked around to the right side of the car. He gave the wheel a lightning glance, taking note of the ragged hole in the rubber. Then his eyes lifted to sweep the sparsely treed road. He walked briskly back around to the driver's side, and yanked the door open.

"We're going back," he said, and immediately reached forward to turn the key.

Racquel blinked at him, and the words clawed at her throat. "Back? What do you mean, back?"

Sean turned the wheel. "Something's wrong. We're going to drive on the flat until we get to the highway. Reach into my pocket and get out my cell phone."

Racquel's fingers fidgeted through his pockets as he fought to get the car turned around.

"What about the two private investigators? Couldn't they help us?"

"We can't wait around to find out. I'll check in with them later."

Racquel pulled the phone from his pocket and quickly punched in the emergency code. Sean glanced into the rearview mirror of the car and swore beneath his breath.

"A car's coming up behind us . . . fast." He gave her a quick glance. "Your belt on?" When she nodded, he said, "OK. Hold on." He jammed his foot on the gas and the car surged forward in a crazy, lopsided manner. Racquel spoke quickly into the phone, giving their exact position on the gravel road. Her voice was surprisingly calm, considering the fact that she was just a baby's breath away from total terror.

The car was upon them now, racing up behind, then pulling out to overtake them. For half a second, Racquel felt herself relax. Thank the Lord, she thought, it was not coming after them, but her moment of relief was short-lived. The sedan turned diagonally and, with deliberate leisure, blocked the entire width of road before them.

Sean reached into his inside coat pocket and removed a blunt-nosed pistol.

"Take this," he said.

Racquel's fingers were ice cold. "I've never used a gun," she stammered.

Sean gave her a firm look. "Put your finger on the trigger, point, and shoot. There's nothing more to it than that."

The man in the sedan was getting out, standing by the driver's door, waiting. He knew that there was no way out. They had to either go past him, or go back. Racquel's breath came in sharp little stabs.

"What're we going to do?"

Sean brought the car to a shuddering halt. "We'll let him come to us. He's probably not expecting us to fight. Don't worry, the police will be here soon."

They sat, peering through the murky darkness at the tall figure standing unmoving at the side of the car.

Racquel's fingers shook. "What's he waiting for? If he's going to kill us, why doesn't he do it?"

The sudden noise of glass breaking had them both spinning in the direction of the sound. Racquel got a quick glimpse of a man swinging something that looked very much like a small log toward them. The wood caught Sean a glancing blow against the side of the head, and in the fright of the moment Racquel lost her grip on the gun in her hand.

She cried out only once before a big hand reached into the car and caught her by the throat. Sean was slumped forward in his seat, his head resting drunkenly against the steering wheel. Racquel scrambled for the gun with her feet, but the man was strong. He yanked her up and over Sean, never once relinquishing his grip on her neck.

The world around her began to go out of focus as she struggled for breath.

Just before she lost consciousness, the man's mouth descended on hers.

Twenty-five

She came out of her stupor screaming his name. "Ralph! Ralph!" She twisted and turned, trying to get free, but her arms were bound in front of her, and the same thick cord was wrapped about her ankles. Understanding washed over her in unrelenting waves. It had been her ex-husband all along—the one tormenting her all these months.

She screamed again, this time for Sean. His name bleated from her throat, hitting the night air and then just fading away like pollen on the wind. Her heart battered heavily against her ribs, and she prayed. She didn't care what Ralph did to her, just please, God, let him not hurt Sean.

She tried to move her head, but found that she could only do so by a mere fraction. She was lying on her back, next to a long, dark shiny box, and the only thing she was sure of was that she was in a car, and the car was moving.

She forced herself to be calm. She had to be. She had to think, and not panic. Where was he taking her? What had he done to Sean? And where were the police?

"Ralph?" she tried again, but got no reply. "Ralph, what're you doing? Where're you taking me?"

The coarse voice from the front seat belted out a

sharp command, and a swell of terror clawed at the back of her throat. This was the voice on the phone. This was the voice that had haunted her dreams for so many months. But where was Ralph?

"What . . . what do you want from me?" she asked.

The man wheezed, then chuckled. "You'll find out soon enough," he said.

Racquel took a breath. At least he was talking to her now. "The man who was with me—what have you done with him?"

There was no response.

She tried again. "Where're you taking me?"

"To the cemetery."

A new burst of terror exploded in her chest, and she turned her head sideways to look at the metal object that she was lying right beside. In the darkness, she recognized it now. It was a coffin. A coffin. Oh, God, they meant to bury her alive. They meant to put her in it and bury her alive.

The man was talking again. "I tried to warn you months ago, didn't I?"

It was several moments before Racquel could manage, "What? When?"

"On the way to the airport. I told you about lying, and what that man had done to his wife."

Racquel closed her eyes, and a tear slid from under a lid. She remembered now. The taxi driver. The man who had taken her to the airport when she left Idaho. The one who had told her about the girl being buried alive.

She strained to break the cord around her wrists. She had to get free. She *had* to. She lifted her hands to her mouth and gnawed at the cord until her lips were raw, but it was thick, and the knot too tight for her to pull loose with her teeth.

The car came to a sudden stop, and she knew that

they had arrived at their final destination. She closed her eyes. Was this how it was to end, then? Would she never see Sean again? Never touch him? Hold him? Tell him how much he meant to her?

The back door of the car opened, and moonlight crept in to light the darkness. Racquel squinted up at the man above her. She could just barely make out the thick scar tissue beneath his neck.

"Why're you helping Ralph?" she asked. "What's in it for you? Whatever he's paying you, I'll double."

The man's mouth twitched upward in a lopsided smile. "Can you give me back the last fifteen years of my life?" He leaned in farther, so that his entire face was now exposed to the light. "You don't recognize me, do you, girlie?"

Racquel squinted up at him. "No . . ."

The man laughed. "Your daddy ran me off his place almost two decades ago. Then he set the law on me. Said I killed the orphan boy." He wiped the side of his mouth with a sleeve. "But, you know what, girlie? It's your daddy who done the deed. I saw him."

Racquel blinked at the man. It was a lie. Her father hadn't been a saint, but he certainly hadn't killed anyone, either. Besides, the only orphan who had lived on the property was Sean, and he certainly had not died years before. He was alive and well. At least, she prayed so.

"I saw him stick the boy in the side with that pitchfork. Drove it right in, he did. Boy told him that he was going to marry you when he was old enough. That got your pappy all riled up. Then he did a frame-up on me, see? So I went to jail for what your pappy did. Now it's time for you to pay, since your pappy can't anymore."

Racquel's mind worked furiously. The scar on Sean's

side. It could've been made by the teeth of a pitchfork. Nothing made any sense. Why was this man saying that her father had killed him, when he had obviously not?

"The . . . the orphan didn't die," she stammered. "He grew up . . . became a doctor."

The man grinned. "Yeah, I found out all that later. Your pappy sent him to medical school. He ran himself into debt to do it."

Racquel's head lifted. "That's not true," she said. "Sean was adopted. He *was.*"

The man reached down to lift her into a sitting position. "Poor girlie. Everyone's been lying to you."

Her eyes ran over the tall man. "How do you know so very much?"

"I've made it my business to find out. Years in the pen with nothing to do but think. Your pappy made your doctor friend promise that he'd come nowhere near you, change his name. It was part of the deal they worked out. The orphan's silence for a paid trip through medical school. Penniman doesn't know all this, but then, Penniman's crazy for you—he always was. So crazy that he'd rather kill you than let another man have you."

"You . . . you killed my parents?"

The man threw back his head and cackled. "Still haven't figured it out, have you? Penniman did that. Your pappy didn't want him marrying you either, so Penniman killed him—killed them both. Fixed the car up, he did, just as he done with you."

Racquel rested her head against the silver casket. It was all too much. Too much. Lies. Lies. Lies. The man was telling nothing but lies.

The man leaned forward. "Come on, little lady . . . it's time for you to get into the box." He turned behind him to look at the headlights of the car slowly approaching. "The boss is here."

He opened the lid of the casket, then reached long arms toward Racquel. She waited until he was close enough, then reared up suddenly, striking him a stunning blow with the blunt of her head.

The man staggered backward, clutching at his right eye. He swore thickly and lumbered forward again. He grabbed Racquel around the neck, placed a hand beneath her knees, then placed her facedown in the casket and closed the lid. Deep, terrifying darkness closed in on her, and Racquel struggled to turn her face sideways so that she might breathe. Panic tore at her when she found that she could not move. Her elbows pressed into the soft velvet, and her toes were pressed right to the length of the space. The air inside was hot, stifling. In less than ten minutes, she knew, she would be gone. . . .

She bit down on the velvet, and cried out to God to save her.

A sudden gush of night air on her back startled her almost as much as the sudden lack of it had. Hands reached down into the interior to lift her out. She opened her eyes and looked into the most welcome pair of eyes she had ever seen. *Sean.*

His eyes were brimming with tears, and he kept muttering over and over, "Oh, babe, what did they do to you . . . what did they do to you?"

Within seconds, her hands and then feet were free and she was in his arms, being pressed close against his wildly beating heart.

"Sean . . ." she murmured. "You're not dead—you're here."

He hugged her close. "Yes, I'm here. I'm here."

"Ralph?" she said suddenly. "Where's he?"

Sean took a breath. "Dead."

Her eyes flicked up to his. "D-dead?"

Sean nodded. "The gun . . . you dropped the gun, remember? I had to. He would've killed me otherwise. I found out from him where you were being taken."

She swallowed. "The other guy? Where's he?"

Sean inclined his head. "Over there. Unconscious."

"And the private detectives?"

"The cops found them both bound and gagged in the trunk of their car . . . alive, though."

Racquel took a deep breath, then released it in a long sigh. "It's over," she said. "It's finally over."

Sean took her by the hand, and over the sounds of approaching sirens he said, "There're a few things I have to tell you."

Racquel wrapped an arm about his waist. "Does it have to do with your not really being adopted?"

A look of surprise came and went in his eyes. "You know?"

She nodded.

A deep frown grooved the skin between his eyes. "Will you marry me . . . still?

Racquel pressed a kiss to the side of his face. "Try to stop me. Come on, let's go home."

And, in the gathering mist of early morning, they walked back toward the car, holding onto their memories of things past—distant memories of pain that could only be completely forgotten in the warmth of each other's arms.

ABOUT THE AUTHOR

Niqui Stanhope was born in Jamaica, West Indies, but grew up in a small bauxite mining town in Guyana, South America. Because her parents traveled quite a bit and always took the entire family along, the summers of her childhood were spent exploring the rich cultures of the Caribbean, South America, and North America. In 1984, she emigrated to the United States with her family. She admits that novel writing never occurred to her until after she had graduated from the University of Southern California with a degree in chemistry.

Niqui Stanhope now lives in Los Angeles. She is also the author of:

NIGHT TO REMEMBER
MADE FOR EACH OTHER
CHAMPAGNE WISHES

e-mail: NiquiJ@aol.com
PO Box 6105
Burbank, CA 91510